ABOUT THE AUTHOR

Batt Humphreys spent 15 years at CBS News in New York, most as a senior producer. As a reporter, he covered hurricanes, executions and more murders than he cares to remember. When he left CBS in 2007, one of his colleagues wrote, "Quite frankly, there's no one other than Batt that you'd rather have in the control room when news breaks. He worked ridiculous hours, through the middle of the night, and somehow managed to be sharper and tougher and more quick-witted than those of us who were less sleep-deprived could ever be."

In 2007, Humphreys returned to his beloved South, but it wasn't long before the lure of the headline drew him to a century-old story.

DEAD WEIGHT

Based on a True Story

BATT HUMPHREYS

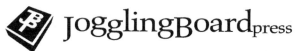

JogglingBoardpress

Charleston, South Carolina

DEAD WEIGHT

Based on a True Story

FIRST TRADE PAPERBACK EDITION, MAY 2010

Copyright © 2009 by Batt Humphreys

DEAD WEIGHT

By Batt Humphreys
Published by Joggling Board Press

Joggling Board Press books may be purchased for educational, business or sales promotional use.

For information:
Joggling Board Press
P.O. Box 13029
Charleston, S.C. 29422
jogglingboardpress.com
sales@jogglingboardpress.com

Library of Congress Cataloging in Publication record applied for.

Trade Paperback Edition ISBN: 978-0-9841073-4-6

ACKNOWLEDGEMENTS

This story came to me as a gift. Much of the historical research was complete. My publisher, editor and friend Susan Kammeraad-Campbell offered a challenge with a weighty responsibility. Take these rich elements, add characters as you see necessary and make this a book that will make a difference.

Fear can be inspiring. A novel was a test I had yet to take. The risk of failure seemed too high. She lent confidence, an occasional insult to my insecurities and a wise hand at editing. This is a journey we have shared.

We acknowledge the contributions of Daniel J. Crooks and Douglas W. Bostick for painstaking research on the State of South Carolina vs. Daniel Duncan. A valuable and ready resource or all things historic in Charleston, our thanks to South Carolina Historical Society and the Charleston Library Society. Photographs and imagery are courtesy of Gary Geboy, Steve Lepre and Stewart Young.

My thanks to my partners in promoting this story, the staff of Joggling Board Press and to my publicist Marjory Wentworth, poet laureate of South Carolina and energy without end, amen.

There is little of this life worth measure or mention that is not in some way connected to Laura. She knows me in ways that I do not even know myself. She remembers much, which I try to forget. She has faith, where I do not and somehow still believes she was not mistaken in marriage.

DEDICATION
For Daniel Cornelius "Nealy" Duncan

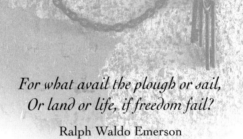

For what avail the plough or sail,
Or land or life, if freedom fail?

Ralph Waldo Emerson

CHAPTER ONE
Sunday
OCTOBER 2, 1910

If you can choose your approach to a city always take her by sea. It makes for a softer entry. Sailing into the harbor, the long slow entrance affords time to savor the change. The city grows large before you, usually showing her best side.

Three days on roiling water has prepared me well for the relief of land. We are meant to walk on solid ground, just ask anyone of my puking shipmates. On solid ground, the smell of salt air has its charms. But I prefer the stench of mother earth more than her kelp. I prefer the scents of Man; he and his women, their progeny and pets.

Charleston Harbor is built of history itself. Over there, Fort Moultrie held the British at bay. Beyond it, Fort Sumter took the first volley of the Civil War, the war of "Northern Aggression" as the natives call it. Over the fort, the bright morning sun illuminates the fluttering banner of the winner of that contest. God, I bet Old Glory irks the hell out of these crackers.

A more European air of the ancient and artful, the city appears beautiful in an un-American way. It is as if the twentieth century took a pass on Charleston. Perhaps that is the problem.

There is a trial in this town, a triangle of animosities – a Jewish merchant murdered, a black man accused and a white populace primed for a hanging. It is what put me on the high seas.

My name is Hal Hinson. I write for the New York Tribune. I've traveled a thousand miles to cover a trial whose outcome is foregone. Be certain I am not happy to be here. Lynching in the Jim Crow South is common enough – local newspapers are loaded with accounts. But they are far from front-page material. The notion is absurd that this one, cloaked in jurisprudence, is any different. I am here for one reason only – punishment for calling an editor an ass. Maybe next time I'll learn.

Last time I was aboard a ship, I was returning from Africa with our esteemed former president. That was something worth showing up for. Now I'm watching the deckhands going through their paces, tossing lines to shore. I hear the engines reverse and the stern pull sideways drawing the lines taut. The engines fall silent. These wharves have seen the hard work of a few hundred years. Dockhands hoist the gangplank into place, and I can see those more eager to get ashore fairly tumbling to get back onto terra firma. And there in swarms is the collection of hucksters, hands held out for coins, buzzing around the debarking passengers. As I make my way down the plank, I can feel it dance beneath my feet and I try to adjust my gate to its rhythm. Finally, I walk onto land.

"Mista, Mista. Take yo bag fo a penny."

The voice came from my waist. I looked down into the face of a young Negro boy looking up. He inhabited a coat that was beyond worn. It more closely resembled a rag, streaked with stains that tracked an urchin's life. Beneath the coat, he wore two shirts, both hinting at their original color – white maybe. For pants, he wore half slacks ending at bony, dirty knees. A length of hemp rope cinched the pants around his thin waist. His bare feet were covered in dirt, calloused and affixed to bandy legs. His eyes met mine. A toothy grin appeared beneath the grime.

"Excuse me, son. What are you saying?"

"Not yo son, Mista. I sez I takes yo poke fo a penny."

"Don't you people speak English down here?"

"'Scuse me, Mista, but yo de one talk funny."

"What's your name?"

"Mojo."

"Mojo? What kind of name is that?"

"De one my daddy gib me."

"You're just full of them aren't you. Why did he name you that?"

"Cause he say, if'n it wernt fer his dam mojo, I wudn't be heah."

"I guess the humor is hereditary. Mojo it is. Here's your penny, throw these bags up on that carriage."

He took the coin and stuck it deep into his pocket, making sure it did not drop through some forgotten hole in its bottom, then heaved my bags up to the luggage platform, struggling with a suitcase that weighed neigh as much as he did.

"Whas yo name, Mista?"

"You're a bold one. You can call me Hal."

"Jes wanna know mo bout da big city man."

"What tells you I'm from a big city?"

"Dem shoes, dat hat ... don't see dem round here."

"So I stand out a bit?"

"Like a ho in church."

"You're a bit young to speak of whores."

"I knows 'em all. You wanna? I take you dere."

"Let's skip that. You know your way around here?"

"Like your back pocket." He held up my wallet, dangling it in front of my face.

"What? Damn you, give me back my wallet."

"Gib me a job. Make Mojo yo boy."

"I don't need a boy."

"Mista, you *needs* a boy."

"I'm from New York but you got my wallet, maybe you're right. God help me. Be outside the Mills House at six."

"Yes, suh, Mista Hal."

I heard the clang of trolleys a block or so away, but the carriage was more convenient, somehow more in tune with the mood of the town, though my own mood was rank enough that pretty much everything grated on it. The horse, a big bay draft, was well groomed and in obvious spirit as he pulled the carriage away from the docks. Time was traced in the streets' trolley tracks, cut into the cobblestones. The combination made for a rough ride.

It was a warm October morning. People strolled along the streets entering and exiting the shops and offices in this part of town serving the port industry. In another block, the mercantile bustle changed. Around a corner, a handsome street stretched out with storefronts displaying the shingles of attorneys, a lane of lawyers. Bastards! This is where the hangings should be held; skip this mock trial. First, we hang the lawyers.

Around another corner the courthouse faced off a church. I'm sure that was someone's idea of a joke. You don't get past this place without someone slapping judgment on you.

The hotel was only a block beyond. No surprise, it was somewhat old and wore that same stately manner that was stamped on this city. The spacious lobby was open and breezy. I introduced myself to the receptionist.

"Good morning, Mr. Hinson. Welcome to Charleston." She was cute, but a few cars back on the fashion train.

"Good morning. I see you have my reservation."

"Yes, sir. How is New York?"

"The baseball season is all but over, and we're kind of excited that Penn Station is about to open."

Her eyes went down to the sleeve of her dress, which she absently brushed with one hand, and then raised both hands to the collar of a dress still of Victorian cut. She was far too attractive to be wearing last decade's castoffs. Her glance came back to mine and her eyelashes went to work.

"Your dress is very pretty. In New York the women have gone a little wild. It seems they've discovered color and they're going quite radical with it. I dare say it might cause a commotion here, but dresses up there are now cut above the ankles."

She looked down at her own hem, then back at me.

"Above the ankles? I'd love a dress like that, but I'd be fired for wearing it."

"I'm sure it would be lovely on you."

Her eyes went bright and she grew a bit more attractive. I snapped myself back.

"Are there any messages for me?"

"Just the one. It's from the office of Chief Boyle."

It was a long shot, but before leaving New York I sent a telegram to the Charleston police chief, requesting an interview with Daniel Duncan, the accused killer. I slit open the envelope and pulled out the single sheet. It contained a single word.

No.

CHAPTER TWO
Thursday
JULY 7, 1910

Daniel Cornelius "Nealy" Duncan woke up in a pool of sweat. It was late afternoon in June. The heat of summer came early that year. Air barely flowed through the tenement where forty other Negroes shared space and portions of their lives. Their tenement didn't face a cooling ocean breeze. There were no high windows on the veranda. It was a cramped, airless sweatbox in summer – life for working blacks in Charleston.

Nealy rubbed his eyes, rolled his feet to the floor to sit up. Waking up in the late afternoon was normal for him. He worked nights. Few understand the difficulties of trying to sleep with the sun up high. It runs against the diurnal rhythm, and you never quite get used to feeling terrible all the time. Nealy worked nights for the money, and for the hope that by doing what no one else wanted to do, he could create his own niche and advance himself in this nasty world. But Nealy had another reason: he was in love.

"What you eatin', boy?" Buchanan Duncan asked his son a few minutes later.

"Rice 'n beans."

Nealy had cooked the southern staple. You could find rice and beans all over Charleston, from the finest of homes to the most miserable of tenements. The only difference was the china.

"There's some middlin' meat over there in the cupboard, thro dat in, have yo self a decent suppa."

"Thanks. This is good enough. I gotta get to work, but I wanna see Ida first."

Ida Lampkin was one of those girls who made the sun shine a little brighter. Her eyes knew nothing but laughter, but even at sixteen she had a serious side. She knew what she wanted, and he was Nealy. He was a rarity – a stable and sensible man at 23.

Nealy cut across one side street before coming to the parade field in front of The Citadel. It was early evening. He would have avoided the ground if cadets were around. Those boys were always spoiling for a fight. At the end of the field stood the imposing statue of John C. Calhoun, a revered figure in South Carolina among whites. Among blacks he was reviled. Nealy's dad told him the facts on Mr. John C. Calhoun, how he thought that Negroes had little purpose other than as slaves.

Although Calhoun died before the Civil War, his staunch belief that slavery was a "positive good" rather than a "necessary evil" helped sow the seeds of secession. Buchanan also told Nealy how, when he was young, the boys would sneak by the statue and smack ol' John C. in the head with rotten fruit or the occasional egg. A few years ago they put the statue on an eighty foot column to make him a more difficult target, but he was still an inviting one.

Nealy whistled as he approached the man of granite. Checking over his shoulder, he reached into his pocket and pulled out a tomato he'd snagged from a garden on the way over. He cocked his arm and pitched the fruit like Cy Young. He heard a satisfying splat.

"Take that, you old bastard."

Nealy jogged the last block to Ida's tenement and jumped the four steps to the porch. She stood at the door, smiling.

"Boy, what you grinnin' bout?" she said sweetly.

"Just paid my respects to Mista Calhoun."

"You better not let them Citadel boys catch you. Wid his blessin' they might jes beat you like des own you."

"They'd have to catch me first and I'm fast."

He pulled her into a dark spot on the front porch, leaned forward and kissed her lightly on the lips, then hugged her close to him. She was so young and lovely. He could almost circle her waist with his hands, her girlish hips well on the way to womanhood. Her firm breasts brushed against his chest and he hugged her tighter.

"Damn right you're fast," she laughed. "You better slow yo'self down, boy."

Their marriage was only weeks away, but there was a line, a limit, to how far she'd let him go. Her mother, Miss Mary, had warned her about boys, warned her that the best way to lose them was to give them too much before marriage. Ida was no fool. She had plenty of friends who made bad choices with bad men, men who took their virtue, then stole off to the gin joints, wasted their money on bad liquor and happy dust. Cocaine was a scourge in Charleston. Too many of her girlfriends ended up with bastard babies with hophead fathers. That wasn't going to happen to Ida. Her life was going to be different.

"You betta get yourself on to that bakery."

"Aw, I'm just looking for some honey to sweeten the loaves."

"Why, Nealy boy, you know that honey pot is full, but the lid's on tight 'til next month."

She kissed him full and hard on the mouth, then pushed him off the porch. He stumbled back, dropped his head and shuffled a few steps like his feelings were hurt, then slowly turned, showing her a face lit with a foolish grin. He made a big sweeping gesture and threw her a kiss.

"Put that in your hope chest, girl."

"You just come back here in the morning," Ida teased. "They might be mo' where that come from."

"Girl, you gonna drive this boy crazy." Nealy walked into the night. He turned onto Calhoun Street. You just can't escape that man around Charleston.

Geilfuss Bakery was where Nealy worked. Rudolph Geilfuss was the second-generation owner of the bakery and store that had been in operation since the nineteenth century. Geilfuss's father emigrated from Germany bringing Old World recipes and baking methods still used in the shop. The old ways worked especially well for fresh bread. Geilfuss did a great business. The bakery ran wide open from eight p.m. until the last of the loaves were finished about mid morning. They sent breads, pies and cakes to Charleston's finest homes and restaurants.

Geilfuss took an early interest in Nealy. He hired him when he was eight years old to work as a cleanup boy. Nealy worked hard and was reliable. Rudolph taught him to read and write and lift his language above streetspeak. He trained him as an apprentice. During that time a drunken baker tripped while carrying a hot tray of rolls and crashed into Nealy, the hot iron tray rammed into his face, searing the flesh and leaving a permanent scar on Nealy, a gash very like a saber scar. Geilfuss fired that baker and gave Nealy his job.

When Nealy arrived at the door that night, Geilfuss sat outside smoking his pipe. "Evening, Daniel." Most people called him Nealy; his boss preferred his formal name.

"Evening, sir."

"Daniel, it's time we had a discussion about your wedding."

Nealy sat on the stoop.

"Daniel, you and Ida will be married soon. You've been almost like a son to me and now you'll be a married man."

"It's not going to change anything, Mr. Geilfuss."

"But it will change, Daniel."

Nealy paused, not sure of what was coming.

"You've been a hard worker and loyal employee. After your wedding, I don't want you to come back into the shop."

Nealy was stunned, "But I don't understand."

"I want you to take a week off, with pay for your honeymoon. When you return, it will be with a raise. You're no longer a single man, Daniel. You need to start thinking like a provider."

Nealy was still stunned, but now tears were forming in his eyes. Geilfuss put his arm around his shoulders.

"And we're baking the cake for your wedding. Congratulations, Daniel."

All of Charleston knew the beautiful cakes Geilfuss produced. No major wedding went without one.

"Mr. Geilfuss, we'd love a cake, but we can't afford one."

The tough old German put his arm around Nealy. "Vas ist das? Daniel, we want the cake to be our wedding gift to you. It would be our honor, and it will be one of the finest cakes we've ever made."

Nealy lowered his head and took two deep breaths, his eyes tearing. "I don't know how to thank you. Ida will be so proud."

Geilfuss lifted his arm and patted Nealy on the back. "Let's get started. It's time to get to work."

Their night began as most of the town finished dinner and got ready for bed. Both had reasons for liking the loneliness of the overnight hours. For all his kindness, Geilfuss shunned the public as much as possible. He suffered from a severe case of rosacea, a condition that deformed his nose and cheeks. He declined to sit for a family portrait. There was no cure, and as his condition worsened he kept closer to the night, avoiding when possible even his best customers.

Nealy preferred the night. Class and racial distinctions were less rigid, maybe because the highfalutin whites were all inside their big homes. Also, he needed the money. With his wedding just weeks away, nearly every dollar he made went to furnishing their new place. Every payday for months, Nealy walked up King Street to Little Jerusalem, where newly arrived Jewish merchants set up shop. Established stores farther down King Street served only whites, but Little Jerusalem catered to crossover crowds, blue collar whites and Negroes. The night hours, coupled with the trust invested in him by his boss, helped keep Nealy out of trouble. Some nights the festive sounds from Market Street floated up like a siren's call to the young men on a smoke break outside the bakery.

"Yo heah dat, Nealy?" The teenage shop boy sat on the stoop with Nealy.

Music came, punctuated by high-pitched laughter, the sounds of fun fueled by cheap gin or cocaine, probably both.

"Sounds like fun," the kid said. "Listen to dem ladies laugh."

"Boy, sounds like the Devil calling his own home."

"But I bet dem ladies know how to show a good time. Ever wish you was down dere, chasin' de ladies?"

"No. Down there you just lose all your money, and those ladies don't run far. They're not trained to run."

CHAPTER THREE
Tuesday
JUNE 21, 1910

Early morning in Charleston arrived to a cacophony of sales calls. There was a rhythm, set by time and tradition. The first cries up from the harbor were, *"swimpy, swimpy, swimpy,"* as shrimp men cried their catch. Fishmongers followed with pitches for, *"porgy, porgy,"* a local saltwater chub. Women walked neighborhoods with baskets of fresh vegetables perched on their heads, calling out to prospects, *"get yo vegetubble."* And, since no Charleston table was complete without a floral arrangement, the flower ladies followed.

Farther uptown, merchants raised shades and hung out shingles, a more quiet start to the day.

Max Lubelsky opened his door on King Street.

At thirty-five, he was part of a new wave of Jewish immigrants to Charleston. After the assassination of Russian Czar Alexander II, the persecution of Russian Jews started an exodus. Max, his wife Rose and his son traveled to Charleston via New York City. Charleston had a reputation for religious tolerance. She boasted one of the largest Jewish populations in the country, large enough to feel the strains of change inherent in an expanding community with diverging theologies.

Newcomers who could afford to do so opened businesses on upper King Street, living upstairs and keeping shop below. The more established Jews had the older stores farther downtown, catering to Charleston's elite. Max and his peers settled for trade with anyone who entered their doors.

That morning, Max was alone. He opened his clothing shop as owner and sole employee. His wife Rose and young son Joseph were off in New York visiting relatives. Max grabbed a broom and swept dust to the doorway, the morning sun cutting a shaft of light through the suspended particles. Sounds of passing trolleys and horses caught his ear, and the whispers of sweeping came from next door. He shook his head and pushed his broom out the door at the same time as his neighbor.

"Well, Max. Another day and we are still with the problem." Charles Levin began with the same issue he'd been harassing Max with for weeks.

"What problem is that, Charles?" They stood in a swirl of dust. "That there is too much dirt in the world?"

"This dirt is God's work, it is not the dirty work of our own people. The president of our synagogue plans to open his store on the Sabbath and you will do nothing?"

Max slowed the stroke of his broom, toying with the small pile in front of him. "Every day. Every day, you talk about Joshua. Every day I say it is not my concern and everyday you tell me I should be concerned. Listen to me, Charles, *I don't care.*"

Levin pushed. "And so today you are no longer a Jew? You're maybe a Methodist?"

"I will keep my doors closed on the Sabbath."

"And defile God's will because you care nothing ..."

Too far.

Max pushed his broom and sent a cloud of dirt across the top of Levin's new brogans. Levin sold shoes; it was no small insult. He raised his broom and for a moment they locked eyes. Max spun on his heel, walked through his door and slammed it behind him.

Joel Posner arrived at Lubelsky's shop just before noon. Joel traded in chickens and pigeons, and he was a friend of Max's. Sometimes Max would trade clothing for a future dinner.

Joel was with his young daughter, Carla, who wanted to pick out a new tie for his birthday. They entered the shop and Joel called for Max. No reply. Rose and his son were out of town, he knew, and Max never left his store unattended. They walked through the store, thinking Max might be in back where he kept his chickens. The birds were there, squawking, but no Max. Joel walked back into the store. The silence felt wrong. It was midday. Even without a customer Max should be there, cutting or sewing.

"Max!" The sound fell flat on rows of neatly folded shirts.

Hackles rose on the back of his neck.

"Child," Joel whispered, "come here and sit on this chair."

"Daddy ..."

"Hush, honey."

He strode to the front and called again. "Max!"

From behind him came a faint sound, a scratching on the floor.

"Max? Where are you, my friend?"

"Help," he heard faintly and rushed to the voice.

In the middle of the shop was a tailor's table where Lubelsky did most of his work. Beneath it, Joel saw a blood-stained hand scratching the floor.

Carla saw it at the same time and screamed.

Joel fell to his knees, grabbed the hand and leaned under the table.

Carla wailed, pulling at his jacket. He pushed her away as he crawled deeper and found Max. His head was covered in blood, his skull dented, flesh torn away, exposing bone. He knew it was his friend only by his trademark handlebar mustache, still curled and waxed to perfection. Joel wretched.

"Max, I'm going to get you some help." He reached to the table above and grabbed a bolt of cloth to put under his friend's head. Joel leaned closer to Max, whose lips moved, making a slight sound, but Joel couldn't make out what Max was saying. All the while, Carla cried in a high, hysterical pitch.

"Carla, please," Joel said sternly. He looked at her, then back to Max. "I'll be right back."

He crawled backwards and hit his head on the table, stood up too quickly and had to clutch the counter to keep from falling down. He grabbed his daughter's hand, felt a wetness on his own but kept moving to the door, to the closest help, to Charles Levin.

He entered Levin's shop panting and dragging Carla. Levin sat in a chair by the window.

"Help, please! He's hurt, bleeding badly. He may be dying."

Levin looked up. "Who may be dying?"

"Max, Max Lubelsky. He's in very bad shape."

No movement. "What's wrong with him?"

"I don't know! We need a doctor, his head is ..."

"I'm no doctor. I sell shoes and I can't leave my store. You go for help and take your daughter with you."

Posner raced to the street and stopped. He looked north, up the street, but saw no one. He looked south, spied a policeman, threw up his hands and started running.

Sergeant Frank Stender had seen a lot in his years on the police force. A man running down the street was barely enough to raise an eyebrow, certainly not enough to break the rhythm of his stroll along his beat. But the crazy man was running straight for him, trailed by a young girl.

Posner almost collided with Stender. Panting, he waved his arms and pointed. Stender had no idea what the man was saying, but he followed Posner back up the street and into Lubelsky's store.

"Hurt. Max. Here. Please look." Joel sucked air as he pointed under the table.

Stender bent down, then sucked in his own breath. A pool of blood spread across the floor from the tailor's severely beaten head. Lubelsky was still alive. Stender moved, but too quickly, smacking his head on the table, as he spun and kicked the table leg, catching a curse just in time to spare the young girl. He reached into his pocket, fishing for the big brass key he carried. He rushed out the door, headed for the closest police callbox. Stender looked all business, but his hands shook slightly. He'd seen plenty of killings, usually knifings or the occasional shooting down on the seedy side of town, but not here, in broad daylight, in a respectable shop. He shoved the key into the callbox, pulled the door open and ripped the headpiece off the hook.

"Dammit, answer the phone." The connection was taking too long.

"Central station, whadda ya got?"

"This is Stender. One of the Jew merchants has been badly beaten. Call for Dr. Pearlstine, and have the wagon sent to 543 King Street. Fast dammit, this man's almost dead." The cop slammed the callbox door closed and spun on his heel. He had to protect the crime scene. He ran back to the shop, pushing his way through the small crowd gathering outside. In the center of them all was Charles Levin.

At the police station, cops and detectives flew out the doors. The first detective at the scene was Clarence Levy, who was riding a trolley up King when he saw the crowd outside the tailor's shop. He jumped off the car and wedged his way through the crowd, to hear Levin holding court before a group growing more agitated.

"It was a black man, I tell you," Levin shouted. "I saw a young black man this morning, just standing in front of the store."

"What reason would a colored man have to attack a man like Max?" shouted one man.

"Hey! You! Shut yer yaps!" Levy bellowed. "Bust it up! Let the police do their business. Make way." His booming voice had the effect of Moses. The crowd parted.

Most of Charleston knew Detective Levy was tough. One night, in a gunfight with a suspect, he took a bullet in the hip, fell to the ground, then took aim with his pistol and shot the trigger finger off his attacker, who promptly surrendered. Levy was an old bulldog with plenty of bite left.

Levy found Stender inside the store.

"What the hell's going on here, Frank?"

"The tailor, Lubelsky, was beaten. I called it in. Dr. Pearlstine should be here any minute."

"Get out there and clear him a path."

Levy got down on one knee to see Lubelsky, who breathed in shallow, raspy gasps. Levy stood up looking around the store. Coins were scattered on the counter and across the floor, along with a crowbar and hatchet, and bloody fingerprints stained the counter. Motion at the door caught his eye. The doctor walked in.

"Over here, Doc. Under the table."

Dr. Pearlstine was a young man, just starting his practice. He wasn't used to a patient with his head cracked open. Bile rose in the doctor's throat.

"Help me get this man out from under the table," he said, motioning to Stender and two others.

The three gently pulled Max into the open. Pearlstine checked his pulse, then pulled out bandages to try to slow the bleeding.

"Whaddya think, Doc?" Levy asked.

"It's not good. There's too much blood to tell how severe the damage is. It looks like he took several hard hits. His skull may be crushed."

"Boys, push that crowd back. Get this man outta here."

A moment later, an ambulance arrived and they loaded Lubelsky into the back. Pearlstine climbed in with him. The ride to the hospital was brutal for the patient. Every rut and pothole jolted the wagon. Lubelsky moaned, but nothing rose to the level of speech. Pearlstine used up the bandages he had, pulled out his own handkerchief and did what he could.

In the hospital, he shaved Lubelsky's head and irrigated the wounds. He'd been correct back in the store, the skull was fractured in three places. Three blows to the head, three severe gashes to the scalp with bleeding from the brain. Pearlstine and a nurse worked to stem the flow of blood, but Max Lubelsky died on the table.

Pearlstine's shoulders slumped as he stood over the dead man. He knew Max and his family. He knew as well that Max's wife and son were out of town. The rabbi would have to be contacted. His report would have to come later, based on the observations he made during treatment. Jewish tradition did not permit autopsies on its people. Also, burial was supposed to be accomplished within twenty-four hours. It was up to the rabbi to decide how to deal with the fact that he was murdered in Charleston while his family was away in New York.

The doctor went to the sink and ran water over his hands and up to his elbows. He was covered in thick, congealed blood. He looked over his shoulder as he scrubbed. He would let the nurse pull the sheet over his patient. It was too much of an admission of defeat for him.

"Nurse," he said, "please send a runner to Lubelsky's store with a note. Tell them Max died at 1:17 p.m."

The entire detective force of the Charleston police department stood in the middle of the store. In the center was Chief of Detectives James Hogan, 62 and past his prime, big, beefy, sweating profusely in the afternoon heat. He was head detective more by seniority than ability.

"Chief!" The shout came from the beat cop controlling the door. "There's a kid here with a note from the hospital."

"Send him in."

A young boy dashed in, breathing heavily, and handed Hogan a slip of paper.

"Boys, what we've got here is a murder investigation." Hogan's voice filled the shop and carried into the street, where it riled the crowd further.

"All right, fellows, gather round. Let's hear some facts. Levy, what you got?"

"It looks like a robbery, Chief. The till is empty. There's small change scattered around and the display window was pried open."

"That it?"

"From the looks of things, the struggle happened near the middle of the store, just about here. We found a hot pressing iron, that crowbar and hatchet and some bloody prints. Looks like Lubelsky tried to get up but couldn't make it."

"Okay, Brennan?"

"I talked with some of the folks around that morning. The fellow next shop over, Charles Levin, is telling everyone he saw a black man carrying a stick, hanging around his store this morning between ten and eleven. He says he approached the fellow, spoke to him, but got no response. Another fellow, Frank Frost, a black drayman, said he was at the store at 11:15 trying to deliver a package. A fellow met him at the door, claimed to be Lubelsky's porter, said he was watching the place while his boss stepped out. The drayman left, said he'd come back later."

"What's the description?"

"Negro male, 25 to 30 years old, clean shaven, about five and a half feet tall, light complexion, possibly mulatto."

"Okay, that's the suspect. I want you boys back at the station. I want bulletins and descriptions out to every department, deputy, train station, tavern, holdup and hellhole from here to Columbia. And, I want it done an hour ago. Work your contacts, boys. We need quick action. Chief ain't going to be happy with a colored killing a white in his town."

By the end of the day the detectives got their first hit. Police in Bamberg, ninety miles from Charleston, picked up a man fitting the description. He was spotted free riding a freight train out of Charleston. He was in custody, heading back to Charleston.

Charleston Police Chief William Boyle was pleased with the quick results. Still, it didn't make the last act of the day any easier. He sat at his desk, pulled out a telegram form and stared at the blank paper. He dipped his pen into the inkwell and started scratching.

Mrs. Rose Lubelsky,

Regret deeply to inform you that a tragedy has occurred. Your husband has been killed. You are needed in Charleston without delay. Return as soon as is practicable.

Chief William Boyle, Charleston Police

CHAPTER FOUR
Thursday
JUNE 23, 1910

The train pulled into Charleston in the heat of the afternoon. Rose Lubelsky stepped off wearing black. The color of mourning was not the color of choice in hot weather, just another burden for the young widow to bear. She was tired. Young Joseph was in a trance. The train trip had been brutally long, with nothing to fill the time but the dread of what lay before her.

"Rose!" It was the rabbi. "My dear Rose. Max was a good man, such a thing should never happen."

"No, Rabbi, murder should never happen."

"Of course. It is against God's laws. We have all been waiting for you to return. Poor Max must be buried today. We will begin sitting *shiva* tonight."

They had delayed the burial to accommodate her return. Sitting *shiva* was another part of religious tradition. Seven days of mourning would begin that night.

"Please take me to my husband, Rabbi."

Max Lubelsky had not been alone since his death. Friends or members of the synagogue sat with him, reading Psalms. When Rose entered, the *shomer*, or watcher, stood up and left Rose and Joseph alone to be with Max. She stepped to the closed casket, touched the cool smooth wood tenderly, turned and hugged her son.

"It's just us now," she said.

She glanced back to the door of the synagogue. People streamed in. Friends and acquaintances offered condolences. The rabbi got straight to the business of the funeral.

Voices were raised. Voices were lowered. She, as if mesmerized by the droning, stared at the box until someone touched her elbow. It was time to go. She followed the casket to the cemetery, watched while they returned her husband to the earth.

Friends brought her home above the store where her husband was murdered. Inside they lit a *shiva* candle. Mourners carried in food and everyone ate. When the last of them left, Rose found her son sleeping fitfully on his bed. She went to her bedroom, to *their* bedroom. His things were still on the dresser, just like hers. His clothes hung in the closet, just like hers. Everything was the same, except that Max wasn't there. Nothing would ever be the same. She lay down on the bed and rested her head on the pillow. Sleep came quickly, a gift from God.

In the days that followed, all seemed the same: somber friends, food, small talk, and always at the end she was alone. She heard from visitors that the police had arrested a string of suspects. One by one they were released. Police Chief Boyle had paid his respects. Charles Levin made a short, uncomfortably tense visit. Mrs. Dora Birlant, owner of the store across the street, told her she had seen Max and Charles Levin arguing on the morning of the murder.

Seven days the *shiva* candle burned, and when the time of mourning ended, Rose blew it out. The next morning, as she brushed her hair from her eyes, the bell rang. Rose looked out the window to see who was calling.

"Joseph, it's the rabbi," she called. "Please go down and let him in."

Joseph hurried down the steps and brought the rabbi into the parlor. Rose stood by the window. "Please go wash up and dress yourself, Joseph," she said. "We have many errands today. And put a comb through that hair."

"Please, sit down," Rose said, motioning to the rabbi.

The rabbi remained standing. "No thank you, Mrs. Lubelsky. I will not be long. There are things I must say and you must listen to."

Rose stayed near the window. The rabbi didn't remove his hat. They looked uneasily at each other.

"Mrs. Lubelsky, I pray God will be merciful to you and your son, but I have already heard many things that concern me."

Rose glanced out the window and fingered the hem of her apron. "What concerns you, Rabbi?"

"What concerns me, concerns all Jews in our city. Someone,

perhaps a colored, has broken the law in a horrible way. To murder a man is to go against the will of God. Yet there is dissension, even distrust among some of our people. Those Israelites, who for generations have lived here, do not understand our customs or habits. Harsh words have passed between many Jewish men over the very sanctity of the Sabbath.

"Mrs. Lubelsky, did Max have an enemy? What I mean is this, did you ever know of another Jew who taunted him or accused him?"

"I stay upstairs with Joseph. I don't know what happens in the shop, and I was away when he was killed."

"So you know of no one, Jew or Gentile, who would have reason to kill your husband?" The rabbi's words finally found meaning. Maybe whoever murdered her husband wasn't a Negro. Maybe he was even white. But a *Jew*?

"Rabbi, please tell me our people aren't at such odds that one could kill another?"

A long silence. Then the rabbi spoke. "Perhaps." He paused again.

"There is another matter, Mrs. Lubelsky, a matter of great magnitude. There is talk that you will run the business. Business is the work of men. Your place is to care for your son. You must reconsider your choices."

Rose looked directly at the rabbi. "I will take care of my son. I will do with the store what I please. Now leave my home."

He stared in silence, then descended the steps, his footsteps pounding all the way to the bottom. A moment later the front door slammed shut.

Rose was angry. But the rabbi's words had served one good purpose; they snapped her out of her sorrow. She would open the shop.

Rose started the morning of July 8 the same way Max started all of his mornings, sweeping the dust out the front door. When the broom crossed the threshold, she saw Charles Levin standing in front of his shop, broom upright and held with two hands so hard his knuckles were white. His eyes black.

"So, Rose Lubelsky, you defy the rabbi and our faith?"

"Mr. Levin, I am here to run my husband's business and provide for our son. If you want to talk about clothing or shoes or the weather, we can chat. If you want to talk about what you think I should do with my life, you can stand here and talk to yourself." She wheeled abruptly and went back into the store.

Rose turned her attention to the inventory in the store and was counting shirts when a man entered the store.

"Good morning," she said. "Can I help you?"

The man said nothing, but picked up some merchandise and brought it to the counter.

Rose wrote down the prices and added them up. "That will be eight dollars." She lowered her head to wrap the purchase in brown paper. Tying the bundle with twine, she looked up just in time to see the man's arm raised above her head. He held a wooden slat. Rose screamed as he smashed the board on her head. The impact drove her to her knees. Dizzy, she felt blood running down her forehead, but she was angry again. She thought of Joseph, and strength surged through her. She would not let this man make her son an orphan. She lunged and pushed the man backwards. It took him by surprise. He stumbled, giving her time to bolt for the door and the safety of the street. The man escaped out the door.

Rose screamed loudly. Holding her head, she collapsed in a heap outside the store, blood seeping through her fingers. She began to shake but forced herself to gain control. People rushed up the street in the direction of the commotion. Dora Birlant ran from her store and dropped to cradle the wounded woman.

Further down the street, Isaac Goldman and Moses Needle were in their tailor shop when they heard the screams. They ran out the door and saw a black man standing in the middle of the street, looking at the crowd growing around Rose. Together, they ran toward him.

At first, Nealy Duncan stood between the trolley tracks, puzzled. Commotion came from Lubelsky's, where he was going. With this morning's pay, he was going to make the last payment on the black suit he would wear to his wedding. Hearing foot falls behind him, he turned to see two merchants running toward him. He saw hate in their eyes, but by then it was too late to run. Both men grabbed him.

"We got 'em!" They shouted together. "We have the colored!"

Several men helping Rose to stand broke away, leaving Dora to tend her. Though wounded and bleeding, Rose had escaped the fate of her husband.

In the middle of the street, between the trolley tracks, the crowd thickened around Nealy, who made no attempt to break free.

"Get a rope! Let's hang this boy right here!"

Someone pushed through the crowd surrounding him and repeatedly punched Nealy on the side of the head. Other men broke from the crowd and dragged him to a lamppost. Another man ran up the street, swinging a length of rope.

Police Officer W. H. Stanley, walking his regular beat, was at the corner of King and Anne streets when he heard the ruckus. He ran to see what was about to be a lynching. Elbowing his way into the crowd, he pulled out his night stick.

"Back, ye heathens! Let go that boy before I smack somebody. What the hell is going on here?"

"That nigger boy attacked Rose Lubelsky." Needle yelled.

Goldman joined in. "I bet he killed Max!"

Another man in the crowd lunged at Nealy and got a night stick to the ribs.

"Back off. He's mine." Stanley knew he needed to get his prisoner off the street. With Nealy offering no resistance, the officer was more concerned about controlling the crowd. Stanley backed his way to the callbox and used his stick to keep the crowd at bay.

"Stanley!" A voice called from the mob. "Let 'em go and walk away! We'll save the city a lot of time and money!"

"Get back," Stanley barked. "This nigger is going to the station with me. Step back or we'll see how many Jews can fit in the wagon with him. Back off!"

The 'Black Mariah,' with its tall and imposing black walls, cut through the crowd. Two men rode shotgun, two others stood on the back step. The drivers spotted Stanley and pulled up near him.

"What the hell is going on here, Stanley?"

"We need to get this fella outta here."

The officers jumped down, clubs in hand, grabbed Nealy and threw him into the wagon, then climbed in behind him. As the wagon began to roll, a man in the crowd leapt up and threw a cobblestone through the bars, hitting the prisoner squarely in the back of the head. Nealy slumped, dazed by the blow. He stared at the floor of the wagon and didn't raise his eyes.

CHAPTER FIVE
Friday
JULY 8, 1910

Nealy winced, his eyes slamming shut as the rear doors of the Black Mariah swung open and the bright sunlight invaded the darkest space.

"C'mon boy, Chiefs got a few questions for you."

They grabbed his arms, half carrying, half dragging him into the police station. Nealy was hustled up a set of iron steps and into a small hot room. The heavy door slammed behind him. With a table and two chairs facing each other, the room was barely big enough to turn around in. He stood facing the door, his back to the table.

The door opened almost immediately. In its frame stood Chief Boyle and Detective Levy.

"Boy, sit yourself in that chair," Levy barked.

Nealy stepped backward to the chair on the opposite side of the table and sat. He was well dressed for a black man. Certainly not a vagrant, probably well employed. They noted some white powder on his pants.

"What's that?" Levy asked, pointing suspiciously.

"Flour."

"What's your *name*, boy?"

"Daniel Cornelius Duncan, sir."

Levy leaned across the table to grab Nealy by the collar.

"Why did you hit the Jew widow?"

Nealy looked at the table. "Sir, I didn't attack anyone."

Levy stood up straight, pounded his fist on the table. "She sure was bleeding, and you were the only nigger on the street, from what I hear."

No response.

"Empty your pockets." Nealy dropped a handkerchief, four coins and several envelopes onto the table.

"What are these?" Levy asked.

"Invitations," Nealy said, barely audible.

"Speak up, boy. Invitations to what?"

Nealy raised his head. His eyes met Levy's eyes. "My wedding."

That set Levy back for a second. He picked up an invitation and looked at it, scratched his head then laughed. "You might be a little late to the party."

The interrogation continued – Boyle barking questions. Nealy responding. The room was stifling hot; all three were sweating. Nealy's head throbbed from the cobblestone that hit him, but that was nothing compared to the terror he felt in the pit of his stomach.

Levy's fist came down on the table again. "Tell me about the attack on the woman."

"I said, sir, I don't know about that."

This time, Levy's hand swept sideways and slapped Nealy on the right cheek. It caught him off-guard, rocking him in the chair.

"Don't fuck with me, nigger. You don't know nuthin' about the woman? Then how about the Jew tailor you killed two weeks ago."

Nealy picked up his head and looked from one man to the other. "I didn't have anything to do with that. It's bad what happened to Mr. Lubelsky. He was a nice man."

Levy drew back for another swipe, but the chief touched his arm, stopping the swing before Levy wound up.

"Let's step outside, Clarence," he said.

"I'll be back, boy," Levy said, "and you better get your thinkin' done quick, because I ain't started working on you." He walked out and slammed the door behind him.

"He's not giving up much," Boyle said. "Get a detail together and take him over to the widow's house. See if she can identify him. But I want you to go out the back way, avoid the main street. That crowd was about to lynch this boy and I don't want your men to have to shoot a Jew to save a nigger so we can hang him ourselves."

Levy went to the top of the steps and shouted down. "Sean, John, pull the wagon around back and grab a couple of shotguns. Grab some shackles, too."

He went back to the interrogation room, yanking open the door with such force it slammed hard against the wall. "C'mon, boy." He grabbed Nealy by the nape of his neck and pushed him to the stairs. Two men stood at the bottom, one with a gun; the other with a pair of shackles. They clamped the chains to his ankles. The metal bit him, hard. Levy shoved Nealy. He stumbled. The two men grabbed him roughly under the arms and dragged him down a small set of steps, fairly tossing him into the back of the wagon.

Inside, the motion of the vehicle smoothed out and Nealy put his head in his hands. He was in shackles, had just been accused of attacking a woman and murdering her husband. He wanted to grab the bars on the window and shout for help, but that would only get him another beating.

He had no idea where he was being taken or what would happen to him. After a few minutes the wagon stopped. He could hear voices, but couldn't make out what they were saying. Minutes later the door swung open. Levy shoved his fist inside and grabbed him by the front of the shirt, pulling him through the shop doorway.

"Is this the boy who attacked you, Mrs. Lubelsky?"

Nealy blinked, looked up at the woman he'd seen run into King Street several hours ago. Her head was bandaged, blood seeped through one small gap at the top.

"Mrs. Lubelsky, please look at this man," Levy insisted. "Is he the one who attacked you?"

She glanced at Nealy and looked away. In a near whisper she said, "I wrapped the package and I thought he was about to pay me. When I looked, his hand was up, way up. Why didn't he kill me?"

Every face went from Rose to Nealy and back to Rose.

"Mrs. Lubelsky, is he the man?" It was as much a command as a question.

Without looking up, Rose Lubelsky said, "Yes."

Nealy was shoved back into the wagon. He heard the padlock snap, then the wagon began to roll. Detective Levy walked back into the store where detective Hogan had finished gathering the evidence.

"You got the weapon, Hogan?"

The cop showed Levy three pieces of wood found near the

counter where Rose was attacked. One was a two-foot length of split pine stove wood with blood and hair strands at one end. Levy took the wood with him and returned to the station.

Nealy was back in the interrogation room when Levy walked in and slammed the wood on the table.

"Seen these before, boy?"

Nealy looked at the wood, saw the blood and felt sick to his stomach.

"No, sir. Never."

Levy wound up. This time Nealy saw it coming, but could do nothing. The blow dazed him, knocked him sideways.

"One of us is either stupid or lying, or both and it ain't me. I got a woman who says you're the one who attacked her. I got witnesses who say they saw a black man outside the store the morning her husband was murdered. Can you do math, boy? I'm adding one plus one. What does that get you?"

"Two," Nealy said meekly.

"No. *One* boy, *one* hanging. That's all we need." Levy burst out laughing.

That night Daniel Cornelius Duncan was charged with the aggravated assault of Rose Lubelsky on July 8, and the murder and robbery of Max Lubelsky on June 21. He was transferred to the Charleston County Jail.

CHAPTER SIX
Sunday
OCTOBER 2, 1910

The hotel lobby was populated with the same oddball sorts you see in any upscale establishment in the world. There is generally a colonel who no longer commands troops, but will command any audience interested in any war in any part of history or the world. You find the professionals, women and men who sell social skills and sex and every game that has a price to play, passion on the discount side. Then there were the usual bird women, ancient crones who watch life's noisy parade like hungry hawks. No one goes unnoticed, no rumor unheard, and she knew something of everyone who passed.

On my way through the lobby, I was stopped by a genteel question.

"Good evening, sir. And how did you leave New York?"

"Missus ..."

"That would be Mrs. Vanderhorst."

She sat in a damask covered armchair, one arm on each rest, poised like a diminutive queen. Her silver hair was precisely coiffed. She wore pearls, was dressed as if headed out for the evening, but the chair was as far as she would go.

"Mrs. Vanderhorst, you would make a good reporter."

"Sir, *good* and *reporter* are two words not often connected."

"You malign my kind, ma'am. However, my compliments to your sources."

"Are you heading out tonight, sir?"

"It is my hope to see something of Charleston this evening."

"Then I hope you see something of its beauty, and not the sordid side you seek."

"Goodnight, Mrs. Vanderhorst."

"Goodnight, Mr. Hinson."

I walked slowly through the lobby, knowing her eyes followed my every move. She was something, right down to knowing my name.

I stepped out into the gaslit evening. Leaving the hotel's revolving door, I heard my name again.

"Mista Hal."

There he stood, all four feet of him. Eight years old and too worldly for his own good.

"Where have you been all day, Mojo?"

"Heah, and theah. Mostly theah."

"Ever the wise guy. Have you eaten?"

"Little biscuit dey hand out back of da bakery."

"Take me down to some place we can eat."

"We? You means both eat? *Together?*"

"Yes, together, at the same table in the same room. Does that happen here?"

"Funny ting bout dat, de white man can eat where he wants, it's jes the udder way round dat don' always work out too good. I takes you down to Miss Mary's."

We began walking. Everything in Charleston is within walking distance. Rich man's world to poor man's world in one easy stroll. Going from the one into the other, the gaslight glow disappeared. Light spilled sporadically from windows, a flash point when someone opened a door. The night signaled the start of entertainment in all forms. Tempting strains of jazz carried us down the street.

"Dis place be smokin' soon, Mista Hal. If'n you wants to have some fun."

"Maybe another time, Mojo. I'm not here to jump straight into the gin joints. It might be an idea to do something like work first."

"Good 'nuf, I's hungry anyway and heah it is."

We walked up the stoop of a simple framed house and through a screened door that banged behind us, no formal announcement necessary.

From the back a voice called, "You a bit late for suppa, but siddown. I'll be right there."

We sat at a table with two mismatched chairs. An oilcloth covered the simple pine plank surface. There was a noise around the corner and a woman whirled into the room stopping in her tracks.

"We don get many white folk after dark. And Mojo boy, what you doin' here?"

"Miss Mary, dis heah ain't no local fella. He's all de way from New York."

"You must be that reporter fella." Miss Mary tucked a towel into her apron. She was probably in her mid thirties but looked older. She was beginning to put on the pounds that come from too much time in the kitchen. She still had an attractive face and an air that commanded authority in her domain. A well-used apron covered her plain cotton dress.

"So, you da one here to cover dat murder trial?"

"Yes, ma'am, though I don't really know what I'm going to cover. From all accounts, the police have a suspect they're confident committed the crime, and all of Charleston seems ready to go straight to the sentencing."

"Dat may be," Miss Mary said, "and dat may happen, but it's too bad you sees it the same way. Cause dat boy sittin' in the jail up there was about to become my son-in-law."

My jaw dropped and I turned my head to Mojo, who sat with an impish grin on his face.

"You knew this?"

"We din come heah jes for da food."

It was the second time in a day I'd been suckered by an 8 year old.

"You two sit here while I get ya'll some food."

She was back in a minute with plates piled high with a stewed chicken and something green and something red.

"Oh Miss Mary, chicken an dumplin, collards and red rice and corn bread. I ain't used to dis."

But Mojo was familiar enough to dig into his food like someone was about to steal it. His fork moved from plate to mouth so fast it was a blur. I started eating as Miss Mary brought three glasses of tea and sat with us.

"Mista ..."

"Please call me Hal."

"Mista Hal, then. Nealy Duncan is an innocent man. I've knowd him since he was a boy and watched him for years, workin' hard, keepin' clean. You tink I let him take my Ida away if he was one of those boys who wasted his time and money on gin and happy dust? I been watchin' him like a hawk ever since he and Ida decided to get hitched. He dun nuthin' but work, save his money and see Ida twice a day, befo' he go to work 'n when he done. Nealy don have a mean bone in his body and he sho' ain't got no reason to kill no Jew. Deys gettin' married. I nevah seen two happier kids. Find da truth, cause nobody heah seems to care and my Ida's fixin' to be a widow befo' she even marries."

'What is Ida doing, Miss Mary? How is she reacting to all of this?"

"Oh, Ida, she jes a child. She don't understand what's happenin'. She don't know her Nealy is probably gonna hang, goin' to be murdered hisself. She bakes him cookies, fixes his dinna every day and sends it along with a note. Poor child, this whole thing will kill them both."

I finished my meal, regretting that such delicious food was spoiled by the story of Ida and Nealy. I took a sip of tea and looked at the long-cleaned plate in front of Mojo, who was now full and happy and maybe a little sleepy.

"Miss Mary," I said, "thank you for sitting with us and telling me your story. Thank you for the dinner. I can see why Southern food is held so highly. Do you think I might talk with Ida soon?"

"You can, if you promise not to make things worse."

"You have my promise. Could we meet tomorrow, perhaps around noon?"

"You come back heah for lunch, might'n be a bit more busy, but that means you keep it light."

"I'll see you then. How much do I owe you?"

"Not a ting. Jes try to help my Ida and her Nealy."

I slipped a few dollars under the plate as I stood. Mojo and I walked out the screen door, which slammed a farewell that sounded just like the greeting. We walked up the street.

"I've got some thinking to do, Mojo, and I do that better alone. Why don't you meet me at nine at the hotel. We've got some shopping to do on King Street. I think you could use a new suit."

"Good food *and* a new suit? You worth stickin' wid, Mista Hal."

"You earned both tonight. See you in the morning."

I crossed the border between black and white, re-entering the streets with gaslights and sidewalks. Here a softer glow painted these homes in perfect splendor. From behind high walls topped with spiked bars and embraced by vines, tall windows released rays that made their way to the street. Walking past Charleston's homes you could feel the barrier that separates *them* from *us*. "Us" being those not tied to bloodlines reaching back to the birth of the nation. It's a defining line of class, a stark separation that seems out of step for this city. In this light she was seductive, a little worn perhaps, a bit past her prime, but still radiating a tangible heat that made you want to fall into her arms.

I walked and began to feel this story turn. Tomorrow it would take on faces. I would meet the tragic, presumed widow-to-be, rather than a blushing bride-to-be. I had to find a way to get to Nealy. His was the face I needed most.

My pace must have accelerated with my thoughts. Moving down a high walled garden, my legs caught the inertia of my thoughts. I came to a corner and looked up just as I collided with a woman. When we bumped, I reached out to catch her hand as she stumbled slightly. Now, I stood back and looked at her face. For a moment, the breath went out of me. Her beauty was of the sort that drives men mad and few would deny the opportunity. I stepped back even more, but as I did I swear sparks flew from our parting fingertips.

"Madame, forgive me," I said. "I was lost in thought."

"I am not a madame, sir, except by insinuation, and you would not be a gentleman except by assumption, since I heard you muttering to yourself like some eccentric as you came around that corner."

I stammered. She gave no ground.

"Sir, you may indeed be mad, or simply have misplaced your capacity for speech. Around here, both are somewhat common, though crazy in Charleston is something of a refined art. Which are you, sir?"

I summoned composure, but barely.

"I am neither, ma'am, neither from around here, nor crazy. I am from New York, here to cover a trial. My name is Hal ...”

“Hinson,” she beat me to my own last name. “I’ve heard of you.”

“I can’t believe it. Does everyone in this town know about the Yankee reporter in town for the trial?”

“It’s a small town, sir, but I happen to know you from reading your newspaper.”

“You honor me. May I have the added honor of addressing you by name?”

“I am more accustomed to dishonor, but, as you wish. My name is Randy Dumas.”

“I seemed to have interrupted your walk.”

“If nearly bowling me over is interrupting ...”

“And, frankly, you returned the favor.”

“Amusing, Mr. Hinson. Walk with me, as long as your wit lasts. It is a rare evening to share engaging conversation.”

We continued down Meeting Street toward the park called The Battery. It was a warm evening, and the breeze from the harbor blew cool against us. I tried to keep my eyes forward, so as not to stare transfixed at her face. As we talked, I glanced at her, stealing the profile of a nose that was refined to the point of being royal, cheekbones set up high, and lips full to bursting. To look any lower was folly.

She wore her sex like a summer dress, lightly, clinging to her, flirtatious yet fixed. She was inseparable from her sensuality. Her breasts teased the material that covered her. My gaze slipped, she caught me and smiled.

“I have followed your stories and travels in Egypt with the former president.”

I was flattered, and intrigued that she seemed to be well-read beyond the bounds of her city. “There were no dull times with Teddy Roosevelt. He cut his own path and was admired by many, but had the occasional gift of rattling even our allies, as in Egypt with his comments on the assassination of Boutros Ghali.”

“But you travel the world, then return to New York only to be sent to Charleston, South Carolina.”

“Yes. That was my own mistake. Call it penance for angering an editor.”

"Join the company of those on the outs."

She stopped talking. I paid attention only to her. We had apparently walked down a lane and were standing in front of a very nice house, not quite the mansion quality of some of the others, but very inviting.

"This is my home," she said. "Would you care to come in for a glass of sherry?"

"I would come in for a glass of salt brine, if that's what you're offering."

We mounted the steps and the door opened from inside.

"Hello, Meredith," Randy said. "This is Mr. Hinson. We'll have sherry in the parlor, please."

The room was nicely furnished, somewhat feminine but not frilly. The floors were covered with Oriental rugs of good quality. The walls were lined with bookcases. They did not appear to be mere decorations.

We sat as the maid brought the sherry and left.

"You're a lovely woman," I said. "I won't risk embarrassing myself by taking that line any further. You are obviously well-read and have a wit that many would find imposing. Yet you invite a virtual stranger into your home. That seems a bit bold for this place, in this time."

"Mr. Hinson ..."

"Hal, please."

"Hal. You flatter me by noticing the things that mean the most to me, and neither have anything to do with my looks. I don't feel you're a total stranger, because I imagine I come to know those whom I read frequently. As to my place and time, I am not of this place and I would prefer not to be of this time. I come from New Orleans. You may recognize the name Dumas. I descend from a quadroon. Here most would consider me a whore, but in New Orleans, we are more like courtesans to the Creoles. It is a dying tradition, raising young girls to become the mistresses of the elite, but tradition in New Orleans runs deep. A young gentleman courted me. He was married, as is generally the case. We became involved.

"These arrangements are part of the working fabric of New Orleans. There was the wife, the husband and the mistress. It is

French. He was a lovely young man who spent a great deal of time with me, more than with his wife. There were said to be horrific fights. Then one day his papa came to visit me. He said his daughter-in-law threatened to ruin his son, to take their children unless he gave me up. Papa was a businessman. He made me an offer: leave town that day or he would make sure I was cast into the street to make a living in the most miserable fashion he could force upon me. It was a powerful offer."

"You took it."

"I had little choice. I came here and bought this house, but no amount of money could buy entry into Charleston. Here, it's okay to marry your cousin, but having a mistress, living with sex as a part of your life is unsavory. My past makes me unfit for Charleston's society."

"So, why do you stay?"

"This is where I am, for now. My circumstances forced me to become a businesswoman. No, I do not sell myself. But there are houses in this town where young women who would otherwise be on the streets have a warm place to stay. They offer services. I collect the "rent." And the pillow talk they collect has given me considerable sway over a number of the city's so-called gentlemen. Now, not only have I been forthcoming, I've been forward. Would you prefer to leave?"

I had never met a woman like her. She controlled her world and then some. I toyed with my sherry and unconsciously tossed back the final half glass. That seemed a signal to her.

"Then I'll show you to the door."

"I believe you're mistaken. I thought I'd pour another sherry, then we would continue our walk."

"I would love to join you for both." She smiled, sending a bolt right through me.

We retraced our steps to Meeting Street and turned into the breeze coming off the harbor. Spanish moss moved with the wind, gray ghosts hanging from the limbs of the ancient oaks. The sidewalks were strung with pools of gaslight like a long pearl necklace, each illuminating a different scene. We walked from light to light, and with each spotlight I stole a look at her. With each stretch of darkness I drank in her voice.

Light.

The lamps illuminate, she glows. There is a color to her skin that is unique, or it may be that it simply encompasses all, like the color white, a combination of all colors. She would not be considered white in Charleston. Her ancestry was far more exotic in texture, brown with a brilliant base. Here they would probably call her *high yellow*, seeing only her past and some crossing of black. Odd that in the visual spectrum, black is the absence of color. She cast her eyes on me, with green sparks like jade and all the mystery natural to the gem. Our eyes locked.

Darkness.

"Keep your focus," Randy said.

We walked in a short stretch of night.

"Tell me about Africa, when you were traveling with the President."

"I believe Africa even impressed Mr. Roosevelt. He awoke each morning like a child at Christmas."

"You mean the chance to hunt?"

"He was there on safari. You can't separate Teddy from the hunt, for game or for politics. He goes after both pretty much the same. He brought back a huge collection of exotic animals, stuffed mainly."

"And what did you bring back from Africa?"

"I suppose a sense of awe. Watching the sun rise over the African plain is like witnessing the beginning of the world. The sun is huge, primal, and rises like a god, awakening all of creation. The great beasts of the Earth are still there, still have some rule over their domain. It gives you a sense of place."

"Were you ever afraid?"

"Oddly, no. There you know almost everything around you can kill you, so you're on guard. It's places like here, where you can't see the teeth on the croc, that you really need to pay attention."

Light.

My words hung in the air as we walked into the lamplight.

I'm focusing, don't you worry about that, Miss Randy. On your hair. Brown, dark with hints of gold, falling to your shoulders. Curls, but something more natural about the way they frame your face than those silly ringlets of the society girls. And, you wear no hat. Your hair blows freely and lightly in the breeze.

Darkness.

"The danger here is disproportionate. If you live behind these walls, the beasts are held at bay. Everyone else is on their own. The only time in this town that all men are created equal is when nature comes calling – an epidemic, a hurricane, an earthquake – when all the petty privileges are put aside and Death has her way."

"Death is feminine?"

"Nature is feminine, like Justice is supposed to be."

As I turned to offer a semblance of wit, she caught her toe in the crack of a sidewalk and began to pitch forward. Instinctively, I shot a hand out to catch her and wrapped my free arm around her waist to stop her fall. As she fell, she spun around and we both froze. She was suspended two feet off the ground, my arm under her waist and our hands clenched above her head.

"You perform an effective tango, Hal."

"I'm only as good as my partner."

I lifted her back to vertical and we brushed and straightened our clothes. I blushed like a stupid kid and kept my head lowered as I offered my arm and we walked into the park the locals call White Point Gardens.

The park sits at the point of the Charleston peninsula. Here the oaks that line Meeting Street and flow to the park spread wide to offer a protective canopy, shielding the cannon and arms placed in tribute to those who defended the city from all foes, foreign and domestic. She indicated the ordinance with a brief nod.

"An indication of how Charleston sees herself in the world."

We arrived at a walkway that faced the water.

"To our right is the Ashley River," she said. "To our left is the Cooper River. If you're a Charlestonian, this point, where the two rivers come together, forms the Atlantic Ocean."

"A tad egocentric."

"Just a bit."

We looked over the railing at the harbor and at the Atlantic. It would have been an amazing place to watch a war begin in April of

1861, the first battle, with no casualties, just the euphoria of shells flying in a day's early light.

I turned to Randy. She gazed at the city, away from the harbor.

"There is so much that is beautiful in this town."

I leaned an elbow on the railing and she bent in my direction. I met her in the middle and our faces came close. I felt her hair on my cheek, smelled her scent. She lifted her head slightly and our lips touched, barely a kiss, but enough for us both to know.

"Perhaps you would be kind enough to walk me home."

"Only if you take my arm. No need for another tango."

We walked back through the park gently touching. At her front gate, we turned to face each other. She lifted on her toes to lightly kiss my cheek.

"I'll drop a note at your hotel tomorrow, Mr. Hinson. I might be able to offer some help in your efforts here."

"I hope a note isn't all I'll see."

"Doubtful."

She turned and walked up the steps.

The next morning I was up early, ordered coffee in the room, and scanned the local paper. When I was done, I went downstairs.

"Good morning, Mr. Hinson. A pleasant night strolling along the Battery?"

"You seem to know a lot about what goes on around this town, Mrs. Vanderhorst."

"There's not much that goes on in this little town that I don't know. You see, Mr. Hinson, I'm like an old spider, my reach is far and wide, and when anything moves in this town, it comes back to me in this chair, at the center of my web."

"You make yourself sound like a Black Widow."

"An unfortunate turn of the phrase, Mr. Hinson. You may have noticed a sensitivity about color around here. But Black Widow it is, if that is your choice, though I don't kill like the spider. Instead of blood, I simply suck information to live vicariously through the misadventures of others. I'm an old woman, Hal. I'm so brittle I can barely stand to walk across this hall, but once I could float a waltz across a ballroom. You may think I'm a bitter old biddy, biding my time, intruding into the lives of others. That may seem so, but I'm not bitter, just jealous of you and your youth. I am jealous of the young lady who shared your night. You walk with a lighter step this morning. They say love is uplifting."

I blushed, unable to resist. "I could give you details if you like."

"Don't taunt an old woman. Now hush up and sit down here. Tell that porter to bring us tea, and ask me the questions no one else in Charleston is answering for you."

I seemed to have little choice and sat like a Schnauzer, motioning the porter over to our public parlor.

"Tea for two, please, and some biscuits or something of that order."

"Yes, sir."

"Okay. Mr. Hal Hinson, Mr. New York City reporter, what have you learned in this lovely little town, about our ugly little murder?"

"Damned little."

"You're surprised even to find your brothers-in-journalism aren't rushing to help."

"I've had more doors slammed in my face than a Fuller Brush man."

"Did you really expect anything different? A *Yankee* comes to Charleston to cover the trial of a black man accused of killing a white man. Pardon us for not expecting a wholly objective observer. We are many things here, but we're not stupid, and we're not the stereotyped crackers you may have expected. Charleston has been here since before this country was a country. We have a history of arts, theatre and music, architecture and design, and religion. Look around you. What of this place is so base that we're perceived as barely evolved? We have endured wars, hurricanes, fires and earthquakes, and we will survive this breach of civility. I only ask you to do your job and report, don't judge. Now, what do you want to know?"

The old woman had me nailed, and she seemed to know a lot about almost everything.

"Let's start with what you know about the crime."

CHAPTER SEVEN
Monday
OCTOBER 3, 1910

The sun was high in the sky when I stepped from the hotel. Mrs. Vanderhorst had eaten up part of my morning, but filled me in on a lot of the details the local papers weren't mentioning. Most important was that, in the weeks after the murder of the tailor, no fewer than eleven suspects were detained, questioned, and then most were released. All were black men, differing in description and degrees of suspicion. Most were drifters and were suspicious for one reason or another.

"You late, Mista Hal."

"You don't get paid extra for being a clock, Mojo."

"Good clock might keep you from sleepin' late, or you get tired wid all dat walkin' down on da Battery las night."

"What the ..."

"Wid Miss Randy."

"Now how do you ... oh, never mind. It's a wonder there are any newspapers in this town. Word flies so fast around here, there's no reason to write it down."

I took a playful swipe at his head, which he dodged like Jack Johnson.

"You're quick on your feet. You ought to be a boxer."

"Nah, I'm too small to be a boxer. Sides, don't see much point in getting beat up for a livin'. I can get that for free."

"Where do you live?"

"Jenkins Orphanage."

"Your parents?"

"Mama died from the 'sumption. Papa, he was nevah around much. Think he might be in da jail."

"What's it like?"

"Deys pretty nice dere. Lotta kids. Dey can't keep up wid me."

"Not sure I can keep up with you, Mojo. You hungry?"

"Always hungry."

"Okay, then. Let's get over to Miss Mary's. We have a lunch date."

We walked back across the Divide, still in sight of Charleston's great mansions and the world that lives in their shadows. The street and houses that looked quaint in the dark now just looked shabby. Miss Mary's plain frame house drooped, its paint peeling. As we approached, the smell of food drew us like coyotes to a kill.

Bang. The screen door announced our arrival. Mojo and I stood in the entranceway. Heads turned to look at us – a portrait, lunchtime in still life. Forks were poised before open mouths, biscuits half buttered were held in mid-air.

"What you folks starin' at? Get 'bout your business." Miss Mary cut the silence like a fog-horn. "You two come on back here to da kitchen. Ida's waitin' for you."

The kitchen was warm. Big pots steamed on the stove. A pile of fried chicken was stacked on newspapers to catch the grease. In the corner by the door was a table for two, and Ida Lampkin. She was one of the prettiest young Negro women I'd ever seen. Her complexion was coffee with a dollop of cream. Ida wore a simple cotton print dress and a sense of composure. Her eyes were older. She looked at me with a steady gaze. Her focus didn't drop as I approached.

"Mojo, boy," Miss Mary said, taking control. Ida smiled. "You go out front and find you a seat. I'll bring you some food. These two need to talk." Mojo scampered away and she turned to me. "You two do your talkin'. Nevah mind me, I've got work to do feedin' these folks."

She stacked three loaded plates on her left arm, grabbed one more in her right and used her foot to nudge Mojo out the door.

"You're mom is quite a woman."

"There's not too many folk mess wid Miss Mary. She seems all business, but running people 'round is just her way."

"You know who I am, Ida?"

"You dat reporter from New York."

"And you know why I'm here."

"To write about my Nealy."

"Yes, to write about Nealy. When did you see him last?"

"The night before dey arrest him. He stop to see me on his way to work. We talked about nuthin'. We talked about the next day. He said he was going to go up to dat tailor's to get his suit. He said it was de next to last thing he had to buy before our wedding."

"What was the last thing?"

"Our wedding bed." She smiled, blushed.

"Oh, sorry." Maybe I blushed, too. "Did he ever talk about Max Lubelsky?"

"Just said he was a nice man. Measured him for his suit, treated him nice, let him pay on time."

"Did Nealy go there often?"

"He did all his bidness there, 'cept maybe for dungarees and his work stuff. He bought all 'is dress up stuff there."

"Did he say anything when Max was killed?"

"He was all upset, couldn't figure why anybody would kill dat nice Jew. Couldn't figure why any Negro man would kill him, 'cause he always let them pay on time."

"What about after he was killed?"

"He din know what to do. He only owed two dollars more on his suit. The store stayed closed for over a week. He thought he lost his suit, den he herd the wife was opening the store and said he was goin' to get his suit."

"That was the morning he was arrested."

"Yes, sir."

"Have you seen Nealy since then?"

"No. They won't let me. Say no women in the jailhouse. I send him a note every day, tell him I love him, I'll wait for our wedding. Mama lets me bake him cookies. I send him cookies. Mama sends him suppa."

"When is your wedding supposed to be?"

"Was suppose to be July 13. My wedding dress is hangin' in de closet, waitin' for de new day."

Her eyes were clear, still hopeful, and I imagined the pretty young girl in a white wedding dress. My thoughts lingered a moment too long, past the pretty scene, to the hard reality of a wedding that wasn't going to happen. I clenched my jaw and looked away. Miss Mary caught the look.

"You two done enuf talkin' for now. Mista Hal, you hungry?"

"Ah, no, Miss Mary. Not just now."

"Okay. You take dis tea and a hunk of cornbread and go on out front there and find that Mojo before he gets into some kind of trouble."

I took both in hand and walked to the door, turning to look back at the little table and the girl sitting there.

"Goodbye, Ida. I hope to see you again soon."

"Thank you, Mista Hal. I hope so, too." She smiled a sweet and brilliant smile that almost gave me hope. Then I started hating the world all over again.

I walked out to the front of the house, matching at least one surly look and feeling like a fight if one came. I wandered through two small rooms until I came to the front. At a corner table I saw Mojo, empty plate to one side, starting to work three half walnut shells on the flat table. A couple men had pulled chairs up closer.

"Mojo! Game's over. Let's go."

"Mista Hal ..."

"No talkin'. Let's get walkin'. You're either with me or you're not."

He swept the shells off the table and into his pocket, slipping past the men. One tried to grab his arm as he passed.

"Hey boy, gimme my money back."

"Mojo, outta here, now." He slipped behind me to the door.

The man moved to stand and I took a step toward him. Two men at the edge of my vision got up. It wasn't looking good.

"Whaddya boys think you're doin'?" It was the voice of authority. Miss Mary, saving my ass. "You dumb niggas, this man here is trying to help Nealy. What good is whippin' his ass gonna do? Since you're on your feet, shake hands with this man. He's Mista Hal Hinson from New York City, here to write about the trial."

My fists went from clenched to outstretched. Instead of trading punches, I found myself shaking hands. I walked out on wobbly knees. I was glad that screen door was the only thing that hit my ass on the way out.

I put my hand on the back of Mojo's shoulder, a little on the firm side.

"If you're gonna be with me, cut the con. You ever pull that kind of thing on me again and we're through. Gimme those shells."

I took them and threw them into the street in front of me, making a show of crushing one under my heel.

"Sorry, Mista Hal. I was jest tryin' to make a little money."

"Money, is it? I think you just like having the upper hand. If it's money, here's the deal. You're working for me now. You get fifty cents a day, and you eat when I do. But you better be on the up and up."

"Heah on out, I straight as a deacon, Mista Hal."

We walked for a few blocks, then hopped a trolley headed uptown. As we moved up King Street, a different kind of city opened up. The storefronts were less ornate, the pedestrians more mixed. It became more blue collar the further north we went. When we got to the 500 block, customers coming in and out of stores were both black and white. I stopped in front of 543 King. The sign still read, "*Max Lubelsky, Clothier.*"

We walked in.

"Good afternoon, sir. May I help you?" A man walked from the back.

"The sign out front says Max Lubelsky. Are you Max Lubelsky?"

"Not unless I'm a ghost. What kind of question is that? Are you here to buy a suit, or here to talk about a murder?"

"Maybe both, my name is Hal Hinson. I'm with the New York Tribune."

"Ah, the big writer. So you're from New York. Where do you live?"

"Upper West Side, on 72nd."

"Columbus?"

"Central Park West."

"Oh, Mr. Fancy Schmancy. So you're no starving writer living in that big apartment."

"Actually, just lucky. When I first moved in, it was considered so far uptown, they called it the Dakota, like it was another territory. You seem to know a lot about New York."

"I used to live there. My name is Abe Price. My brother Sam owns a bakery on Columbus."

"Up on 85th?"

"You know the place?"

"Best knish in town."

"*Oy vey*! What a small world. Okay, Mr. Hal Hinson, sit down and let's talk."

"Why don't we talk while my young friend here gets a suit."

"Excellent. Young man, what would you like?"

"Sumptin' make me look tall."

"Ha! Then we should try something in a stripe."

As he measured Mojo, he filled me in on the area of upper King Street, Little Jerusalem and the merchants who ran the shops. He had taken over Lubelsky's after Rose was attacked. She had moved away from town to recover. She tended chickens and sold the eggs.

"It was pretty tough," Price said. "All Negroes were under suspicion. Regular customers weren't so regular. I heard the cops pressed the darkies pretty hard to find someone. Then Rose was attacked and they picked up that Duncan fellow. Things have quieted down now."

"What about in the Jewish community?"

"What about it?"

"There is talk of tension in the community."

"Our people go back to Abraham. It is an ancient religion. God is perfect. Man is not. We all suffer for that. But Jews do not kill Jews. It is against God."

"Murder isn't *kosher* in any faith, but it happens."

"The police have a man, caught by two men right on the street. He's a Negro, not a Jew. Let the law have its way."

"That seems to be the sentiment around here."

"God's law, Man's law, who am I to judge? Now, your young friend here is all set. I've got his measurements and his suit will be finished in two days."

"That's pretty quick. Thanks. How about we get some pants, shirt vest and a pair of shoes for him now."

He gathered up the different items and put them on the counter.

"Go put these on," I said to Mojo. "Let's walk out of here in style."

"Yes, suh!" He headed for the back.

"How much do I owe you?"

"Suit, pants, shirt, shoes ... twelve dollars, and you can pick up the suit on Wednesday."

"Thanks. The trial begins Thursday, and I'll be a bit busy after that."

"You'll find a lot of shops on this street closed that day, too."

Mojo sauntered from the back of the shop, proud in his new clothes. He tried to suppress a smile, but it broke free before he got to me.

"Lookin' good, Mojo," I said. "We'll make a gentleman out of you yet."

"Not sure I wants dat, fum what I seen round heah. But now we looks like we belong together."

And we did, in a strange way. A lanky, strawberry blond of English descent and a short, street-smart descendent of slaves. I put a hand on his shoulder and we walked out the door together.

The afternoon sun softened the edge of the day as I walked back into the hotel. In the lobby, the cute girl with energetic eyes called from behind the desk.

"Mr. Hinson! A message for you."

I smiled, which pleased her, took the note and opened it. A faint, familiar scent drifted up to my nose and my heart picked up a few beats.

Dear Hal,

If you would be so kind as to join me for dinner at my home this evening. I have something of interest to offer.

Seven o'clock.
Randy

A few thoughts shot through my mind. I dismissed most of them. I was smiling when I looked up. The desk clerk watched me, a little less sparkle in her eye and a pout on her mouth.

"Thank you, Miss Pope."

"You know my name?"

"It's on your name tag."

"Oh." The pout appeared again.

"But thank you very much. It's very kind of you to help me."

Bright Eyes was back. She was a puppy who needed petting.

In my room I stripped and climbed in the shower, alternating blasts of hot and cold to jolt my senses. When I stepped out, I was ready for a few rounds in the ring with a heavyweight. I pulled on my best double-breasted sack suit coat and topped it with a burgundy repp tie. It was about the best I could do at the moment. I didn't pack formal wear to cover a murder trial. I poured sherry from the decanter by the window, and looked over the rooftops at the setting sun. This town was taking hold of me.

I didn't have time for a cross-examination tonight, so I dodged the parlor perch of Mrs. Vanderhorst. Outside, the evening breeze held a hint of autumn. It was hard to keep the pavement beneath my feet as I walked the few blocks down Meeting Street. I flew up the stairs and rapped with the brass knocker. The door opened by a trim Negro woman.

"Good evening, Mr. Hinson. Miss Dumas is waiting for you in the parlor."

Randy stood next to the fireplace. To most people, her pose might seem affected, but standing or sitting made little difference. She could neither create nor escape her aura. She wore a Poiret gown, loose and flowing with a high waist, appropriate in Paris, probably unseen in Charleston. Her dress was as free of corsets and confinements as her mind was of conventions. The neckline was cut off her shoulders, leaving a brilliant expanse of skin from neck to breast. Her hair was worn up to enhance the view. She smiled devilishly. She knew what she was doing to me.

"Hello, Hal. Cat got your tongue?"

"Excellent, Randy. You're playing me like a Stradivarius, and you know every note. For my next act, I'll strap myself to the mast and you can sing enchanting songs."

"Fair Odysseus, I mean you no harm."

"Nevertheless, don't expect me to try to resist your charms."

She flowed across the room and kissed me lightly on the cheek.

"Please don't resist," she said and I didn't. "Now let's walk into the dining room. Meredith has been working all day on our dinner."

I caught a flash of heaven, and this was it. She took my arm and led me from the parlor across the main hall and into the elegant but simple dining room. A mahogany dining table, that could easily seat twelve, was set for two. Instead of sitting at opposite ends of the table, our places were set side by side. A candelabra glowed from the middle of the table. Candles in sconces along the walls shed added illumination. Light reflected off the wine glasses. Each place was set with three glasses and flatware for several courses, not settings for a simple supper. At the head of the table, I pulled the chair out for Randy, but she walked to the other chair, pulled it out for herself and sat. I was just in time to help ease her chair up to the table, just in time to help myself to a very brief scent of her cologne.

"You should be sitting at the head," I said. "It's your house."

"It is, and so it's my choice where I want to sit. Please take your chair. Meredith has oysters Rockefeller and champagne to start."

"You've gone to too much trouble. We could have dined out."

"I'm from New Orleans, remember? Eating is not trouble, it's life. And dining out was no option. The food here is barely evolved from the Civil War. They have great ingredients, from the earth and the sea, but they don't have the French touch."

Meredith came in from the kitchen with two plates and placed them before us. A young man followed, wearing a dark jacket and white shirt, carrying a bottle of 1899 Perrier-Jouet. I sat up a slightly in my chair. He poured with a tentative hand.

"Thank you, Markus." When he left, she explained. "He's Meredith's son and helps around the house. Wine service is something he's still learning."

"He's learning with a very good vintage." I sipped, savored and smiled.

"Tell me what you learned today."

I told her about lunch with Ida, about the hope in her eyes and the plans she was still making, and the notes and cookies sent to the jail. Even in the telling, it all sounded so innocent, and that was without Ida's sweet smile. Randy was not smiling.

"I know Miss Mary's protecting her," she said, "but that's going to make the reality a crushing blow when she finds out she'll never see Nealy again this side of the river Styx. They'll never let her inside the jail and God forbid anyone lets her see him after he's hanged."

She went silent for a moment. Something was going on inside her head that she wouldn't talk about, and I wasn't going to ask. Her eyes narrowed a bit and her finger traced a tiny circle on the top of the crystal flute, making a harmonic note which she prolonged without paying attention. After a moment, she lifted her finger and came back, a slight smile on her lips.

"Excuse me, Hal. Something came to mind. We can discuss it later. Let's move on to the next course."

As if on cue, Markus appeared and removed the plates and champagne glasses. Meredith followed with the second course.

"This puts a little Creole on the table, Mister Hal," she said. "It's crawfish etouffee. Finding enough crawfish around here for a proper etouffee isn't easy. Markus finally found some Cajuns who set up a little stand in the market."

"It looks lovely, Meredith, and the smell is wonderful. It fills the room with an earthy perfume."

She smiled at the compliment. Markus followed with more wine, this time a sturdy burgundy that held its own against the seasonings. His hand was a little more steady on the pour.

Randy ate with delicacy, enjoying her food. I had to show restraint. The food was so good, I was close to fanning it into my mouth, Mojo fashion. I described our trip to Lubelsky's and Mojo's shopping excursion.

"It sounds like you're growing fond of your little man."

"He's an amazingly sharp fellow. It's hard not to like a kid who is surviving on his wits at such a young age."

"Seems like he's touched something in you."

"The most frightening thing about a woman is her intuition. Yes, there is a common cord. He's an orphan, growing up without a father. I wasn't an orphan, but my father was not very involved in my life. He was brilliant and dedicated to his job, building his buildings and his empire. He gave me everything, except his time."

"It would be kind of hard to compare the life of a young street urchin to yours."

"All children have the same basic needs, and the most important of those is love."

"Don't let the little thief steal your heart. Others may want a part of that."

"You needn't worry."

I went on to describe the talk with Abe Price, the tailor who now ran Lubelsky's shop. She laughed at the New York connection, but her eyes took on a narrow look as I described the tension in the Jewish community.

"That's a hard one to figure." Her finger went back to the rim of her glass. "They're a very tight community, as hard to penetrate as any other part of Charleston society. This whole business-on-the-Sabbath thing has sparked talk, even outside the Jews."

"He certainly went cool when we were talking about that. I don't know what to make of it. Tension, yes, but I'd have to agree with him on one point: Jews aren't in the habit of killing Jews."

"Religion has killed more people than money, Hal."

She had a point.

The kitchen door opened and Meredith entered with our third course, a serving dish she presented first to Randy and then to me.

"Chateaubriand, Mister Hal. It's not necessarily New Orleans, but it's one of our favorites."

She served us plates of small slices of tenderloin, then spooned *sauce bernaise* over the meat, and finished the dish with small potatoes roasted to perfection. Though we had each only sampled a glass of the Perrier-Jouet, Markus followed with another bottle of wine, which he presented to Randy first. I looked at the label. Chateau Lafite 1899.

"I am not worthy, Randy," I said. "This is marvelous and a tribute to your taste and wisdom if you've laid in any of the '99 or '00 vintages."

"I saved some for rare occasions, or rare people. Tonight matches both."

Murder is a topic unfit for so fine a wine, so we talked of more pleasant things. Randy favored Impressionism in art, and the classics in novels. She had read Homer, and was also fond of Flaubert, Frankenstein, Hamlet and, to blush, Tom Jones.

"The prudish would call it pornography," she said, "but most homes keep a dog-eared copy, thumbed by generations of men in the household. It's hypocritically hush-hush, but in fact it's just a silly romp."

No argument.

She dismissed the New Age notions spun by Madame Blavatsky, the theosophists and the so-called Spiritualists. "In Louisiana," she said, "trying to get, or stay, in touch with the dead is an old rite. Voodoo, occultism, whatever you want to call it, is simply acknowledging that there is a life spirit, an energy that exists after death. *There are more things in heaven and earth, Horatio, than are dreamt of in your philosophy.*"

I sipped the wine, savoring. The door opened again. Meredith and Markus swept the table clear and returned with dessert and a silver coffee service. I groaned.

"Now, Mister Hal, you can't end a New Orleans dinner without something sweet. Cherries jubilee and chicory coffee is the best way to end a meal."

Randy glanced from Meredith to me and smiled.

"So," I said, "is this what your note suggested? *Something of interest to offer?* Four courses of the finest dinner I've had in years. Meredith, my compliments to you and Markus. You are truly amazing."

Both Meredith and Markus smiled broadly at the compliments, then left us alone to our coffee.

"Actually, Hal, dinner tonight was just dinner. I hope this is not a rare occasion in the future. It, of itself, was not the 'something of interest.' *That* is an interview. I have arranged for you to talk with Nealy Duncan at the jail tomorrow morning at 10 a.m."

My eyes grew to saucer size. Only clenched teeth kept my jaw from dropping. Randy smiled.

CHAPTER EIGHT
Tuesday
OCTOBER 4, 1910

I woke up early. The sun backlit a grey morning. Clouds hung low, threatening rain. It was a perfect day for a foul mood. The opportunity to interview Nealy Duncan was nothing short of a miracle. Randy must have thick files on key politicians to have such clout. It didn't make me feel any better. Coffee was brought early and I downed enough to make my hands shake. It was too soon for the interview, but I threw on a topcoat in case it rained and headed for the lobby. My hands were deep in my coat pockets, my mind was buried just as deep in thought as I walked through the lobby.

"Good morning, Mr. Hinson."

If I could have spun around and kicked myself, I would have. Twice.

"Good morning, Mrs. Vanderhorst. I'd love to stay and chat, but I'm off to an important interview."

"Yes. With that Duncan boy."

I paused, looked straight at her and saw a hint of a smile, then turned, smacked my forehead with my palm and walked on.

Mojo saw me come out the hotel door and caught his hello halfway. He saw it was no morning for jokes and fell in beside me. We walked in silence for several blocks before the solemn little man began to amuse me.

"Good morning, Mojo."

"Good morning, Mista Hal."

"You seem to know where I'm going."

"Yes, suh."

"I'm not even going to ask."

"Mista Hal, I got sumpin' for you." He reached into the pocket of his new vest and pulled out an envelope. On the front, in a feminine but informal hand, was written, *Nealy*.

"What's this?"

"A letter from Miss Ida. She asked me to gib it to you to gib to Nealy."

I took the envelope, thought about Ida sitting at Miss Mary's table, and put it in my breast pocket.

Nealy's trial was two days away. I hadn't met any bookies in Charleston, but the odds were not in his favor. He'd been in jail just shy of three months and had yet to see his lawyer. The prosecutor, on the other hand, was well ahead of the game. John Peurifoy was well-connected, handpicked for the case because of his almost perfect record of convictions. He began working his case just days after Nealy was arrested. According to the local papers, he held weekly meetings with his staff to canvass witnesses and review evidence. He was smart enough to let the local papers in on his progress, and made sure everyone knew that a conviction was all but guaranteed. Peurifoy played this case for all the publicity he could get. He had political aspirations.

Nealy's attorney was just the opposite. He shied away from the press. Brice Matthews was a Charleston lawyer with a good reputation among his Broad Street brethren, but had been assigned this case over his protests. He was odd man out in the selection process. At best, the case was considered indefensible, acquittal was political suicide. Matthews performed no preliminary interviews, met with no witnesses and refused to answer all reporters' questions.

Then there was the reward. Right after the murder, offers from the city, the business community and even the governor, for the arrest and conviction of the killer grew to seven hundred and fifty dollars. All sentiment favored giving it to the arresting officer and detectives on the case. Even split up, it was a sizable sum for a city cop. It would also throw considerable weight to ensuring the police produce the evidence needed to make the case stick.

I didn't need a bookie. I'd be more likely to bet a lame horse in the Derby than to lay money down on Nealy's future.

Mojo tugged on my sleeve.

"Mista Hal, you's 'bout to walk pass de jail house." Mojo pulled me out of my trance and pointed to a three-story building cast from the mold of dungeon architecture inspired by centuries of incarceration. It was tall, stone and had bars in every window. Clouds drifted across the sky and the building seemed to descend from their grayness.

I walked up to the open door. Inside, a guard sat at a desk.

"I'm Hal Hinson, here to interview the prisoner Daniel Duncan."

"Yeah, I know who ya are," the guard said. "Go on up, third floor."

It seemed a bit casual, but I went up. It was an odd mix of metaphors: you ascend into heaven, descend into hell. I walked upward, coming closer to the depths. By the time I got to the third floor, I could barely breathe from the stench of confinement. Okay, that's being polite. The fetid stink of unwashed men, acrid urine and worse. I retract any aforementioned preference for the stench of Man. The only thing missing in the jailhouse air was rotting human flesh. But then, you stand in the presence of rotting lives.

"Nealy." I called. "Nealy Duncan?" Heads in a half dozen cells turned, one didn't. I walked to him.

"Nealy?"

"Yes."

"I'm Hal Hinson with the New York Tribune." He was a well-built, lanky young man in dirty clothes and in need of a bath.

"Mr. Hinson, I apologize for my state and poor furnishings." Nealy motioned to a chair in the corner.

I pulled the chair up next to the bars and sat. Nealy had little for comfort in his cell. He appeared to sleep in a hammock; there was a chair and a small table. On the table was a Bible. He turned to face me and I noticed a scar that ran from his ear across his cheek. He noticed my stare.

"It's a burn from a clumsy baker years ago. He was drunk. After the accident he was fired. In a way it opened a new door for me. My boss gave me the baker's job."

"Sounds like a painful but positive twist of fate."

"I'm not big on fate right now."

"Of course. You speak like, ah, you don't sound like most folks I've heard here."

"You mean I don't sound like a Negro?"

"To be frank, yes."

"What you hear, Mr. Hinson, are Negroes speaking Gullah, an odd blend of languages from the islands of our past. What you hear now is, again, thanks to my boss, Mr. Geilfuss. He taught me to read and pressed me to speak what most consider a better form of English to our customers at the bakery. I guess you can say I'm bilingual." He paused. "Oh, Law, I sho don know bout killin' no Jew, suh. I ain't ah-tack no one."

"I see. That must make you stand out somewhat."

"It's a matter of choosing when to use which. In some quarters, my use of proper English could earn me a beating."

I reached inside my jacket. "Nealy, I brought you a letter from Ida." I handed it to him through the bars. He opened the envelope carefully, held it to his nose, then pulled the single sheet out and began to read. It was a short note. His eyes went over it once, then again. My eyes went to the floor, the ceiling, the other cells, anywhere but his face. I looked back when he folded the letter and placed it between the pages of his Bible.

"She said you are a good man and that I should be honest with you. So, Mr. Hinson, what does New York City care about this poor boy in Charleston?"

We started at his beginning. He was born in 1887 to a father who had been born into slavery on a Charleston plantation. After the war his father migrated to the city, working in the stables to support his family.

"My father always had a way with horses, even the mean ones. Some horses would come into the stable, whipped and with the white showing in their eyes, they were so afraid of humans. He could calm them. There was one horse that had been in a stall for weeks. The owner would just walk in the front of the barn and the horse would go crazy. If he went close to the stall, the horse would turn into a demon, ears back, teeth bared. Once the man went into the stall. He carried a whip with him. The horse shrank into the corner, trying to be as small as it could, as the man raised his hand and went to raise the whip. The horse lunged out and sank his teeth into the man's shoulder, picked him up and threw him against the wall. My father pulled the man out just before the horse's hooves came down where his head had been. The man told my father he could shoot the horse or sell him, he didn't care which. Day by day, he would stand outside the stall until the horse no longer shrank to the corner. Then one day he went inside and stood in the corner. After a couple of weeks the horse would come to him for the grain he held in his hand. My father saved that horse and sold him to a nice family."

"Sounds like your father knew the value of patience."

"I never saw him angry. He always said that anger was a luxury only rich men could afford, because in the end it always cost you."

"He worked hard in the stables taking care of other people's horses. Sometimes he would take a hard luck horse and save it from itself, or its owner. People came to hear about his ways and he made extra money fixing horses. It helped our family, he was able to buy a small house on Society Street where we lived."

"Then why were you both living in a tenement on Vanderhorst Street?"

"When I was a young boy, the fever hit Charleston one summer. It had been hot and rainy for weeks. Most of the whites would leave town and go up to the mountains. They say it's cooler up there and almost always free of the fever. Charleston could be a ghost town in the summer. That year the fever started in July. When it came, most of the remaining whites fled. Those who stayed were those who had no place else to go, the Negroes and poor whites. For a short while, everyone became almost equal. Those who were well took care of those who weren't. Days went by and we thought we were going to be fine. First my sister got sick, then my mother. We sat with them and tried to keep them cool. After a couple of days, they seemed to be getting better. One night we were sitting on the porch, there was a light breeze and the evening felt almost nice. My mother stood up, then fell to her knees and vomited. It was black. She and my sister both got very sick, very fast. What happens to a person at the end, I won't even say. To this day, I try to forget their last hours."

He fell silent. His eyes focused on the floor, then to the window and upward to the sky.

"There wasn't any proper burial. So many people were dying. We wrapped them and put them on a wagon to carry to the cemetery. My father and I buried them ourselves. All the gravediggers were too busy digging big pits. A lot of people were just heaped in a pile and burned. Those pyres were set at night. When the wind shifted and blew the smoke toward Charleston, it was a smell straight from hell."

"We returned home. My father spent two days cleaning the house. Then he packed our bags and we moved to rooms in the tenement. He never went back to the house, but rented it to another family. He went back to work, back to his horses, but people seemed to mean less to him after that. A year or so later I got the job at the bakery and Mr. Geilfuss became a second father to me."

"Did that happen from the beginning?"

Nealy laughed, it echoed oddly through the jail, "No, Mr. G. can be a tough boss. I swept floors and did all the dirty work for over a year, before he really started noticing that I paid attention, showed up on time and did my work, and then some."

"So, you didn't really have a childhood?"

"It's a little different for colored folk. Having food and a place to sleep comes first. I was lucky to have a job with a man who took interest in me. He taught me to read, that took me places where most of the kids I knew never went. I worked, went home, read books and saved my money. I was a loner until I met Ida."

"How did you meet?"

"At a church picnic. My father continued to go to church after my mother and sister died. Sometimes I wasn't sure whether it was God or the horses that gave him the strength to go on. He tried to get me to go, too, so that I would have some life outside of work and books. This one Sunday in spring, just over a year ago, I went to a picnic down by the river. After the baptizing in the water and service was over, the women started setting food out on tables beneath the oak trees. There was one young girl fussing over the food. Her laughter seemed everywhere. It floated from the branches and carried down to the river. I couldn't take my eyes off of her. She was Ida. When I got the courage up to walk up to her, she just looked me in the eye and smiled. We both knew at that moment that we'd be together always."

He stopped talking, reached over and picked up the envelope that carried her note, pressed it to his nose and then kissed the paper. I kept my silence.

"That Miss Mary," he smiled and started talking again. "She wasn't too sure about me. We all rode back that first night in my father's wagon. The moon came up full and Ida and I sat in the back. We couldn't stop talking. The moon was almost as bright as day and I watched her face the whole way home, how her laughter came not just from her mouth, but from her eyes. From that night, I knew all the sadness in my life was in the past, at least until a few months ago."

That statement hung in the air, as real as the fetid jail cell where he now sat.

"Can you tell me about the day you were arrested?"

"Oh, I could describe it in more detail than you'd care to hear. I've thought about that day, every day, since I landed in this jail. What was different? But mainly, why was it any different? The morning was the same as thousands before it. We baked all night, got the early deliveries out and set the display counters and baskets with the fresh breads from the later batches. Some mornings Mr. G. makes some of what he calls 'small bread' that he and his wife like for breakfast. He and I sat just before sunrise at a small table and ate the rolls with coffee before the first customer arrived. I went back into the bakery and mixed the dough to be ready for the evening baking. After that, I cleaned the kitchen and stepped out the door. That was the morning I was going to pick up my wedding suit. The store was open again after the murder of Mr. Lubelsky. The sun was already hot. I was walking on the east side of the street in the shade of the buildings. Part way up King Street, I slipped my jacket off and folded it over my arm. I always put my jacket on to leave the shop. Mr. G. expects me to look respectable. When I was coming close to Lubelsky's, I stepped off the sidewalk and walked to the middle of the street. That's when I heard screams and stopped dead in the middle of the street. I saw a woman run out of the shop and fall in the street. People started rushing toward her, then I heard a man yell and saw two men running toward me. Everything else happened so fast, it's all a blur. I remember getting hit a couple of times and then being thrown into the police wagon."

"Did the police interrogate you?"

"Some big Irishman came into the room with the chief, called me nigger this, nigger that, smacked me a couple of times, then accused me of killing Mr. Lubelsky. They threw me back in the Black Mariah and took me to the store. When they pulled me out, Mrs. Lubelsky was there all agitated. Her head was bandaged and eyes looked strange, like she was dazed. The cop asked her if I was the one who attacked her. She was talking some nonsense. Then he almost yelled, 'Is *he* the man?' She said yes.

"Until that point, I thought the whole thing was some terrible mistake and the authorities would see it for what it was. But riding back to the jail, I looked out the window like I was seeing the street for the last time. That night they charged me with murder and brought me here."

"Have they questioned you since?"

"No. They've taken me out to stand in a line with some other men."

"Did they treat you any differently then?"

"They made me put on a hat and a coat."

"Were the other men dressed like that?"

"No."

"Have you seen a lawyer since you've been here?"

"No."

"How have they been treating you?"

"Since I've been here, not too bad. They let food come in and I get Ida's letters. Which, if you don't mind Mr. Hinson, could I borrow your pen for a moment?"

I handed my fountain pen that I'd been using to make notes through the bars. He took a scrap of paper from between the pages of his Bible and wrote a couple of lines.

"If you would be kind enough to get this note to Ida. It's been a bit difficult for me to get messages out to her."

"Anything I can tell her for you?"

He thought for a moment, "To have hope, not hate."

DATELINE:
Charleston City Jail, October 4, 1910
Hal Hinson | New York Tribune

In an eight by eight foot cell in this old city, a young man sits.

His name is Daniel Cornelius Duncan, a 23-year-old black man accused of murder and assault. The component of the crime that bodes ill for young Duncan is the fact that the victims were white. In this Jim Crow South, segregation is the law of the land. Negroes do not eat with whites, drink with whites, marry whites or, as young Duncan will find in the days to come, lightly stand accused of killing whites. The crime would be no less heinous if he had, but his future would be less in question "if" he had killed a person of his own race.

The bars that separate him from society are not as much to protect us from him, but to protect him from us. A mob came close to providing the citizens of this fair city with a lynching on the day of Duncan's arrest.

Here is a young man who has risen in the respectable trade of baker, who reads and speaks in an educated manner, and who, but for a costly morning stroll, would lead a far different life today.

On a June morning in Charleston, a Jewish merchant was murdered. Witnesses reported seeing a Negro near the store at the time of the killing. The murder of a white man by a black man sent scores of police out in search of suspects. In the following days, they came up with many and released as many. Seventeen days later, the murdered man's wife was herself attacked, according to her own account, by a Negro. As she ran bleeding into the street, the gathering crowd spied the one Negro standing. He was Daniel Duncan.

I make no case here. The full facts, such as they will be represented, will unfold in two days time. What is different in this trial, what is both perplexing and tragic, is that the city, its populace, and the man accused are acting in an exceedingly polite manner. The initial anger is to some degree restrained. The lawyers speak of justice, but the accused speaks very little. The prelude to this trial unfolds with the stylized motions of kabuki theater.

Daniel Duncan sits in his cell facing a trial that could end with his hanging. He shows neither anger nor angst. He is a picture of quiet dignity. In his eyes is a simple sadness, in his voice there is no hatred. He only speaks of a love unfulfilled.

On the morning of his arrest, he went to the tailor shop to pick up his wedding suit. Five days later he was to be married.

This morning his bride-to-be sent a letter to his jail cell. She is still planning on a wedding. She is sixteen.

I filed the report at the telegraph office. I could have called it in, but I didn't want to talk to anybody in New York. They clamored for copy and the trial hadn't yet started. There were things I didn't write, not yet. It's hard to describe the stench of the cells, the sight of a man wasting in body and heart after three months locked in a box. The furnishings were sparse, his only comfort were the meals and notes that came daily from his family – the food was roundly pilfered and the notes, through simple neglect, often didn't get to their destination. He showed sterner stuff than I, because I felt rotten through-and-through.

It was late afternoon and I walked back to the hotel, a drink was on my mind.

"Mr. Hinson!" called Bright Eyes from the desk. "A message for you, sir."

I took the envelope. My name was written in a masculine hand. I read the note and she read me. My eyebrows went up.

Mr. Hal Hinson
New York Tribune
c/o Mills House Hotel

Dear Sir,

If you are not too busy to join me for a drink this evening, I will send a car by the hotel at 4 p.m. to pick you up.

John H. Peurifoy

CHAPTER NINE
Tuesday
OCTOBER 4, 1910

I grabbed a piece of paper and scribbled a note to Randy. I would rather see her, but couldn't refuse a chance to interview Peurifoy. I stuck my head out the hotel door. Mojo was there, keeping watch over the sidewalk.

"Take this note to Miss Randy," I said. "It explains everything. I'm not sure what time I'll be back this evening. You don't need to stick around."

"Yes, suh, Mista Hal."

There was just enough time to wash up to remove the lingering foulness of the jail. It's not a cologne you want to wear. I walked out the hotel just as a Model T approached. Evidently the Tin Lizzie was still a novelty in Charleston. A small gathering of passersby collected around it at the curb, well-dressed people from the neighborhood and a bedraggled gaggle of street urchins, who were being herded away by Mojo.

"Git outta de way! Look out for de gentleman!"

"Thank you, Mojo. Did you see Miss Randy?"

"Yessuh. She look at your note, her eyes get worried. She says you bess see her whenever you gets back. She tells me to wait here for you."

"We both have our orders. I'll see you in a bit."

A distinguished black man in driving livery held the car door for me.

"Mr. Hinson," he said, "Mr. Peurifoy sends his regards. Please relax. We're going to his country home. It should take about a half hour."

I climbed into the back and settled in as the car drove away, the excited group of urchins in a hot pursuit that lasted two blocks, until we turned toward the Ashley River. The flivver made good time through town. Other forms of conveyance cleared a path, except for a few horses, who snorted at us in contempt. When we crossed over the river, the roads became more rustic. Pavement dropped away, the roadway turning to packed sand with an odd, gravel-like consistency.

"What are these roads made of?" I asked.

"Oyster shell, sir."

"Folks must eat a lot of oysters around here."

"Yes, sir."

He wasn't very talkative, by choice or order. The landscape transformed into a long avenue of huge live oak trees. Even more than the stately homes, the ancient oaks defined the look of the area. Branches, crooked with age, twisted into a fantastic canopy over the road. I found myself thinking of Randy, my mind wandering on pleasant paths as the road wound farther and farther from any point of human contact. We passed an occasional entrance, grand gates suggesting something even grander beyond the view from the road. I checked my watch, wondering if this was a long trip to nowhere, when the car slowed and turned. Framed by brick columns, a wrought iron sign hung above old iron gates.

Peurifoy Plantation.

We drove through the gates and down a wide driveway that was better manicured, but of the same oyster shell base as the road. Here the oaks were just as magnificent, but the grounds were planted, trimmed and pruned to create a portrait-worthy scene. I understand why these Southerners were once considered American royalty. They cling to their baronies. We drove through an immense piece of land, finally passing through two more brick columns that were only slightly smaller than the Pyramids. Beyond them, the drive formed an oval that led to a huge, handsome home with gabled roofs and a wide, covered porch that wrapped around the sides. The porch was framed by columns that gave it a stately look without being imposing. The buildings were covered with a native stucco of oyster shells engineered into an integral part of life. We arrived at the front steps, where a man dressed in a tweed sporting suit waited at the top.

"Mr. Hinson, welcome. I take it our avenue of oaks is a bit different than the canyons of New York City."

John Peurifoy was a man in the prime of his life and comfortable with his world. He was in his late forties, with a distinguished dash of grey at his temples. I mounted the steps to an outstretched hand and a firm handshake.

"I'm glad you could come on such short notice," Peurifoy said. "I imagine we will all be a bit busy over the next few days and I wanted a chance to show you a little Southern hospitality. Please, let's walk down the veranda. There are drinks there at the table."

There was a reason for the veranda. It overlooked a great lawn framed by oaks and flowering tea olives that carried an aroma more pleasing than the finest French perfumes. The sun was setting, and the low autumn angle of the light added a softness to colors that cried out for a canvas to capture the beauty. It would not be a bad place to spend a lifetime watching the seasons change.

"Mr. Hinson ..."

"Please call me Hal."

"Then Hal, I took the liberty of making a pitcher of what we call Plantation Punch, a little bourbon, a few mulled spices, a few bitters and a splash of tonic, all mixed up. A refreshing end to what must have been a trying day for you."

So he knew about the interview. He might be the one who approved it.

"Jail interviews are rarely fun because, frequently, the end isn't very pleasant."

"There will be a trial. You must let justice have her way. But I'm sure you didn't come here with the expectation that I could, or would, discuss a case before trial. I merely take the evidence the police provide and make my best case."

"And you are very prepared for this case."

"It is my job to be prepared."

"I hear Brice Matthews has yet to see his client."

"I can't speak for Brice. He is a capable attorney and I'm sure he will do his best. But really, Hal, there is not a lot I can discuss about the trial."

I took a sip of my drink. It was very good, better than the straight bourbon I'd expected from a bigot. I was half wrong, so far. I gazed over the veranda at the vegetation lining the driveway.

"Those are camellia bushes," Peurifoy said. "Their stock has been on this plantation since the 1600s. I apologize that you're just a few months early to see them bloom. This is the oldest garden in America. There are a number of species that we have cultivated over centuries. If you look across that reflecting pond you'll see an arboretum, where we keep our subtropical species. Perhaps another time you'll indulge me by listening to a discourse on orchids."

We got up and strolled the length of the porch, over the grand lawn to the front and past the gardens. Opposite a reflecting pool on the other side, a beautifully arched bridge led to the arboretum. We strolled back to the house, overlooking a raised lawn that led to the river.

"It is the river that connects us all. For centuries it was the highway, the means of moving all goods to Charleston. This very house came down that river. The main part was built upstream after the Revolutionary War. After the Yankees, excuse me, Hal, burned our original home here, this one was floated down the river in one piece to replace it."

"Your place certainly is magnificent, Mr. Peurifoy."

"Please, call me John. Now while we're back here, let's walk into the house. I've laid out a light supper. If you have the time, we'll have a quick bite, then I'd like to show you something."

"I'm interested in anything you have to demonstrate, and I'm certainly available for supper."

"Good. I'm glad you're hungry."

Light supper was an understatement. On a handsome table in the dining room, illuminated by a chandelier just smaller than Rhode Island, was a small feast for two. Cold chicken and ham, several blocks of cheese and freshly baked bread, served with a hearty burgundy, completed with pecan pie and a strong cup of coffee.

"John," I said, "I'm not sure I would want to see what you might consider a heavy supper."

After eating, Peurifoy stood up, walked to a highboy and produced two long cigars. We lit them and returned to the porch.

As we stood smoking in quiet appreciation, a groom came around the corner leading two horses, tacked and ready to ride.

"Do you ride, Hal? I know it's probably not popular in New York City."

"Actually, I do ride a bit," I said. "I play polo with the Meadowbrook Club out on Long Island. I usually manage not to fall off."

"I'm impressed. I've played on occasion with the Aiken club. I hope you'll appreciate these two mounts."

They were both thoroughbreds of obvious good breeding, one a large black bay stallion, sixteen hands high with a long sleek neck, muscular shoulders and powerful hindquarters.

"He's called Stonewall, a descendent of Iroquois, the first American-bred horse to beat the Brits at their own sport. He came from Kentucky. Hopefully he'll send offspring back there someday to win a race. We've run a couple of his colts at the Charleston races."

"How'd they do?"

"One won, one placed."

"He's a very handsome fellow. You must be proud of him."

"They say pride is one of the seven deadly sins, but I'll risk it in this case. Yes, he is more than just a horse to me. He represents the qualities that some humans only hope to attain – strength, spirit and nobility."

"That's some horse. I understand and agree with the final point. I have known several horses who seem beyond human in their capacity to give."

The other horse was a chestnut gelding with a white blaze and white stockings on the front. He had a strong, curved neck and agile build. I would take him home in a minute.

"This guy's not too bad himself," I said.

"He's a good fellow. He's fast and has a good attitude. Funny thing about geldings, sometimes they're caught in a state of arrested development. They seem to keep the attitude of a teenager all their lives. This guy's got a sense of humor. The ladies love him."

I took the gelding by the reins and moved to the mounting block, put a foot in the near side stirrup and lifted myself into the saddle. It was a nice English-made piece of work, comfortably broken in and suitable for either hacking or jumping. Peurifoy mounted, took the reins from his groom in both hands, and we lined up walking away from the house. The day quickly faded from dusk to dark. It was late enough in the year that light didn't linger long once sunset approaches. I was curious why we would begin a ride at dark.

"This plantation is about 1200 acres, some of that is acreage in the river, where we still grow some rice. Years ago we produced enough rice for my ancestors to live comfortably. Actually, it made them rich. Much of Charleston's wealth was built on rice. Since the war and a loss of labor, we only grow enough to keep the tradition alive. Fifteen acres produces about fifty to sixty thousand pounds a year. It's a small cash crop, but the demand for Carolina Gold rice isn't what it used to be."

We rode away from the river, up the oyster bed driveway, took a right turn and headed down a narrow lane that cut straight into the trees. It was even darker in the woods. The path was barely visible. This didn't make sense. A quarter mile down the trail, two mounted riders suddenly broke out of the forest carrying lit torches and heading for us. The hair on the back of my neck stood up. I pulled my horse up short, ready to turn and ride like hell.

"Easy, Hal. That's our escort."

They cantered up to us, blazing torches held high. A dozen strides out, they checked their horses in unison and performed a perfect pivot, a pair of hooded, ghost-white riders of the Ku Klux Klan. "Peurifoy," I hissed, "if you've got some idea of hauling my ass down for a Yankee hanging ..." I raised one fist as if to get one hit in before making a break, and the masked men reached for their hips.

"Stop, both of you." Peurifoy was in control. "Hal, if I wanted you dead, I could've done that without leaving Charleston. You're here to see something, witness something most New Yorkers are not likely ever to see. You're a reporter. You might find this educational. Now let's ride on."

I fell in beside him and behind the Klansmen. We picked up a canter back to where our escort had appeared, checked our horses and broke down to a trot. The well-worn path led deeper into the woods. Dimly, in the distance, I saw more flickering light. We drew closer and our escorts cut to a side path that took us up a slight rise. They separated for us to ride between their flank. In front of me were a hundred torches illuminating a hundred men wearing the insignia and rank of the Klan. A tall cross burned in their center. My skin crawled, goose bumps rose on my arms and my mouth went dry. It was a flight reaction and, if I could have, I would have run like a rabbit. All that hit me at the same time my rational mind took hold. I was a white man, I told myself. If I were black I wouldn't be scared, I'd be dead.

Across the crowd, a voice rose. "We will have our justice. A nigger will hang for killing a Jew. We get *two* for the price of *one*, and *we* don't have to do a *thing*!"

Torches were raised and waved, along with voices and a few laughs. My skin went back to crawling. The fear in the pit of my stomach was replaced by nausea as I listened to the vile speeches. I looked closer at the crowd. They looked like popes at some devilish gathering. But the scene was nothing to be smug or superior about. There was real power here. This scene wasn't chance, it was *made* to strike fear, and it worked. There is the legend of the Klan, and there is the reality. This, *this* was real. Their robes were white, pure and clean, but their motives were sordid. I glanced at the man to my right. He stared straight ahead. His peaked mask covered his head except for two holes. He turned toward me. Our eyes locked. I focused on what I could see through those holes. They were not dark eyes that matched the common hatred, but were a surprisingly bright blue with a hint of humor. I imagined him smiling beneath the mask, enjoying my discomfort. He turned away and I burned the image of those eyes into my brain. I glanced at his hands resting atop his reins. He wore an ornate, expensive ring. Torchlight reflected off a big, well-formed ruby. He was no backwoods bigot.

The crowd broke up, most of the men moving deeper through the woods to tether lines where horses were tied. A few rode slowly past us as they left their little gathering. A pair rode out in front.

"Hey, Peurifoy," one said. "Sure we can't hang that there Yankee tonight? Kind of quiet back here."

"You boys keep on moving," Peurifoy said. "There won't be any of that tonight." He turned his horse's head and our robed escorts did the same. I cast a last glance at the group drifting into the forest, then turned to ride in the relative safety of my group. Away from the torches, I could see the moon had risen. It lit the woods so bright that it cast shadows. In different company, it would have been a beautiful night for a romantic ride, but there was no romance in this equation. We rode out to the lane that ran through the woods and Peurifoy pulled his horse to a stop.

"Thank you, boys," he said. "I appreciate the escort. There's moonlight enough from here. We'll go on alone."

"Okay, John," the bigger one said. "Thanks for letting us use your land tonight."

They turned right and picked up a canter. When their speed blew out the waning torches, they dropped them in the road. We turned left and walked along a moonlit trail in silence. We came to the break in the forest, moved into the open of the plantation and turned left again onto the main drive. The silvery moonlight glittered off the ground oyster shell drive like a lighted path.

"What did you think of the gathering tonight, Hal?"

"For dinner theater, I'd say it was poor comedy, and the musical numbers left a lot to be desired."

"I'm not joking."

"Okay. I won't apologize. It was my first Klan meeting. I don't have much of a point of reference. Your demonstration showed the restraint of not stringing up some poor unfortunate just for my amusement, and that includes me. The Klan still has the capacity to create fear, at least they did for me. I can only imagine what a horde of hooded horsemen does to a poor family isolated out here in the country. Can fear be a weapon? Certainly."

"I'm sure you're aware of *some* of the history of the Klan. It was formed after the war by some of the generals of the Confederacy. Reconstruction wasn't pretty here. The pendulum swung pretty far after the war, and those who once ruled were pretty harshly ruled over. The Klan did use their ... *influence* to push the pendulum back, to defend against egregious breaches of law and civility."

"Riding in like white knights," I said, shaking my head. "Not much of a fairytale ending for a lot of people. The litany of violence is long. Cloaking the Klan in the 'defense of honor' is a nice story, but even Nathan Bedford Forrest saw the group go wrong and couldn't stop them. There's not a lot to brag about in the Colfax massacre."

"I'm impressed with your knowledge, but I'm not here to defend the Klan. The point of this evening was to give you an opportunity to see them, hear them and, yes, feel the fear. They still exist. Some of them are well-respected members of the community, and many are more than willing to hang people to make a point. You are aware, I'm sure, that in the days after the murder of the Jewish merchant, many Negroes were arrested. Arresting them, innocent or not, making a show of a massive police effort, was a part of the investigation, a show to make sure the Klan didn't take matters into their hands. That control was unraveling about the time the wife was attacked. If that boy Duncan hadn't been arrested then, I wouldn't want to speculate on the number of coloreds that might have been found hanging from trees. You heard them tonight. In their less than eloquent way, they are satisfied at the moment."

"'At the moment,' meaning if they get their hanging. If Duncan swings, everything will be just fine. Innocent or not, he dies, or the Klan kicks off a roundup and massacre. That's perverse."

"As for Duncan's innocence, that's up to the trial. There is convincing evidence that he committed the crimes. As for the potential were he found innocent, yes, that could be bad. His hanging would prevent the death of perhaps dozens of other innocent men."

"It seems to me that the failure here is in the law not controlling the Klan. Why should a place like this still be under the influence of a lawless mob? You're a prosecutor, why do you tolerate them?"

"Now you're being naive, Hal. They wore hoods and robes tonight. You don't know who they are, but I do. Some of the leading citizens of Charleston were with us tonight."

My horse stopped. I had run into a metaphorical brick wall of reality, and the horse took his cue from the way my shoulders and seat had set back in the saddle. I leaned forward and loosened the reins. We walked in silence back to the house and dismounted.

"Would you like to come into the house for a drink?"

"Ah. Thank you, John, but no. I want to go back into town. You've given me insight, and I find it unsettling, albeit illuminating."

"Hal, if I thought you were not a man who is capable of objective evaluation in writing your stories, I would not have invited you. As I said, I'm a prosecutor. I work with the facts at hand to make my case. So do you. I just wanted to give you an opportunity to see the bigger picture."

He turned and called, "Pinckney!" The driver came around the corner. He opened the rear door as I walked his way.

I turned to Peurifoy.

"I won't wish you good luck in court," I said, "but perhaps after tonight I should. You should try defending some day. You did a good job tonight in creating a reasonable doubt in my mind. Good night, John."

"Goodnight, Hal. Thank you for coming."

I climbed into the car and we set off down that beautiful moonlit driveway. I could not get the images of the evening out of my head. The Klan by torchlight. It's an image I wish I could send back to New York. But photographs rarely capture the feel of fear. The flivver picked up speed on the roadway. The moonlight was bright enough to see for some distance ahead, even beyond the headlamps. An occasional rider appeared in the distance and I studied each to see if I recognized the horse, and wondered if it was the second time I had seen them tonight.

My spirits lifted as we crossed the bridge over the Ashley and drove back into Charleston. The lights were gay after the torches and shadows that were now miles behind me. In the front of the Mills House, my four-foot sentry was still on duty.

"Mista Hal, sure glad to see you. Miss Randy had me all aworry over you."

"I'm back in one piece, my young friend. We'd better go see her so we both don't get in trouble."

I opened the car door.

"You wan *me* to git in dat ting?"

"Sure, why not?"

"Umm, Mr. Hal," Pinckney said, his first words since leaving the plantation. "I don't think Mister Peurifoy would like that."

"To hell with Peurifoy," I said. Moonlight glittered on Pinckney's big smile.

"Yes, sir. He told me tonight to treat you like a guest. Guest is always right. Come on up, little man!"

Mojo climbed up into the front seat beside Pinckney, barely controlling himself as the car pulled away from the curb. He slid back and forth across the seat, looked out the front, then the side, waved like royalty at people passing. We pulled up in front of Randy's and I asked Pinckney to honk the horn. He gave it a couple of beeps and I thought Mojo was going to explode. Randy came out on the porch, saw the commotion and started laughing. Her laugh sounded like music. I opened the door and stepped out.

"Pinckney," I said, "if you think Mister Peurifoy won't mind too much, how about taking Mojo on a lap around the block and then back to the orphanage?"

Pinckney leaned across the front seat and said in a whisper, "To hell with Mr. Peurifoy." The laugh that followed echoed through the neighborhood. Pinckney and Mojo joked with each other as they pulled down the block.

Randy stood in front of the open door. She took my hand as I came to the top step, pulled me inside and closed the door behind us. She grabbed me by both arms and pulled me close. This time the kiss wasn't glancing, but full on the mouth, her lips parted, her tongue dancing with mine. The full length of her body pressed against mine, and I pulled her closer. The feeling had potential. She fell back in my arms for a moment, then leaned forward and kissed me again, briefly, on the lips.

"I was afraid for you," she said.

"If that's my reward, let me step back outside and try something really dangerous."

"Don't be funny." She took a step back. "I know John Peurifoy. I know the company he keeps. You're lucky they didn't give you a Yankee necktie party."

"It was my first Klan meeting."

She took another step back. "Let's go into the parlor. I think whiskey is in order."

We moved into the house and she went to the bar, took glasses, poured two fingers of bourbon and handed me one. There was much to love about this woman.

"Tell me every detail," she said.

DATELINE:
Charleston, S.C., October 4, 1910
Hal Hinson | New York Tribune

In the Devil's Den they performed their play. Torchlight in the deep woods was the footlight for evil. I was the fortunate Yankee to witness a backwoods gathering of the Ku Klux Klan, fortunate not from a particular desire to be there, but because the party didn't include me as the evening's entertainment, the main act, a sacrifice to the twisted Southern code of honor.

There is much in America, this great and diverse nation, that is little known to those who inhabit the island of Manhattan. There are the great plains of grain in the Midwest, the harvest season of sweat, dirt and hope. There are the sounds of ducks on the wing, the smell of spent powder and the splash of a favorite dog retrieving dinner. In rural America, there are the smells of pies cooling on windowsills and the sounds of a church choir calling the faithful down a dusty lane. These scenes are part of the everyday richness of this country. And then there are the forgotten scenes of our ignored inhumanity.

The relative quiescence of the Klan in recent times has allowed us to forget the lynchings and massacres of just a few decades ago. Occasionally stories of roughneck riders in white will surface, or not, depending on whether the editor himself puts on a peaked hat for torchlight rallies. We in civilized canyons smirk at these rubes in robes. I have lost that smugness. After a good supper and atop an expensive horse, I rode into the heart of darkness.

These so-called Knights gather with impunity,

by invitation, on the great plantations of the South. They still carry a chip on their cloaked shoulders and they carry the power to influence, through fear, through their secret society.

By the light of a burning cross, I saw glimmers of gold on their fingers, edges of expensive clothing peeking from beneath their cuffs. There is terror here, robed in respectability. There is a threat that this type of violence could be reborn in America.

The Klan here is spoiling for a little night dance at the end of a rope.

A trial that starts in a day's time is all that restrains this town, these men, from a fury of murder. Someone will hang here and either way he is likely innocent.

In the torchlight, in their eyes, I saw the Evil and he is among us.

CHAPTER TEN
Wednesday
OCTOBER 5, 1910

The waiter topped off my coffee as Randy entered the dining room. She wore a simple dark dress with a matching jacket, a lace blouse wrapped across her front. On another woman, the outfit might look plain, but on her it was enough to make men stand when she came into the room. She walked straight to me. I rose to accept her hand.

"Good morning, Mr. Hinson."

"And good morning to you, Miss Dumas."

I was about to sit when one of the men from another table approached us.

"Good morning, Chief Boyle," Randy greeted the smiling visitor.

He was tall and strong in a suit trimmed in the military style. He wore a thick mustache, and as he turned and smiled I saw his eyes, the striking blue eyes behind the mask from the night before. Now I knew what the hidden smile looked like.

"Mr. Hinson," Randy said. "May I introduce you to Chief William Boyle of the Charleston Police?"

"Hinson? The newspaperman from New York?"

"The same, Chief Boyle," I said. "But I believe we've met before."

He smiled again. "I don't see how that's possible."

"Odd, Chief, the things that go bump in the night. Perhaps I'm mistaken, but since we've been introduced officially, how about I drop by your office later today. We could chat about good times on the ol' plantation. Or not."

"I'm sure I don't know what you're talking about, Mr. Hinson, but I'll be in my office all afternoon. Miss Dumas, a pleasure to see you."

"Thank you for stopping by Chief," Randy said.

He walked back to his table, where three men were finishing

breakfast. I wondered if they were at the gathering last night, too.

"Old friends?" Randy smiled.

"A wolf in Knight's clothing. He was one of my escorts last night. Those eyes are a dead giveaway."

"I seriously doubt if he cares you know. He probably prefers it that way. But he *is* one of the ones who you should beware of. He likes to keep a tight lid on his town, and he's never been fond of reporters. Cops who talk to the newspapers don't get too far. Try not to annoy him with your charm."

We tried to act like acquaintances, but frequent knowing glances were thrown our way. Randy was right about her preference to spend time in her own home, but these people could think what they wanted, and they could get used to seeing us together. We had coffee and talked about matters unrelated to the trial. She read the papers and was not shy with her opinions. President Taft, the big man, was not big on her list of favorites. She called him a "bloated conservative." Teddy Roosevelt, like any great actor and too few politicians, knew when to leave the stage and for that he still held the hearts of many. Randy was not enamored of the 'Rough Rider' image of T.R., but his progressive politics appealed to her.

"For all his bullish persona," she said, "I think Mr. Roosevelt will be remembered as one of the great presidents. He was certainly what we needed at the beginning of this century, a man with vision. He saw the need for the Panama Canal, and to bust the trusts. Taft can't see past the end of his nose."

I asked if she had seen Haley's Comet earlier in the year.

"I climbed onto the roof one night, very late, after the gaslights were dimmed, and watched for hours as the tail traced its way across the heavens. I imagined it as the trail of Apollo's chariot and wondered where he headed in the heavens. It was so close. I wanted to reach up and grab it, to ride across the universe. It was a magnificent sight. It made this Earth seem small."

"That is one night I wish I'd shared with you."

"There'll be others. Counting shooting stars can be just as romantic."

It was time to leave before the conversation went further afield.

"Let's walk out to the lobby," I said. "We might as well say hello to Mrs. Vanderhorst."

We found the parlor where the old woman held court.

"Good morning, Mrs. Vanderhorst," I said.

"Mr. Hinson, Miss Dumas, good morning."

"I see you two know each other," I said.

"We are aware of one another, Mr. Hinson, and that is not quite the same as knowing someone. I have not had the opportunity to meet Miss Dumas before this. Perhaps you two could join me for tea sometime soon."

Randy offered a smile that would melt taffy.

"I would enjoy nothing more, Mrs. Vanderhorst. I will let Mr. Hinson make the arrangements."

"Then I look forward to seeing the two of you." We walked to the main lobby.

"That old woman has talked *about* me for long enough," Randy said. "I suppose it will be interesting to talk *with* her for a change."

"She seemed pleasantly disposed to you."

"I'm sure it's because of you. She seems to like the lad from New York."

"I have that effect on women."

"So it seems."

We walked through the lobby, right past Bright Eyes and the young girl fixed her gaze on Randy. I wouldn't have thought she could shoot daggers with those eyes. Randy matched her, returned the look with bigger daggers and Bright Eyes withered.

Randy turned her gaze to me. "Your charm is affecting the entire hotel."

"I'll do my best to stop it."

We went through the doors and onto the sidewalk. Randy took my hand.

"I'm off to do a bit of shopping," she said. "I won't bore you by dragging you along. I know tomorrow's a busy day, but why don't you join me for a light supper tonight? About seven?"

"Thank you. It gives me something to look forward to, after the interview with my favorite Klansman."

"You'd better watch yourself with him. Save that charm for later." She turned and walked up Queen Street, headed for the fashionable shops on lower King Street.

I turned around and found Mojo standing there, grinning. He had been watching us.

"Mista Hal, she sho is one ..."

"You better watch yourself, Mojo."

"One fine woman."

"Yes, she is that. Now let's walk on up to Lubelsky's. It's time to pick up a suit for you." He took off, his little legs pumping. I had to break into a brisk walk to keep up. We hopped a trolley and rode for a few blocks before jumping off at upper King Street, about where Nealy had been collared. I stood for a minute, looking up the street at Lubelsky's and then back down in the direction where the merchants would have seen him. I was stuck in the moment, thinking how I stood here in one life, looking forward to dinner and Randy's company tonight, while totally beyond my reach or control, Fate could turn completely and my life and dreams could be as shattered as Nealy's.

"Mista Hal, where you at? You looks like you seen a ghost."

"Maybe so, Mojo. The ghost of lives past, of lives that will never be. Let's get outta here."

We moved on up the street to the tailor shop and walked in the door. Abe Price looked up from his tailor's table.

"Mr. Hinson. Good morning, sir."

"Hello, Mr. Price."

"I wrote my brother yesterday to tell him his knishes are famous and talked about as far south as Charleston. He'll be happy to hear that."

"Tell him they could use his knishes in Charleston. These biscuits every morning get a bit old."

"Deys nuthin' wrong wid biscuits ebery mornin'," Mojo said, "wid little honey, maybe wid little graby, deys hunnert ways to eat a biscuit."

"Maybe you just need one of my brother's knishes."

"Perhaps, but while you might take the boy out of the South, I doubt if you'll ever take the South out of the boy. Maybe we'll see. But first, let's take him out of these clothes and into a new suit."

Price reached behind him and grabbed a hanger with a child's suit. It was well-cut and well-pressed, a nice piece of work.

"Go put it on, Mojo!" He grabbed the hanger and headed for the back. I lounged against the counter and made small talk with Price about the end of another season of "dead ball," New York baseball, and the more risqué acts in vaudeville. After a few minutes Mojo fairly pranced out of the back.

"Anybody seen Mojo?" I said. "Who's this young man here?"

"Don't joke on me, Mista Hal. How's I look?"

"You look great, Mojo. Dignified. Why, I'd say you look august."

"Shoot, I can't be August. It's October. How can I look like August?"

I let him ponder that one.

"Thank you, Mr. Price. Very nice work. Tell me," I said as we walked out, "do you speak much with Charles Levin next door?"

"Sometimes we say hello in the morning, not much more."

"So he's not too friendly, even with a fellow Jew?"

"Not all Jews are the same, Mr. Hinson."

"Of course not. Thank you, sir."

At the door, I looked back to where Max Lubelsky had lain, mortally wounded. I glanced around the store at the rows of neat shirts, racks of pants and bolts of cloth. As in the street, I saw where one life had been, and how a single act of fate had erased it from the picture. I looked down at a beaming Mojo and found a reason to smile. Outside Lubelsky's, I paused and turned left, glancing into Charles Levin's store. He sat in a chair watching the door. We stepped through the entrance.

"Good morning, sir," he said. "A fine morning. Are you looking for the finest shoes in Charleston?"

As Levin greeted me, Mojo stepped into sight.

"Hey, you, boy!" Levin said in a coarse voice. "You get on outta here."

"He's with me," I said.

"I don't care if he's with the mayor. I don't let coloreds in my store."

"That's odd. He just bought a suit next door."

"Abe Price can do what he wants in that store, just like Max Lubelsky did and look what it got him. Killed by a darkie."

"So you stopped selling to Negroes after the murder?"

"After the police dragged me through more lineups than I can count? I don't want to have anything more to do with their business, don't want the wrong crowd coming through here."

"But the police claim they've caught the killer."

"And they have. Rose Lubelsky identified him herself."

"But you didn't."

"No. I was out of town when they caught him for attacking that poor woman."

"So you didn't see him that morning?"

"No. Who are you, a cop?"

"A reporter."

"You take yourself and your boy outta my store, Mr. Reporter. I've already answered all the questions I'm going to until the trial starts and I get to help send that killer to the gallows."

"Business been a bit light, Mr. Levin?"

"My business is my own, Mister What-did-you-say-your-name-was?"

"I didn't." We headed through the door, but Mojo stuck his head back in.

"His name is Mista Hal Hinson. Rememba dat." He cut around the corner as a broom flew out the door.

I tried not to laugh as he caught up to me on the sidewalk.

"One of these days that quick mouth is gonna get you in trouble."

"Nots long as my feets is faster."

We strolled on down the street for a couple of blocks, looking like dandies on parade.

"You want to go down to Miss Mary's for lunch?" I asked.

"I'm always wantin' to go to Miss Mary's."

We caught a trolley back downtown, riding together on the back. We entered the front door at Miss Mary's, and received a different reception than the last time. Several men stood to shake my hand, and more than a few made gentle jokes at the expense of Mojo's new suit.

"Little Man, where you get dem clothes?" "You preachin' nex' Sunday?" "You little young be gettin' married."

Mojo stood proud, and stood his ground. Miss Mary walked

into the room with plates lined up her arms. "Why, look at the two fine men! We don't usually get such well-dressed men in here. Who's that short gentleman?"

"Don't be messin' wid me, Miss Mary," Mojo said. "Mista Hal says I *am* a gennleman now."

"A suit don't make a gentleman. Plenty proof of that around this town. Now you two sit down over there. I'll get you some lunch."

Ida came out with glasses of tea.

"Did you see my Nealy, Mista Hal?" she asked.

I nodded. "He looks pretty good. Jail's not a nice place to be, but the food you're sending and those letters, they help him a lot."

"He liked my letter?" She was thrilled.

"I think it's the only thing that keeps him sane. Here, he sent this for you." I handed her the folded piece of paper from my pocket. She read it once, then again.

"I just can't wait for this trial to be done so he can get out and we can get married."

She smiled that smile again, sweet and full of hope. She left the room and I scowled. That girl was too sweet to have her heart broken.

Mojo worked the room like a pint-sized politician. That ended when Miss Mary came back with our plates and Mojo was on her like a hound on a scent.

"Fried flounder, butter beans and rice and collards! Miss Mary if you needs a son, I's available."

"I gots enough trouble in my life widout you." She let out a big, room-rattling laugh and went back into the kitchen.

Mojo lit into his food like he'd win a dollar if he finished first. He tore through the flounder, devouring meat, fins and tails, leaving nothing on the plate but bones. I was barely halfway through my food when he pushed his chair back and patted his belly.

"I's gonna get fat stickin' around wid you, Mista Hal."

"A few pounds won't hurt you. Besides, you're still a growing boy, or you'd better still be growing."

"I's two inches taller since last spring."

"Good. I was starting to think I was stuck with a midget."

Miss Mary tried to refuse my money again, but this time I was more insistent. We wound through her house, small rooms filled with people enjoying their food. The place had a good, friendly feel to it. The screen door slammed behind us, all but saying, "Come again."

We headed back to the center of town and I was struck again by the dichotomies of this city, the civil and the uncivil, the beautiful surface and the ugly undercurrent. It was a warm afternoon and I was in no real hurry to confront Chief Boyle. Mojo and I poked along the promenade of a small, lovely lake that was surrounded by large homes. Two young white boys placed elaborate toy boats on the water, sloops rigged fore and aft, one fitted with a keel, the other without. The boys lined them up with the wind to their backs. Mojo and I settled on a bench to watch. Both boats caught a gust and were off. The boys jumped and yelled, encouraging their imaginary crews. The boats sailed to the middle of the lake as the boys ran around the edge to the other side. Three quarters of the way across, as the boys were directly opposite us, cheering their boats to the finish, a cross-wind gusted across the lake. One boat took a tack in the direction of the wind, the other tipped and capsized. The apparent winner, the one who stayed afloat, jumped up and down in celebration. The loser reached into his pocked, pulled out a ball of string with a hook on one end and began casting for his overturned boat. Maybe he learned the lesson of the keel. Mojo watched with a keen eye. I wondered if there would ever come a day when the three boys would play together.

We got up and started along Broad Street, which was dotted with shops, until we came to King Street, where the high dollar merchants clustered. A few affluent shoppers strolled through the neighborhood, ladies heading to their homes south of Broad, their servants carrying packages that might otherwise tax their delicate nature. We went past the shopping district to the police station. Mojo made idle talk, acting as my personal tour guide. Outside the police station, two men of heavy brow and rough cut loitered, paying special attention to us. I walked past them and into the station.

A desk sergeant looked up.

"Is Chief Boyle in?" I asked.

"And what would be your business with the chief?"

"He's expecting me. My name in Hinson."

"Ah, the reporter. He don't have much time for your sort."

"He might want to open up a bit. We're generally known for our wit, good looks and ability to hold our liquor."

"Smart Alec, huh?"

"That too."

"Chief's expecting you. Go on in."

I went through a doorway and into a hallway. At the end was an imposing door marked with a sign no one could miss:

William Boyle, Chief of Police. I knocked knuckles on the solid wood door.

"Come in," Boyle called from inside.

His office was larger than I expected, and not unattractive. Bookcases filled with legal-looking materials lined one wall. On other walls were several attractive paintings, a masculine oil of ducks and dogs, a hunting scene in early morning light, and a nice landscape of large oaks hung with moss, a dirt road and a rustic but inviting hunting cabin.

"Nice paintings," I said.

"Thank you. A friend of mine did those. That one with the cabin is my hunting lodge up in Berkeley County."

"Nice place. There are a lot of nice places out in the country. Peurifoy's place isn't too shabby."

"I don't get out there too often."

"Last night?"

"I was at home with the wife last night, not that I need to give you an alibi for my whereabouts. Want to try another subject?"

"How about Nealy Duncan?"

"He goes on trial in the morning. Pretty much out of my hands now. My officers and detectives worked hard to find the person who attacked those Jews. She identified him herself, and that's good enough for me."

"That might make him an assailant, but not a murderer."

"Others identified him as being in the vicinity the morning of the murder of the Jew tailor."

"How many suspects did your department detain during the course of the investigation?"

"About a dozen."

"Were you holding two at the time Duncan was arrested? What did you do with them?"

"I released them. After Duncan's arrest we had the evidence and the man to make a case for murder."

"What you have is a man cornered by a mob and handed over to you."

"If my men hadn't performed their duties like professionals, that nigger would have been hung from a lamp post and we wouldn't be sitting here having this pleasant conversation."

He had a point, and was pretty damned smug about it.

"Chief, how many Negroes have been hanged by mobs in Charleston?"

He leaned back in his chair and glared at me. There was no humor in his eyes now. "In spite of what you might think, we don't make a sport of hanging niggers down here. I'm not saying it doesn't happen, in isolated parts of the county or in other counties, but in Charleston we don't let hooligans run our city."

"Hooded or not?"

"You're not very amusing, and you're damned close to insulting me. It might be a good idea for you to take your New York ass out of here before you stumble on something and break a city ordinance and I have to throw you in jail up there next to your nigger friend Duncan."

We shared a moment locked in each others' eyes. Maybe, just maybe, I had pushed old blue eyes too far. Too late to do anything about that now.

"Thanks for your time, Chief." I got up, walked slowly through the doorway and left the door open behind me. His eyes on me all the way down the hall, I felt them, until I turned into the squad room. The sergeant looked up.

"Guess you weren't talking about hunting. Chief's always got time to talk hunting."

"It was hunting of another sort."

I went outside and Mojo came running up.

"Mista Hal, les go. Don' like hangin' round dis place. Dem two ober dere been axing questions."

"About what?"

"'Bout you mainly."

We headed into the street and the two loafers drifted off in another direction. I watched them until they disappeared around a corner.

"Looks like they had nothing else to say. Let's go."

The afternoon ebbed as we moved down Meeting Street.

Walking past a church cemetery, the unusual circular design caught my eye. The gate was open and we strolled in. The pitted gravestones bore dates going back two hundred years. Some looked even older than that, marked with strange skulls and crossbones, as if they might be pirates' graves, if pirates ever landed in such a respectable place. Mojo looked uneasy.

"What's wrong?" I asked.

"Why you wants to walk in here? Ain't nuthin' but dead folks. I ain't wantin' to see no haints here."

"What's a haint?"

"Dead folk. Haints. Ghosts. Dis place ain't good fer nuthin' but bad luck."

"It's just a graveyard."

"Sum time the dead ain't so dead. I gots no use fer dis place."

"Okay. Let's go."

We left the cemetery, crossed the street and were at the hotel. I told Mojo to wait for me at the front door so we could walk down to Randy's together. Something wasn't sitting right with me, and I wasn't sure if it was Mojo and his 'haints' or the two men outside the police station. I skipped a shower and just freshened up, changed shirts and was back in the lobby in fifteen minutes. The revolving door was in motion and I slipped in without having to put a hand on it. Out on the steps I looked around for Mojo, but he wasn't there. I rushed down to the curb, looked up and down the street and then hurried back into the hotel and found the porter.

"You see a little black kid in a suit at the door?"

"Yes, suh. He was there a little while ago."

"Did you see where he went?"

"Don't know where he went, but two white gentlemen came up and I saw him go off with them."

My heart sank. It made no sense; Mojo was far too smart to walk off with the two men who were threatening enough to scare him a short while ago. I forced myself to stay calm. There was no use going to the police. The only person I knew in this town who had any influence was Randy, so I hit the sidewalk at a trot, heading to her house. The light faded from dusk to dark and the gaslights cast their circles of light as I ran down Meeting Street past Broad. A few people cast curious looks at me. A man in a suit running through the neighborhood probably wasn't a common sight. I turned the corner into the lane leading to Randy's house and came upon a small park, not much more than a garden. In the middle were the two men, with Mojo between them. The bigger one had him by the collar, suspended off the ground, his feet kicking wildly, trying to find a target.

"Hinson, got your little monkey here," the short one called. "He's been a real bad monkey. We might have to hurt him."

Mojo was gagged and his eyes bulged in fear, but he didn't give in. I moved in at the two and Mojo's big eyes looked past me and got bigger. I glanced over my shoulder and saw two more thugs moving in. I rushed the two nearest. As we closed, the big one laughed, smacked Mojo across the face and knocked him to the ground. I went for him first. He pulled a blackjack from his pocket and took a short swing at my head and missed. I stepped into him, caught his arm in a block and brought my right up to deliver a sharp blow above his elbow, and heard a satisfying snap as his humerus broke. He groaned in pain, dropped to his knees and cradled his arm.

His pal moved next. I dropped low and kicked his kneecap hard, which bent him over with a howl. I brought my knee up to smack his nose and he went over backwards to the ground. The other two came at me together. I dropped low and ducked between them, spun and sent a kick to the back of the knee of the closest thug and knocked him off balance. I slipped in behind him, grabbed his neck in a blood choke. He went limp and I dropped him.

The last one gave me an evil smile. He dropped his baseball bat, reached into his coat and pulled out a pistol.

"Don't think yer fancy fighting can handle this, Yankee boy." He pulled the hammer back and raised the barrel to my chest when an explosion went off behind me and a red spot burst on his shoulder. His pistol fell to the grass and I spun around to find Randy with a smoking Browning semi-automatic in her hands.

"When I invited you for dinner," she said, "I did not expect extra guests."

"We were just getting acquainted."

"Let's get un-acquainted, shall we?" She raised her voice, aiming it and the Browning at the battered thugs. "You boys have ten seconds to pick your lowly asses up and get out of range before I unload the rest of this clip into you. And don't think about going for that gun. You're not dead right now only because I don't want to waste the night explaining your body to police. Now move!"

The two less wounded helped the others hobble off into the darkness. I went over to Mojo, who was squirming on the ground. I untied his gag and picked him up. His eyes went from unfocussed to wide open and he threw his arms around my neck.

"Mista Hal, dem men tole me if I didn't come wid dem dey was going to kill you. I din know dey was going to use me fer bait."

It came on slowly, but once he started to cry he couldn't stop. He hugged me hard and sobbed like he hadn't done it in a long time. Randy walked to us and I looked at her over his heaving shoulders. She wore a comforting smile on her lips, not amused, but damn near saintly.

"I thought I'd seen you looking as lovely as I could ever imagine. Who would have thought that a gun would make you a goddess."

"You don't fight too badly for a city boy. I was just watching the fun until the last one pulled the gun."

I stood up, holding Mojo tight against my side. Randy came closer and I used my free arm to take her shoulders and pull her closer. When my mouth was next to her ear, I whispered, "Thanks."

She kissed my cheek, took my hand and we walked back to her house. Mojo was done crying, and was returning to his normal, animated self.

"We taught dem a lesson, din we, Mista Hal?"

"We did, but will the lesson stay learned?"

At the door, Meredith met us with a worried look.

"It's okay, Meredith. Take young Mojo back to the kitchen and clean him up a bit. I'm sure you can find something for him to eat and then, if you don't mind, get Markus to fix that davenport up downstairs in the carriage house. He won't be much trouble for a few days."

Mojo headed down the hall. "Mista Hal, we movin' up in da world."

I smiled at him. As soon as he was out of sight I slumped against the wall.

Randy grabbed my hand. "Let's get a drink."

We went into the study and she poured whiskey and led me to the divan.

I took a long sip, looking at her eye to eye.

"That was frightening," I said.

"Four on one isn't exactly fair."

"Not the fight, not that I do that every day, but Mojo. I had a feeling something was going to happen, but I didn't think it would happen in the fifteen minutes I left him alone."

"Had you seen those men before?"

"Yeah. Two of them were hanging around outside the police station when I went to talk with the chief."

"Then he had a hand in it. How much of a lesson he wanted to teach you, I guess we don't know. I don't think he wanted you dead, just roughed up."

"He made his point."

She sipped whiskey. "That fighting, is it a little something you learned from Teddy?"

I nodded. "Never thought the day would come when I'd appreciate being tossed around by a President learning jujutsu."

"I think we need to adjust the plan here a bit," she said. "After he's settled Mojo down, I'm going to ask Markus to take a note to the orphanage so they'll know where he is, and then have him go by the hotel and pick up your things. You're staying here."

"That may not be the best idea. I'm already on the short list for beatings from the police department. Besides, I don't want people whispering about you, or us, or whatever."

"I'll send a couple of notes out tomorrow that should stop Boyle from doing anything else stupid. And you must know by now that I don't care what people think about me. I want you here. You're staying here. I waste too much time worrying about you when you're not near me. It's just more ... convenient."

"I'm not going to argue with a girl who has a loaded pistol and knows how to use it."

"Good." She leaned over and kissed me, her lips lingering for a moment before she sat back and set down her drink. "Now that's enough excitement for one night. Let's go into the dining room for that simple supper that we mentioned a few hours ago."

The room was just as inviting as before, candles lit, places set. We settled into our familiar spots in a way that made me wish it might go on forever. Meredith entered the room, smiling, pleased with herself again.

"Bouillabaisse, Mister Hal." She said. "Clams, oysters, fish, shrimp and crab cooked with herbs out of my garden. It's one of our favorites."

She put the tureen down, brought out two large bowls with a hearty piece of crusty bread in the bottom of each and ladled in the precious stew of the sea. The scents of seafood and spices made me forget the past few of hours. Markus entered with a bottle of cassis. I sipped wine, realized how hungry I was and then dug into the stew. Randy didn't hold back either. We both picked the shells clean and sipped the marvelous broth. When we were finished, the shell bowl was stacked high and the wine was gone. Meredith walked in.

"Dessert?"

I groaned. "This was supposed to be simple, but you continue to outdo yourself. I am perfectly content. Is Mojo settled down?"

"I gave him a bowl of soup and put him down. Little man was asleep before I finished folding his suit. They ripped a little place on his sleeve. I'll sew that up tonight."

"You're very kind. Thank you."

"Mr. Hinson will be staying with us as well, Meredith. He'll stay in the guest room."

"Yes, ma'am. It's all ready." She smiled at me, cleared the table and left.

"So this whole situation was preordained," I said to Randy.

"Let's just say those hooligans have hastened my plan."

I leaned back and mused. "Maybe Boyle didn't send them."

She laughed and took my hand, led me into the parlor where she poured short brandies. We sat next to each other, sipping and gazing at the fire. Nothing needed to be said. We finished the brandy, the fire burned low and Randy turned to me.

"Mr. Hinson," she whispered, "it's time for bed."

We mounted the stairs together. At the top she stopped.

"Your room is to the left," she said. "Mine is to the right. Sleep well." She kissed me lightly on the lips. "Goodnight."

She walked down the hall and disappeared behind her door.

There were a half dozen ways I could have handled that, and five were better than the one I took. I shook my head and walked down the hallway and into my room. It was lit by a small lamp by the table. My bags sat at the foot of the bed. When Randy wants something done, it gets taken care of.

The room was of good size and decorated in an understated style. In the center was a large four-poster bed, called a rice planter's bed. The floors were covered with Oriental carpets of fairly simple design. One wall contained bookcases, the other was outfitted with a small writing desk, over which hung a brightly-colored painting of a Charleston street scene.

I unpacked my bag and hung my suits in the wardrobe next to the bathroom. I scrubbed my face and dried it, went back to the bedroom and looked around, feeling uneasy. There were plenty of books. I grabbed one and got into bed. The words didn't work. My mind kept wandering down the hall to Randy. After a few minutes I turned off the light, hoping for sleep. Old houses have their own noises. I listened to the creaks and sounds of Randy's house settling down for the night. One sound, a hushed padding, came down the hallway. The door opened silently, and candles peeked around the edge with Randy behind them.

"If you aren't coming to me," she said, "I guess I have to come to you."

She closed the door and stood in a robe that revealed enough to know there was nothing underneath. She set the small candelabra on the writing desk, turned and dropped her robe to the floor. Backlit by the candles, the perfect flare of her hips was outlined in light. Her hair was down on her shoulders. She stood at ease, unashamed and breathtaking. I reveled in a long look, silently thanking my ancestors all the way back to knuckle-dragging Neanderthals for bringing me to this moment.

"Should I mention that you are stunningly beautiful?" I was a breath away from being a stammering fool.

"You should invite me into your bed before I freeze."

She moved beside the bed. I raised the covers and she turned slightly, enough to reveal her perfect profile, breasts full with nipples erect, belly flat, legs long and willowy. She slid into the bed and her heat warmed me.

I leaned over, slipped an arm under her waist and drew her closer. Her lips went to mine and we kissed hungrily, deeply. I moved my hand down and stroked her smooth belly, and she arched her back at my touch. She moaned lightly, kissed me with a new fever and then in one swift move flipped one leg over my body and pulled herself on top. We looked at each other and smiled. She bent down, her hair tumbled over her shoulders and onto my chest, kissing me slowly, as though that was all the motion needed in the world. She reached down and touched me, raised up and lowered herself on me in long slow caresses, catching her breath lightly as we probed each other's depth. I slid my hands down her legs, around her hips and traced my fingers up her spine and around her buttocks. I flipped her onto her back. She was taken by surprise and laughed lightly. Now I bent over and kissed her as I moved, pulling her hips up and onto me. We moved closer to the edge of ecstasy, our rhythm quickened, her moans increased and the very sound of them drove me deeper into her. As our moment approached, as we neared the center of the other, I pulled her head up and face to face we watched each other's eyes as our bodies formed that perfect fusion. Her face was lovely by candlelight. She kissed me lightly. We didn't separate, but simply slipped together back to the bed. We murmured of many things and nothing, relishing the sound of the other's voice. The candle burned to a flutter and we were in darkness. Once again I reached out for her, found her again filled with desire. We kissed and caressed and loved and collapsed in that feeling that has fueled the ages. Late in the night we slept until the dawn came and we awoke in our newly created world.

CHAPTER ELEVEN
Thurssday
OCTOBER 6, 1910

For the past three months every morning started the same for Nealy Duncan, gray light and the sounds of birds. They reminded him that he was the caged one. He ate cold biscuits, listening to the usual morning chatter. Nealy rarely took part in the talk. Most of the men in jail had been there before. He wouldn't associate with them on the outside, and he wouldn't change his ways on the inside.

If not for the Ida's letters, he would not know this day was different.

My dear Nealy,

Your trial starts tomorrow. Finally your chance to be free. Look for me when they bring you to the courthouse. I'll be outside on the curb by the corner.

All my love,
Ida

Nealy didn't share Ida's optimism, but any hope of getting out of the jail cell was good. Just after eight, the jailers came in with a pair of shackles. Bound and under guard, Nealy was led down the stairs and out into the fresh air for the first time in weeks. He paused just long enough to squint and fill his lungs with clean air. For that, he got a shove from the butt-end of a twelve-gauge shotgun. The guards pushed him into a wagon for the ride to the courthouse. He looked out the barred windows as it moved through the town. The streets and buildings seemed very different from the ones he took for granted as a free man. If he ever walked down that street again he would kiss every damned building on the block.

The wagon neared the courthouse and he pushed his face close to the bars. There, on the opposite corner, was Ida, wearing a plain print dress and looking like the excited young girl she was. As the wagon turned the corner he squeezed his face against the bars of the window to see the last fraction of her frame, then he slumped back to his seat.

The guards dragged him back into the dazzling daylight and ushered him through a back doorway and up some stairs. He was taken to a small room and told to sit. When the door opened again, the guard let two men enter. One was middle-aged, his hair swept back and dressed formally in a dark suit and a white shirt with a banded collar. The other man was younger, wore a suit that could use pressing and a tie on the edge of bold.

The men took seats opposite Nealy and sat silently for several seconds. The older one broke the stillness.

"Mr. Duncan, I'm Brice Matthews. I am defending you in this trial. This is Paul MacMillan. He will assist me in your case."

Nealy didn't respond. Matthews studied Nealy. He got up and walked around the room, scrutinizing Nealy from every angle, then took his seat again.

"Mr. Duncan ..." Matthews began.

"Please call me Nealy, everyone does, except Mr. Geilfuss. He calls me Daniel."

Matthews was surprised to hear him speak so well.

"All right. How long have you had that scar on your face, Nealy? There was no mention of it in any of the witness statements."

"About seven years. I was sixteen."

"A fight?"

"An accident in the bakery. I've never been in a fight. And since you're taking notes there, I've never killed a man or attacked a woman, either."

"That's what the trial will determine. You are presumed to be innocent."

"I am? Then why am I stuck in a stinking jail cell for three months when I should be working and going home to my new bride?"

"Let's be honest from the beginning," Matthews said. "This is not going to be an easy case. The widow identified you as her attacker.

Witnesses put you in the vicinity on the day of the murder. I'm not here to give you hope, son, but I will give you a defense. Now, about your manner of speech."

Nealy cut in, "What a strange fascination you folks seem to have with this second language of mine. Surely I'm not the first Negro whom you've ever heard speak with a voice different than the streets of Charleston. I would imagine you've heard and read of Booker T. Washington and Mr. Du Bois. It's amazing what education can do."

"Mr. Duncan, Nealy, my interest is less in the evolution of education in your society, but more in what makes you different, or distinguished in this case."

"So a scar on my face and manner of speech are important to you?"

"Not to me Nealy, but perhaps to the jury."

Both men paused. Their eyes met and held. The angles of their jaws raised an inch, the measure of men measuring each other.

Brice stood and stepped back a few paces, thinking, as he might in a courtroom.

"How well did you know Max Lubelsky?"

"We were friendly. I've done business with him for several years, more perhaps after I started dating Ida. Funny how a girl can get you to spend money."

"That's the truth. Did you ever spend time hanging around the shop?"

"Sometimes when he wasn't busy we'd talk about things. He liked to talk about sports. We had a little thing about the big fight last summer."

"The Johnson-Jeffries fight? Guess he never found out who won."

"No, sir."

"Was he friendly?"

"More than most white folks. He was a businessman, but he wasn't concerned about talking to Negroes. We were his customers. He kept an icebox in the back of the store. Once he offered me a soda."

"Did anyone ever see the two of you chatting, acting friendly?"

"Probably, there were usually a few folks in and out of the store."

"Nealy, you ever been in any trouble?"

"No sir. I started working early, never had any time for trouble."

"Do you have any money saved?"

"Some. I've been buying things for me and Ida, so a little less than when I was single."

"Do you go to church?"

"Yes, a little more of late," Nealy smiled with that.

"Since your arrest have you been in lineups in front of different witnesses?"

"Yes, sir."

"In any of those lineups, in any questioning or statements has anyone mentioned the scar on your face?"

"No, sir."

"Thank you, Nealy."

Matthews got up and went to the door. MacMillan followed. Matthews knocked to alert the guard, who unlocked the door and stepped inside.

"You done, Mr. Matthews?"

"Yes, deputy, but I need you to do something. Mr. Duncan is second on the docket today, which means we won't start until after lunch. Before that I want him taken back to the jail, showered and changed into the suit of clean clothes I sent up there. I do not want this man brought into the courtroom in this condition. If you have any concerns, have the sheriff call me at my office."

"Yes, sir."

"I'll see you this afternoon." Matthews said to Nealy, who wore a hint of a smile as the door closed.

"Is he innocent?" MacMillan asked Matthews in the hallway.

"That's not the issue. We're here to put up a defense against testimony that Peurifoy submits to the jury. That's all."

"Can Peurifoy prove he's guilty?"

"He was found guilty the day he was arrested. Our job is to probe the prosecution's case. All these people expect is a good show. They may just get one."

CHAPTER TWELVE
Thursday
OCTOBER 6, 1910

Randy sat across the breakfast table from me. No light fell on that woman that made her anything but beautiful. Mojo had eaten and made a run for the morning papers. Meredith served eggs Benedict as if she knew it was my favorite. My new world order was falling into place and it suited me just fine.

Nealy wasn't first on the docket, but I wanted to get to the courthouse early to poke around, and to make sure I was present and seated when the gavel fell. The local newspapers were full of the trial. They rehashed the cruelty of the crime and the witness' stories, each with their own embellishments, and also Peurifoy's playing to the press. Randy looked up from her paper as I got up to leave.

"Don't get your hopes up for any miracles," she said. "This will likely be a quick trial and a quicker hanging. The whole town would rather just put this behind them."

"That inconvenience is going to cost an innocent man his life, not to mention leaving a killer running free. I have no real expectations, certainly not for justice. Frankly, I don't think Nealy expects to walk away from this, and that in itself bothers me. There's something noble about the way he's bearing up under all this. But there's something about this easy acceptance in him that just doesn't feel right."

"Justice here isn't even-handed. That's part of the reason you're here. The Negroes are barely one generation removed from slavery. Freedom itself is still a novelty to some. Justice is dispensed by whites for whites, and what is handed out for blacks is something else entirely."

"But where's the anger? Where's the outrage? Where's his fight?"

"Where would that take him, or anybody, in this town, at this time? You saw the Klan in person. Nealy is a dead man either way, but at least this way there is a chance, even if only a small one. Much is changing here, but the changes are painfully slow. Some day justice will be for all, but not in our lifetime. Now go. You have a part to play in this, in making this change happen. Go do it."

I walked away from the house and turned the corner on Meeting Street. A couple blocks up, at the so-called "Four Corners of Law," a crowd had gathered, a mix of blue-collar and blue blood. In an odd display of equality for this town, each would have the same chance at the limited seating in the courtroom. Across the street, Ida waited on the corner. I headed for her.

"Mista Hal." She smiled, excited and full of hope. Under the circumstances, it was the part of seeing Ida that hurt the most.

"Hello, Ida. Are you going in?"

"Oh, Mista Hal, I don't know. No other black folks is goin' in. Momma tole me not to, but Nealy, he needs me. My Nealy needs me. Nobody goin' be pullin' for Nealy but me."

"There's lots of tension about this trial, and a lot of evil people may be looking to do harm. Some men tried to hurt Mojo and me last night. I'm not going to tell you not to go in, but be aware that someone might want to hurt you, too."

Her face changed. The youthful smile faded and the light left her. She looked at me, suddenly older and wiser than I thought possible. Even her voice was somber.

"Mista Hal, when I first saw you in Miss Mary's kitchen, dere was things I didn't tell you. Dere are things I don' say in front of Mama. She tries so hard to keep dis pain from me. I'm sixteen, Mista Hal, but I'm no chile. I knows Nealy will probly nevah be free. I knows he might die. But I'm all he got to hope for and no cracker in a Klan suit is goin' to scare me away."

I was impressed. Ida stood defiant before me, the cute young girl replaced now with a fearless, beautiful woman with fire in her eyes.

"Let's go in," I said.

We filed in together, public, press and participants. Ida was at my side, attracting glances and an occasional heated stare. The crowd climbed the stairs and walked down a short hallway to the main courtroom. We moved into the room and down the main aisle before splitting, me to the section reserved for the press, Ida to a small section marked "Coloreds Only," where she sat alone.

The courtroom filled quickly. Windows were opened to admit the breezes one hoped might cool the crowd. The room rustled with idle chatter, some on the topic of the trial, some on the usual small town gossip. For the most part, the din had the tone of a party, not the trial of a man facing the gallows.

From the back, Nealy entered, accompanied by two deputies. The courtroom fell silent. He was dressed in a dark suit and white shirt, looking much better than the last time we met. He looked straight ahead, the only sound came from the chains dragging as he shuffled slowly to his place. Ida saw him and offered only the slightest of smiles. As he walked past the widow of Max Lubelsky, Rose swooned against a friend. Nealy passed by and took his seat, directed by Matthews to the far side of the defense table, closest to the windows.

Judge Richard Watts entered through a door at the back of the court. Watts was fifty-seven years old, from upstate South Carolina. He was elected circuit judge in 1893 and still traveled the courts. Rumor had it that Judge Watts was unlikely to make it to the state Supreme Court, but he was respected for his knowledge of the law and his control in his court.

"All rise," the bailiff called. "The Court of General Sessions is now in order. The State of South Carolina vs. Daniel Duncan."

Watts banged his gavel and Nealy's trial was under way. Jury selection was first. The *voir dere* process itself brought back Randy's words. Justice wasn't even-handed in the selection of a jury of Nealy's "peers." Prosecution and defense each dismissed a few prospective jurors, but when the panel was seated and sworn, the twelve jurors and both alternates were all white men.

"Solicitor," Judge Watts ordered, "Call your first witness."

"The State calls Dr. K. I. Pearlstine," Peurifoy said.

The young doctor took the stand and raised a shaking hand to take the oath. I hoped his hand was steadier in surgery.

"Dr. Pearlstine, were you summoned to Lubelsky's store on the morning of June 21st?"

"Yes, sir."

"Please describe what you saw on entering the store."

"Mr. Lubelsky was lying on the floor. He was unconscious and bleeding. He was moaning but not speaking."

"Describe the wounds, if you please."

"I found several wounds to his head. It was too hard to examine him very carefully there, so I sent him to the hospital."

"And what did you find there?"

"When I got to the hospital, I had his head shaved and found three large lacerations in his scalp."

"Did you treat him at the hospital?"

"He lived about half an hour after we got him to the hospital."

A wail erupted in the courtroom and all heads turned to Rose Lubelsky, who rocked back and forth, keening. Watts pounded his gavel.

"Order! Bailiff, remove that woman if she can't calm down."

A friend threw an arm around Rose's shoulders.

"Continue, Mr. Peurifoy."

"Doctor, in your opinion what was the cause of Max Lubelsky's death?"

"At the *post mortem* examination we found a fractured skull and hemorrhage of the brain, half a dozen or more fractures, as if the skull was beaten into a pulp."

"The wounds caused his death?"

"The hemorrhage caused by the fractures was the cause of death."

Matthews waived cross-examination. Peurifoy called his next witness, Joel Posner.

A small man stood, walked to the stand, was sworn in and took his seat.

Under Peurifoy's questioning, Posner told of the morning he went to visit Lubelsky with his daughter and how, finding no one in the store, they prepared to wait and subsequently found Lubelsky lying on the floor, soaked in blood.

"What was his condition?"

"He was laying in blood. I was so excited and I went and tried to feel his head and I tried to talk to him, and then he started to wipe his blood."

"Did he say anything?"

"He could not say anything. At the time I found him he was most like dead. When I started to feel his head, he moved."

"Did you see anyone in the shop?"

"I didn't see anyone. I went out the door and called Mr. Levin."

"Where does he keep his store?"

"Right next door."

"What happened then?"

"He told me he didn't have anyone to leave in the store, and then I went and called a policeman."

"Thank you, Mr. Posner."

"Mr. Matthews," Watt said. "Any questions?"

Matthews stood and walked to the witness.

"When you went in, you say you didn't find Mr. Lubelsky?"

"No, sir. I thought he was maybe outside talking to someone, and it was when I was resting against the counter that I found him on the floor."

"Did you hear any noise?"

"He didn't make any noise. He was most like dead. He was lying down. He was sleeping."

"Was there much blood?"

"The whole body was in blood."

"Did you see any more blood?"

"No. I went out and called Mr. Levin."

"And he was too busy to come?"

"No. He wasn't busy. He said he could not leave because he had no one to leave in the store."

"You didn't see anybody or hear anybody upstairs or downstairs around Max Lubelsky's place?"

"No, sir."

"Was the store in disorder?"

"I was never looking to see if it was out of order. I was just looking for a person in the store."

"If it had been in disorder would you have noticed it?"

"I don't understand."

"If everything was thrown around you would have noticed it?"

"Yes."

"And you didn't notice anything?"

"No, sir."

"Thank you, Mr. Posner."

The testimony of Frank Frost followed. He described seeing a man in front of Lubelsky's the morning of the killing and identified him as Duncan.

Next, Peurifoy called Viola Gibbes to the witness stand. She testified that she collided with a black man running with a bundle of clothes the morning of the murder. She identified Duncan as the man who ran into her.

Charles Levin was next on the stand.

"Mr. Levin," Peurifoy began," did you see this man, Duncan, the morning of June 21st?"

"Yes, sir. It was him that morning."

"Are you sure he is the same man?"

"Yes, sir, I am sure. I know it. I saw him by the door for almost three quarters of an hour. Until I walked up to him, he had a wire eight-penny nail, a piece of wood with a nail in it. He had it standing that way."

"In this piece of wood?" Peurifoy held up a piece of split oak.

"Yes, that one. I walked up to him and asked him what he was doing there. He didn't answer me anything. He walked up to the window and looked in there and then went in the store."

Peurifoy questioned Levin on a blue coat and stiff bowler hat, which Levin said was the clothing worn by the suspect.

"Mr. Levin, did you see Daniel Duncan at the jail?"

"I saw him, but he was not by himself. They put him among five others."

"Who were the other five?"

"I don't know. I knew his face and I identified him as the one who had that slat in his hand."

"Did you have any hesitation?"

"No, sir."

"Were you called by the police to identify others suspected of killing Max Lubelsky?"

"Yes, sir. I was to the station house and they brought a good many to me, I believe it was between fifteen and twenty that I looked at, and I told them no, that was not the one."

"So you never identified anyone but Duncan?"

"No, sir."

Peurifoy turned from the stand and looked to the defense table. He didn't quite smile, but had the air of a man with the upper hand.

Brice Matthews stood and walked to Levin.

"Mr. Levin, you testified you saw the defendant outside Max Lubelsky's store."

"Yes, sir."

"Did you suspect he was up to something?"

"I don't know."

"You saw him go into Mr. Lubelsky's shop and you were looking for something?"

"I said that thing looked suspicious."

"So you saw a suspicious man go into Mr. Lubelsky's store?"

"I don't know."

"Didn't you say he went into the store?"

"Yes."

"Was he suspicious?"

"No, he was not exactly suspicious. If you passed me with a thing like that slat, I would suspicion you."

"And if I put that hat and coat on, you would recognize me?"

A chuckle went through the courtroom.

"No."

"You don't remember how many men you tried to identify?"

"No."

"Did they all have that hat and coat on?"

"Some of them, two or three. I don't recollect."

"I ask you, did they have that hat and coat on?"

"Yes, sir."

"If I put the hat and coat with a thousand others, could you pick it out?"

"I could pick out his face."

"Could you pick that hat and coat out of a thousand in a pile?"

"I don't think so." Matthews walked to the big windows at the end of the defense table where the defendant sat. Facing Nealy, with his back to Levin, he addressed the courtroom and the jury.

"Mr. Levin, you have twice stated in your testimony that you recognized Daniel Duncan by his face, but neither in your initial description to the police, from which they posted descriptions for their manhunt, nor in your testimony in the preliminary hearing did you mention anything peculiar, in particular about Mr. Duncan's face." He turned to Nealy. "Daniel, please stand up and face the jury."

I leaned way forward on my seat, my heart racing. I looked to Ida, she shot a glance back at me, then turned to Nealy.

Nealy stood and turned the right side of his face, which had been toward the windows, to the judge and then to the jury. He pivoted, exposing his scar to the courtroom and a low murmur rippled through the room.

"Mr. Levin," Matthews pounced, "how is it that you never mentioned that obvious and fairly dramatic scar that runs across the face of the defendant?"

The gallery gasped and chattered. Several spectators pointed at Nealy.

"Order!" Watts called, pounding his gavel.

"Objection, Your Honor!" Peurifoy was out of his seat.

"Quiet, or I will clear this courtroom," Watts said loudly.

"No further questions, Your Honor."

Matthews walked back to the defense table and sat. Peurifoy shot him a hot look.

"Gentlemen," Watts said. "It's too late in the day to call another witness. We stand adjourned until nine o'clock tomorrow morning."

The courtroom cleared like a small church on a hot Sunday, led by the local press eager to file their stories before deadline. Hot on their heels were spectators who acted as town criers, spreading the details of the testimony across Charleston like wildfire. I lingered, watching the room clear. Nealy was led away, staring fondly at Ida until the door closed behind him. The lawyers packed up their papers and walked out in tandem.

"What do you think you're doing, Brice?" Peurifoy pressed

Matthews as they approached me.

"Defending my client, John."

"Don't do anything foolish. You understand what's at stake here."

"I'm not sure Judge Wells would appreciate this sidebar discussion. I'll see you in the morning."

They went through the door and turned in opposite directions.

I sat back for a moment, alone in the empty, quiet courtroom. This town had the capacity to surprise. Just when you think you can predict a course of events, somebody deals a fade-away pitch and you're swinging and missing. Maybe there was hope for Nealy.

Outside the courthouse, the crowd had drifted away except for one lone sentry. Mojo ran up the steps to meet me.

"Miss Randy says you's suppose to meet her at de hotel for tea."

"What's it all about, Mojo?"

"She sez sumptin' bout Missus Vain de Hoss."

"Vanderhorst, Mojo. She's no hoss, just an old bird."

"Miss Randy sez it yo fault, so you bess shows up."

"Guess I've been told then."

Tea wasn't exactly what I had in mind. Something with a little more punch was called for. The opening day left me feeling a little better about the trial than I expected. We were nowhere near the champagne stage, but some spirits seemed appropriate.

Back at the hotel, I slipped through the revolving doors and Bright Eyes flagged me down.

"Mr. Hinson, I'm so sorry you checked out of the hotel. I hope it wasn't any failure on our part."

"Certainly not. The hotel, and you, are lovely. I merely had an offer to stay in a private home."

"We hope to see you again." She meant it.

"That seems likely. Mrs. Vanderhorst can command an appearance."

"I believe she's waiting for you in the bar."

"Thank you." I walked through the hotel thinking Bright Eyes could stand to get out a little more. In the bar, I felt like I was in another court, but instead of law, this one had more the royal feeling. Randy and Mrs. Vanderhorst were elegantly ensconced.

"Good afternoon, ladies," I said.

"Mr. Hinson, good afternoon to you," Mrs. Vanderhorst began.

"Since you come directly from the courtroom, perhaps you can fill us in on these rumors of an uproar just awhile ago."

Randy winked at me and smiled.

"I'm not sure which of you has the better sources," I said, "but Brice Matthews is giving this trial more than just a cursory run at justice."

I explained about Nealy's scar, and described how Matthews made a telling and significant point that could create doubt in the jury's minds about Levin's testimony. I also described how the point went over with Peurifoy.

Mrs. Vanderhorst sniffed. "A lot of people don't give Brice the credit he's due. He doesn't play politics the way Peurifoy does and he may not be the flashiest lawyer, but he's smart and doesn't back down easily. I imagine he will pull a few more tricks out of his hat before this trial is over."

"The important thing," I said, "is that Nealy may actually have a real defense."

"Don't get your hopes up," she cautioned. "You can lead a jury to the facts, but you can't make them think."

"Well said, ma'am." I glanced at the tea service set in front of the two ladies. My face must have shown my disappointment.

"Tea doesn't suit you?"

"Tea is lovely, but frankly I'd prefer a Manhattan."

"Frankly, Hal, I hate tea." She raised a hand and immediately caught the attention of the waiter, who stepped quickly to the table. "If you please, Robert, remove this tea and bring us each a Manhattan."

Randy and Mrs. Vanderhorst talked of their acquaintances, fashion and where to find the latest in shoes. For two women who were at odds a few days ago, they were chatting like old friends. The drinks came not a moment too soon. Randy raised her glass.

"To new friends and alliances." She winked at Mrs. Vanderhorst and we sipped.

"Would someone care to share the story behind the toast?" I asked. They smiled.

"Just because you're a reporter," Randy said, "doesn't mean you get to have all the answers."

Our talk returned to the trial. I gave them Levin's testimony, and where he contradicted Posner's testimony by claiming instead to have rushed to the aid of his fallen neighbor.

"That man Levin is more involved in this whole affair than meets the eye," Mrs. Vanderhorst offered. "I hope Brice probes more weak points of his testimony tomorrow."

"You are a keen observer of the law, Mrs. Vanderhorst."

"It runs in the family. My grandfather served in the Revolutionary War under Francis Marion, then turned to politics, first as mayor of Charleston, then as governor. He helped revise both the state penal code and prison system to make it something other than a medieval system of harsh sentences and cruel imprisonment. He's buried a block down the street, at St. Michael's."

"I see now why you're sensitive about injustice, or the presumption of injustice, in Charleston."

"I am proud of what my family has done to make the justice system better in this state. No system of justice in which Man is allowed to pass judgment on his fellow Man is going to be perfect, but it annoys me more than a little when humanity, at its more base level, interferes with the law."

She paused and looked at us. "You two have been more than kind to indulge me. It has been some while since I enjoyed a cocktail with young people. It has given me a mind that it might be something worth repeating. But for the moment, you two might find better use of your evening than spending it with an old woman, so run along now. Do the things I wish I was still young enough to do."

She stood slowly, and with all the grace that age allowed, walked out of the bar and into the lift.

Randy shook her head. "Mr. Hinson, I must thank the man from New York for bringing me together with this woman of wit and substance. I believe we will be close friends ."

"What was all that about allies?"

"You'll know, at the proper time."

"The thought of the two of you together frightens me. Someone should alert the press."

"Hal, you are the press."

"Exactly."

Outside on the street, I immediately looked for Mojo and panicked when I didn't see him.

"Don't worry," Randy said. "He's back at the house."

"How did you know?"

"How did I know what you were thinking? It was in your eyes."

"There you go, scaring me again. How did he know where to go?"

"I told him this morning that when he's not on a specific task he should be at home, out of harm's way."

"So we're both under your care and protection now?"

"So it would seem."

"Excellent."

We strolled down Meeting Street arm in arm, and turned into her lane. Randy on my arm and the warm October evening made it seem that everything in my life prior to this had been out of order. There was then and there was now. Now was good. Up the steps, Meredith met us at the door as though she'd been doing it for years.

"If you would like to freshen up a bit," she said to us, "dinner will be ready in a half hour. A bottle of champagne is in the parlor."

She must have read my mind from blocks away. There was a lot of intuition going on around here. This web of women was woven in a wonderful way.

"I'm going to run up," I said, "throw some water on my face and change shirts."

"I'll wait with the champagne until you come back."

I raced up the stairs and tore off my shirt. Time spent up here alone was wasted time. I threw cold water on my face to shock the senses, toweled off and opened the closet. All my shirts were clean and pressed and arranged neatly in a row. Meredith at work. I put on a shirt and a fresh tie, added my coat and arrived at the top of the stairs in time to hear a cork pop. Bubbles were settling in the glasses when I walked into the room.

"Good timing," Randy said.

She gave me a glass and we sat together in front of the fire, sipping wine and discussing the trial. Randy's mind was keen on points of law, and she pointed out several irregularities in the police presentation of suspects, and commented that it didn't help Nealy to be presented to the witnesses dressed in the clothes matching those of the alleged suspect.

Meredith appeared. "Dinner is served," she said. "Tonight we have baked porgy over our own local rice."

"Sounds delicious," I said. "Is this the Carolina Gold rice I've heard so much about?"

"Where did you hear about our rice?" Randy asked.

"Peurifoy."

"Then I guess everything about him isn't bad."

I wondered how much longer Meredith would continue to impress me with her creativity in the kitchen, hoping it would take some time, a very long time. Dessert was hand-churned ice cream, and it was wonderful.

"Mister Hal," Meredith said, "I hope you're not going to want seconds on the ice cream. Markus was teaching Mojo how to make it and we barely saved enough for the two of you. He ate until he almost exploded, then fell asleep."

"He had the right idea." I turned to Randy. "Court starts early tomorrow. I better get some sleep."

Meredith smiled and left the room. Randy got up with an intriguing look in her smoky eyes. I grinned, the last one to get the point. We went upstairs together, and at the top Randy took my hand and led me to her door. Inside was a room alight with a dozen candles. She undressed slowly and stood in her glory in the glow. I joined her and we looked at each other as if for the first time. We didn't rush, our lovemaking was slow and sure, an ecstasy of discovery. When we were spent, all but one of the candles had guttered, their fuel spent.

CHAPTER THIRTEEN
Friday
OCTOBER 7, 1910

The morning papers were filled with the first day's testimony, and the courtroom was even more packed than the day before. Much was made of how things had ended. Ida was still alone in the "Negroes Only" section separated from the rest of the public seats. Without a press pass, I would have been lucky to find a place to stand in the back of the room.

Nealy was seated at the defense table with Matthews and MacMillan. Peurifoy and his assistant also were seated.

"All rise," the bailiff called. Watts entered from his chambers, took the bench and spoke without looking up. "Be seated."

Peurifoy began by calling detectives to the stand. First was Clarence Levy, who described the wounded tailor and countered the testimony of Posner, stating that the store had been ransacked. Next came John Hogan, whose description of the scene on the day of the murder precisely matched Levy's. His testimony touched on some clothes and costume jewelry found in Duncan's apartment on the day of his arrest that matched similar types found in the store on the day of the murder.

On cross-examination, Matthews turned his questions to the arrests.

"How many men have been committed to the County Jail in this case?"

"Only two that I remember. Two besides Duncan were held with probable cause for murder."

Matthews took a different tack.

"Are you aware that among nearly all of Lubelsky's kind there has been a factional fight for years?"

"I never knew of any of them fighting each other."

"I mean a feudal disturbance among them."

"Feudal, sir? I cannot say. As a general rule they are loyal people, at least to one another."

Peurifoy jumped to his feet. "Objection, Your Honor. This is irrelevant."

"Overruled. You may continue, Mr. Matthews."

Brice changed direction again. "Did you take the defendant to Mrs. Lubelsky's house the day she was assaulted?"

"Yes, sir."

"At the order of the chief of police?"

"Yes, sir. He told Detective Levy and myself to do that. He thought she'd been assaulted severely."

"Was she notified of the impending visit?"

"No, sir. She didn't know anything at all until I rapped at the gate, and when the nigger confronted her she flew at him."

"Where was she?"

"In the shop."

"Her wounds had been dressed?"

"Yes, sir. There was a good many people came up there then, and some of them did make a slight attempt to assault him."

"She knew Duncan was in the charge of an officer when you carried him up there?"

"I expect she knew."

Matthews nodded as though he had scored a point, then turned to the day of the murder and the description put out on the suspect.

"What was the description you received?"

"Said he was a Negro."

"Didn't the order at the station house call him a mulatto?"

"No, sir, I never heard that. I didn't look for a mulatto."

"But you arrested two other suspects during the course of your investigation, and held them until after the assault on Mrs. Lubelsky."

"The two we had committed to jail, we didn't turn them loose until this man was arrested and we had sufficient evidence to commit him."

"Sufficient in whose opinion? Yours?"

"The magistrate thought it sufficient."

"Who committed the other two?"

'The magistrate committed them pending a further investigation."

"But he committed them."

"Yes."

"Thank you. That's all."

Hogan sat silent for a moment, staring forward.

"You are dismissed, detective," Judge Watts prodded. "Solicitor, your next witness, please."

"Detective John Brennan."

A burly Irishman stood and walked to the stand, glancing at Duncan and the defense desk on his way to his seat. Peurifoy began the questioning.

"Detective, did the defendant say he was on King Street to buy more clothes from Lubelsky's shop?"

"Yes, sir."

"So he admitted to being in the store."

"Yes, sir."

"When you searched his pockets on the day of the arrest, what did you find?"

"In searching his pockets, we found some invitation cards he had issued to a number of different parties. He said he was going to get married. He admitted to being at Mrs. Lubelsky's store the same day."

"Are these the invitations?" Peurifoy held them up for the jury and the courtroom. Ida leaned forward in her seat, the invitations were only a few feet away, she could have reached out and touched them. Peurifoy handed the simple card to Brennan. "Read that to the court, please, detective."

Brennan squinted. "'Mrs. Mary Lampkin requests the honor of your presence at the marriage of her daughter Ida to Mr. Nealy Duncan on Wednesday evening, July thirteenth, one thousand nine-hundred and ten at eight o'clock at home No. 4 Palmetto Street, Charleston, S.C.'"

The invitation meant to bring Ida and Nealy together was being used in evidence against him, to send him away from her forever. Ida looked to Nealy and for once he turned toward the court and caught her eye. They were both in tears.

"Thank you, detective. Now, I believe you said you questioned a number of people about the killing."

"Yes, sir."

"But none of them were identified positively until after Mrs. Lubelsky was assaulted and Daniel Duncan was arrested?"

"Everyone that answered the description given us by the three witnesses, everyone who was arrested for suspicion, was brought before the three. Each one said the parties we had under arrest were not the party. Two suspects, for reasons of our own, we committed to jail. Immediately after Duncan's arrest and positive identification by all three parties, we released them."

"No further questions."

Matthews walked to the stand. "When you arrested Jones, did you think you had the man who had killed Lubelsky?"

"I might and I might not."

"Isn't it true, detective, that you stated at the corner of Columbus Street and the railroad track, in the presence of a number of railroad men and one Nettie Aiken, that your source of information had satisfied you that you had the right party?"

Brennan shook his head vigorously. "I never spoke to Nettie Aiken in my life on Columbus or the railroad track."

"Did you ever state to anyone that you had the proper party?"

"I might have."

Matthews shrugged, and shook his head and changed the subject.

"How much reward was being offered?"

"I don't know. That had no effect on me."

"How much was offered?"

"I don't know."

"Do you know the governor offered one hundred dollars?"

"I remember reading it in the newspapers."

"Do you know the mayor offered two hundred and fifty?"

"I read it in the paper."

"Do you know the Israelites offered five hundred?"

"I heard it but I don't think it was true."

"So eight hundred and fifty or a thousand dollars is no inspiration to a detective trying to work a case?"

"The detective don't expect to get even one dollar."

"That's a very high concept to take, but does everybody follow that?"

"They do."

"And have you ever been the recipient of any reward?"

"Not offered by the city."

"How about by private parties?"

"In the case of escaped convicts we are allowed to take it."

Matthews walked to the window, hoping, as I was, that the jury would grasp the significance of the point that the police had an incentive to close the case. He glanced at Nealy and turned to walk back to Brennan.

"Now detective, when you had these other men in charge, you say men were brought down to identify them. Were these suspects rigged up with a blue coat and a stiff hat?"

"No, they were just brought in."

"Well, how were they clothed for the occasion?"

"I don't know. According to whatever clothes they wore when they were arrested, the same as Duncan when he was identified in his shirt sleeves and bare headed."

"But when the detectives got ready for Charles Levin's identification, did they garb up Duncan in a hat and a blue coat?"

"Yes, sir."

"Thank you."

Peurifoy rose. "Detective, counsel asked you about a conversation you had with Nettie Aiken where you stated that you had gotten the right party. Did you ever tell anyone that you had gotten the right party until this man Duncan was arrested?"

"I may have said that I *thought* I had the right party, but about swearing that I had the right party or committing anyone to jail as being the right party, that is not the case."

"You say witnesses Frank Frost and Viola Gibbes refused to identify anyone you brought up until this man Duncan?"

"Yes, sir."

"And they promptly identified this man?"

"Yes, sir."

"Was this man rigged up in a blue coat and derby hat when Frost and Gibbes were called to identify him?"

"No, sir."

"Thank you, detective."

"Gentleman," the judge said, "with the conclusion of that testimony, we're approaching noon. Court will stand in recess until one o'clock this afternoon."

Everyone in the courtroom was riveted to the testimony and it took a moment for the notion of a recess to sink in. Slowly, people stood and stretched and headed for the door. Nealy was escorted out, and Ida lingered to catch his eye. I waited until most of the court was cleared and walked to her.

"Let's go down to Miss Mary's for lunch," I said.

"I'm not so hungry, Mista Hal."

"But you need to eat, and don't worry, I'm sure Mojo will finish what you don't."

We left the courthouse and found Mojo waiting on the steps.

"Mista Hal, is dat thing over? Folks came outta here just buzzin'."

"No, Mojo, we still have a ways to go. But we do have a break for lunch. Let's hurry down to Miss Mary's."

"Now dat's the way to do business!"

We walked past restaurants where the white court audience ate, back across the divide, back to the familiar framed house. The crowd was thick, but Miss Mary met us at the door and steered us to a corner table.

"Din expect you folks today. Thought you'd be in dat courthouse all day."

"We got a short recess for lunch," I said.

"Betta get yous something quick, den. Sit down, I'll be right back."

She was back within five minutes with three plates. Mojo's eyes went wide, his mouth followed. He didn't take time for his usual exclamation over dinner.

"You're not going to explain what we're eating?" I asked him and he tried to talk, but it wasn't pretty.

"It's chicken purlo," Ida translated. "Chicken and rice dat you cook long and slow."

"I'm not sure I've ever seen so many ways to cook a chicken."

"Down heah," Miss Mary said, "we gots six ways to Sunday to cook a chicken, but on Sunday you bess bet it's gonna be fried."

"Widdout da blacks," Miss Mary said, "dees po white folks in de South wuld still be eatin boiled meat and taters."

It was nice to hear conversation that steered away from the trial and Nealy's plight, but the topic hung like a low cloud and finally broke into rain.

"Mista Hinson," Ida turned those doe eyes on me, "seems like Nealy's lawyer takin' his side."

Whatever hope I might have with Matthews' fairly spirited effort to defend, there was no point in raising anyone else's expectations.

"I've covered a number of trials over the years," I said, "and they always mystify me. What seems certain can change in an instant on one person's testimony, on one lawyer's smart turn of a phrase, or on a single point that sticks with a jury. Brice Matthews is actually making a case for the defense. He hasn't rolled over on this. Where it will go, I can't say. Peurifoy is holding his key witness for the end of his case, and that may come this afternoon."

"I don know nuthin' bout courts," Ida said, "or trial or lawyers an such, but I do know a little about people. Dere is good and bad, in both black and white. I know my Nealy is good. I tink Mista Matthews is good. He's tryin' to help Nealy. He's de only hope Nealy's got now, so I'm prayin' for him, I'm prayin' for Nealy and I'm prayin' God's gonna get dis one right."

"Child, don't you go blasphemin'."

"Momma, you tole me all my life to put my faith in de Lord. All I got is in his hands now. It's up to him, and dose white men, and I hope he got some sway on dem." She had a defiant look in her eye, and I hoped it would help carry her through the next few days. Some hope is worse than none at all.

I made sure Miss Mary took some money and we set out, launched by the slam of the screen door behind us. As we walked to the courthouse, I saw Brice Matthews coming up Broad Street. I sent Ida and Mojo in one direction and set an intercept course for Matthews.

"Mr. Matthews! Good afternoon. I'm Hal Hinson, with the New York Tribune."

"Good day, sir. I heard of your articles from a few days ago."

"From New York?"

"Friends, Mr. Hinson, on the phone. We're not all cloistered here in the city of Charleston. I've been keeping track of you. I'm a bit surprised you haven't been in touch."

"I've been a bit surprised you're making such a run on this case. I just had lunch with Ida. You've raised a sense of hope."

"That may be premature."

"Any more surprises in store?"

"You're far too smart than to think I'd comment during trial. Perhaps we can talk after testimony ends."

"I'd like that."

"I'll be in touch."

He took the courthouse entrance for lawyers and lawmen. I walked up the front steps with the rest of the crowd. The desire to be in the courtroom led to some minor jostling on the way in.

The gavel went down with a bang.

"Court's in session," the judge said. "Mr. Peurifoy, call your witness."

"Your Honor, the State calls John Shuller."

An old, lanky Negro came forward and was sworn.

"Mr. Shuller, what do you do?" Peurifoy asked.

"I'm a porter, carries things for people."

"Do you remember the 21st of last June, the day Max Lubelsky was killed?"

"Yes, suh, I remember that. I don't remember what day it was."

"Do you know this man, Daniel Duncan?"

"Yes, suh, I know him by sight. I don't know his name."

"Did you see him the day Max Lubelsky was killed?"

"Yes, suh."

"Where did you see him?"

"In the store."

"Whose store?"

"Max Lubelsky's store."

"What was he doing in there?"

"Leaning on the counter with his hand in his hip pocket."

"What time did you see him?"

"About half past nine."

"And what did you do after you saw him?"

"I left shortly after. I left him and Max in there, them two."

Peurifoy nodded with satisfaction. "No further questions at this time."

"Mr. Matthews?"

"What were you doing in there, old man?"

"I always go in there, talking to Max, first one thing then another."

"You say you knew Duncan?"

"I knew his face, but I didn't know his name. I saw him on the street on and off."

"You saw him in the store that morning?"

"He was all the time in there, on and off."

"Was he having any talk with Lubelsky?"

"No more than they were laughing and joking about the fight that man had that time."

"What man?"

"Jack Johnson."

"Did you join in the conversation?"

"Yes, suh, I said one or two words."

"With Duncan?"

"With Max and Duncan. Max was this side in a chair, drinking a cup of coffee and eating a piece of bread."

"So, the three of you were in the shop, talking about the upcoming fight that was the sporting event of the summer, the 'Fight of the Century.' Just three men chatting."

"Objection, Your Honor, leading the witness," Peurifoy didn't like where this was going.

"Sustained. Mr. Matthews, you know better. Get to your question."

"I will, Judge. Mr. Lubelsky was sitting in his chair, sipping coffee and eating bread. Did he indicate he was in any danger?"

"He seemed okay to me."

"When Mr. Duncan was leaning against the counter talking about Jack Johnson, was he carrying a stick with a nail through one end?"

"That I could see?"

"He was not carrying a stick, then."

"No, suh."

"Thank you. No further questions."

Peurifoy watched the old man walk away from the stand, and looked over at Matthew's desk as the witness walked past. He pulled his notes up in front of him and made a few quick scratches.

"Mr. Peurifoy," the judge prodded. "Your next witness?"

"One moment, Your Honor." The prosecutor leaned and whispered a word to his assistant, then stood. "Your Honor, the State calls Mrs. Rose Lubelsky."

The buzz shot across the courtroom.

"Silence!" Watts pounded his gavel. "I'll have quiet in here or I'll clear the room."

Rose Lubelsky was the witness most people were waiting to hear. She stood slowly and nervously approached the stand and was sworn In.

"Mrs. Lubelsky, do you live in Charleston?"

"Yes, sir."

"You are the widow of Max Lubelsky?"

"I am, sir."

"Did you go to New York any time this year?"

"In June."

"When did you come back?"

"I had a telegram my husband was killed."

"Do you remember the 21st of June of this year?"

"Yes, sir."

"Was that the day your husband was killed?"

"That is what the telegram said."

"Was your husband dead when you came back?"

"Yes, sir."

"Did you ever see this man, the defendant, before?"

"As soon as I came back I buried my husband. I didn't care any more for myself. I tried to keep up for the little boy, so I opened the store and as soon as I opened the store that fellow used to come in all the time."

"Are you sure he is the one?"

"I am as sure as I am sitting here that that is the devil."

"Now Mrs. Lubelsky, you remember the eighth of July?"

"Yes, sir, he opened my head. I have a mark right here."

"What did he hit you with?"

"I was fixing up a bundle and waiting for the eight dollars, and when I was waiting for the change and talking about my troubles, telling him my husband was so young ..."

"Objection!" Matthews was on his feet. "Your Honor, this is irrelevant."

"Sustained. Mrs. Lubelsky, you can tell the court that you saw the defendant that day, you can answer direct questions, but as much as we regret the loss of your husband you cannot describe the details of your life."

"Now, Mrs. Lubelsky," Peurifoy continued, "what became of this man after he struck you?"

"While I was waiting for the eight dollars I lifted my eyes up and he struck me."

"Where did he go after he struck you?"

"As soon as I got struck I don't know what happened to me."

"Where did he go?"

"I didn't see anything. I wished he would kill me." Her voice rose in pitch.

"Where did he go?"

"I tried to run to the front," she was nearly hysterical, "and he opened his eyes so big I thought he was going to tear me in pieces and I got to the front and he got off."

Matthews was back on his feet, "Your Honor, I object to all of the testimony in regard to the eighth of July on the grounds that it is irrelevant to the murder charges this man is facing."

Watts thought for a moment, then leaned to the jury. "Gentlemen, she has a right to tell whether she saw him on that day and she has a right to state that he struck her, if he did, without going into the details of it, and she can tell what became of him, if she knows. You must disregard any other testimony on the matter of the attack on her that has been brought out here."

Peurifoy turned to the witness. "Mrs. Lubelsky, did the attack you describe take place in this city on King Street?"

"Yes, sir."

"And the defendant was your attacker?"

"He was."

"Your Honor," Peurifoy said, "the State rests."

"Mr. Matthews, call your first witness."

"Your Honor, the defense calls Mrs. Dora Birlant."

She was sworn in by the bailiff and Matthews asked questions to establish that she owned the shop directly across King Street from Lubelsky's store.

"Mrs. Birlant, what did you see the morning of June 21?"

"It was early," she said, "before the stores opened and I was at the door of my shop when I looked across the street and saw Mr. Lubelsky and Mr. Levin talking."

"Just talking?"

"They were talking. At first it seemed normal, then their voices got louder and louder, almost shouting. Mr. Lubelsky was sweeping his stoop and at one point he swept his dirt onto Mr. Levin, then both men raised their brooms like they were going to come to blows."

"What happened then?"

"Mr. Lubelsky went back into his shop."

"What did Mr. Levin do?"

"He closed his door and walked down the street."

"Did you see him return?"

"No. I went in my store to start my day."

"Mrs. Birlant, you're acquainted with Mrs. Lubelsky?"

"We are friends."

"Do you belong to the same place of worship?"

"Yes, the B'rith Shalom synagogue."

"Is there tension among your people over opening on Saturdays, the Jewish Sabbath?"

Peurifoy stood. "Objection, Your Honor. This is irrelevant."

"Counselor, I overruled you the last time on this subject, and you are overruled again. Continue Mr. Matthews."

"Is there tension, Mrs. Birlant?"

"There is. Some merchants want to open, after all it's the day many people do their shopping. Others, the more conservative, say it's against the Torah, against God's will. It threatens to split the synagogue."

"After the murder of her husband, did the rabbi warn Mrs. Lubelsky not to open her husband's shop?" Peurifoy pounced.

"Objection, Your Honor! Hearsay. If the defense counsel wanted to ask that question, he could have asked Mrs. Lubelsky herself."

"Sustained. Move on, Mr. Matthews."

"Thank you, Your Honor. Mrs. Birlant, are you a widow?"

"Yes, sir."

"Were you advised not to open your shop after your husband died?"

"Yes, sir."

"By whom?"

"The rabbi."

"But you did."

"I had no choice, like Mrs. Lubelsky, I have no family here, I have to support my children."

"Do you attend the synagogue?"

"Not so much anymore."

"No further questions."

Peurifoy approached the stand. "Mrs. Birlant, how long have you operated the shop across the street from Lubelsky and Levin?"

"About a year. Since my husband died."

"During that time did you ever see them argue?"

"Just the once."

"During the year that you have been a shop owner, have you ever had a disagreement with another shop owner?"

"Maybe a minor one, over deliveries."

"Have you ever killed anyone?"

There were a few chuckles in the courtroom, a few jurors smiled. Matthews stood. "Objection, Your Honor."

"Sustained. Mr. Peurifoy, we are not here for your amusement."

"Yes, Your Honor. No further questions."

"Mr. Matthews," Wells said. "Next witness."

"The defense calls Mr. Rudolph Geilfuss."

The back door of the courtroom opened and the baker walked in. His face went red, emphasizing the signs of his rosacea, and he lowered his head and walked quickly to the stand in an obvious state of discomfort, avoiding eye contact with everyone.

"What is your business, Mr. Geilfuss?" Matthews asked.

"Baker."

"How long has your family been established in Charleston?"

"Since 1856."

"Do you know the defendant in this case, Daniel Duncan?"

"Yes."

"How long have you known him?"

"Fifteen years."

"How long has he been in the employ of your family?"

"You mean for the family or me?"

"Both."

"Fifteen years."

"Is his general reputation one of peace and quiet, of respectability?"

"Yes."

"Is his reputation good or bad?"

"Good"

"No further questions."

"Cross, Mr. Peurifoy?"

"No, Your Honor."

Baker Geilfuss was up and out of the chair as though his seat was on fire. He made a beeline for the exit and was gone as quickly as his testimony. I wondered whether his short support of the young man he practically helped raise was due to discomfort from being on the stand, or from the fear of reprisal from the community for lending support to an apprentice now sitting accused of murder.

"Next witness," Judge Wells said.

"Your Honor, the defense calls the defendant, Daniel Duncan."

The gallery went on point, like a dog on a bird. There was little doubt that Duncan was the last witness, and the last stand for the defense. After months of newspaper articles, street talk and posturing from the prosecution, the public would finally hear from the mouth of the accused. It was what they came for, to see and listen to a man who may soon be swinging from a rope.

Nealy stood tall and straight, his features composed. When the bailiff came to "so help you God," Nealy answered "I do" with firm, clear conviction.

"Daniel," Matthews began, "how old are you?"

"Twenty-three years old."

"What is your business?"

"I am a baker."

"Where have you worked and for how long?"

"I worked for Mr. Geilfuss for 15 years."

"Where were you working on the eighth of July, the day you were arrested?"

"At the bakery."

"Now, Daniel, you've heard witnesses testify that you were on King Street in the neighborhood of Mr. Lubelsky's store when you were arrested. Were you on King Street?"

"When I was arrested, I was standing in King Street near the tailor."

"Was anyone else around you when you were arrested?"

"Yes, sir, there were three of them. I can point them out if you like."

"White men?"

"Yes."

"Did they strike you?"

"Yes."

"How did you come to be in the neighborhood of Lubelsky's store?"

"I went to pick up my wedding suit."

"So you shopped there?"

"Yes."

"Have you purchased other goods from there?"

"Yes."

"So you were a regular client of Mr. Lubelsky?"

"Yes."

"How did you pay for your clothes?"

"On time. One dollar a week."

"You had a good record of payment with Mr. Lubelsky?"

"He always called me a good customer."

"Did you and Mr. Lubelsky ever socialize?"

"We talked, in the store. That's about it."

"What did you talk about?"

"Just things, the weather, sports, about that fight last July."

"The Jack Johnson fight?"

"Yes, sir. He was joking with me about it. Said Mr. Jefferies was the 'Great White Hope' and he'd take care of Johnson."

"Guess he was wrong about that."

"Yes." Nealy half grinned.

That didn't help. I looked at the faces of the jurors and none were smiling over the defeat that sparked race riots across the country. It was the most famous fight of all time, and cemented Jackson's place as world champion, but the country wasn't ready for a colored champion, or for any sign that Negroes were equal or superior to whites.

"So you two were friendly?"

"Yes."

"What did you feel when you heard he had been murdered?"

Peurifoy jumped up. "Objection, Your Honor. His feelings are irrelevant."

"Overruled. He may answer."

"Daniel, what did you think?" Matthews asked.

"It was bad. He was a very nice man. He let me, let other Negroes buy on time. I thought, 'who would kill this man?' It made no sense."

"During that time did you walk up King Street?"

"I walk up there every day. It's part of what I do after work. After he was killed, I walked past the shop a number of times to see if it would open, to see if I could still get my suit."

"So, between June 21st and July 8th you would have walked past that area more than a dozen times."

"Yes."

"And no one tried to arrest you?"

"No. Nobody."

"On the morning of July 8th, as you crossed King Street, you were arrested on the sidewalk?"

"I was crossing the street and that same lady on the stand, the tailor's wife, was hallooing and as I got half way across the street, a short man not as high as you ran up and took me. As he took me, three or four of them others hauled back and knocked me in the head."

"Did they talk of hanging you?"

"Yes, sir."

"When were you going to be married?"

"July 13th."

"Did you buy other things from merchants on King Street in preparation for your marriage?"

"I bought a parlor set and a bedroom set."

"How much did you pay for it?"

"All together, 33 dollars."

"Where did you get that money?"

"I saved it up from my pay."

"From working for 15 years?"

"Yes. Fifteen years."

"Did you kill Max Lubelsky?"

"I did not." Nealy's voice rang with the conviction of a church bell.

"No more questions, Your Honor."

Peurifoy stood and walked slowly to Nealy, distant and wary.

"Your name is what?"

"My name is Daniel Cornelius Duncan."

"The wedding invitation called you 'Nealy?'"

"That's what my friends call me."

"What did Mr. Lubelsky call you?"

"Nealy."

"What did Mr. Geilfuss call you?"

"Daniel."

"Why would the man who practically raised you call you by a different name?"

"Mr. Geilfuss is always a little formal. He taught me to speak better English. He wanted me to be better."

"How do you think he felt about you this morning?"

"Objection, Your Honor. Argumentative."

"Sustained. Mr. Peurifoy, don't test me again. Keep your questions on point. Proceed."

Peurifoy barked out a lengthy series of questions that had no purpose beyond trying to trip up Nealy, to catch him at odds with any of the previous testimony about what specific clothes he owned and minutia of his personal life. After peppering him with more than a hundred questions, Peurifoy finally got to the morning of the attack on Mrs. Lubelsky.

"Where did you see Mrs. Lubelsky?"

"I saw her in the door hallooing."

"Was she standing up?"

"She was standing up, she was moving at the same time."

"Which way was she going?"

"She was going outside the door."

"How many times did she scream?"

"I could not tell you."

"What was her condition? Was there any blood?"

"They grabbed me so quick I didn't see anything. All I know is this lady was hallooing and when that man grabbed me and two or three of the others struck me, one gentleman took my coat away from me."

"You didn't see anything of Mrs. Lubelsky when the screaming took place?"

"I saw a fellow running out of the store."

"And you walked over to see what the trouble was?"

"Yes, sir, and when I got halfway there they took hold of me."

"No further questions, Your Honor."

"Redirect, Mr. Matthews?"

"Yes, Your Honor. Just a couple questions." He walked to Nealy. "Daniel, you said that at the same time your attention was directed to Mrs. Lubelsky, you saw another man running out of the store."

"Yes, I did."

"Did anyone grab him?"

"I didn't see that."

"Did you ever see that man again?"

"No, never."

"Thank you, Nealy. Your Honor, the defense rests."

Silence fell over the courtroom. The whole of the gallery seemed to be collecting itself. Watts looked at the witness stand.

"You may step down, Mr. Duncan." He glanced at the clock at

the back of the room and turned to the jury. "Gentlemen, it's too late in the day to start closing arguments. Be prepared to start first thing Monday morning, at nine o'clock. I apologize for carrying this over the weekend, and for the inconvenience, but you will be guests of the State for the next two days. We'll put you up and feed you, but you are under a court order not to discuss this trial, or read accounts in any newspaper until we reconvene on Monday morning. If you do, I'll hold you in contempt. Court is adjourned."

Everyone got to their feet. Reporters sprinted out and the rest left more slowly, as though it was the end of a long sermon and just moving again was good. The jury was led out by deputies for transfer to their hotel. They didn't look happy. Watching their faces, I wondered whether it was a matter of timing, or a matter of influence that led Watts to sequester the jury for the weekend. An angry jury would be in the wrong mood for a magnanimous verdict on Monday, and maybe that was part of the plan. Matthews packed his briefcase slowly. Peurifoy smiled at him on his way past. Part of the plan.

DATELINE:
Charleston, S.C., October 7, 1910
Hal Hinson | New York Tribune

There are surprises in Southern justice. That the courthouse might be described as Federal style architecture and that anything so-called "Federal" might be so incorporated into the Southern judicial texture is a surprise. That a jury of 12 white men might be considered a jury of one's peers for a black man facing death is a surprise. But bigger than those is the surprise that there might actually be hope for justice in this trial after all.

We have been witness to two days of testimony here in Charleston. I say "we" because the court-room here is packed like a Protestant church at Easter – every bench filled, shoulder to shoulder seating, with hands beating funeral home fans that send a scant breeze through the lily-white crowd, except for one lone black girl who bravely watches her hoped-for groom, whose fate hangs on a court-appointed lawyer.

Brice Matthews came to the party late. He never met his client until the day the trial began. But as testimony began some unknown trumpet, unheard to the rest of us, must have sounded and Henry the Fifth echoed in his ear, for he "disguised fair nature with hard-favored rage" and entered the battle.

Even the police had trouble counting the number of suspects rounded up in a net woven and cast by three "eyewitness" descriptions of the killer. Those witnesses testified that they positively identified Daniel Duncan as the man they saw on the day of the murder. But none of the witnesses, and none of the police suspect bulletins, described what was written on the defendant's face. When Duncan stood to face the court, not one had described the obvious scar that runs across his cheek. That scar produced a gasp that was heard through this fair town.

In the police's desperation to bring somebody to trial, all the suspects (and all save Duncan were eventually released) faced line-ups before the witnesses. All were hauled before witnesses dressed as they came, all except for Daniel Duncan. He was trussed like a Thanksgiving turkey in an exact replica of the suit and hat described in the police bulletins. That got him an express ticket to trial.

To give the prosecution their due, they have a case and they have a witness, in the form of the unassailable wailing widow, who positively identified Duncan as the man who attacked her. But were that true, if for reasons that seem unapparent, Daniel Duncan had attacked the widow, the slender thread tying him to the murder of her husband could be broken like a spider's web.

The mystery that has gone uninvestigated is the account of another man slipping from the tailor's shop after the attack on his widow. That man was unchallenged by anyone at the scene at the same time Duncan was being manhandled by a mob, with an eye on lynching. That man has yet to be found.

There is doubt in this trial and only one juror has to find it a reasonable doubt to spare the life of this young man.

On Monday Brice Matthews will offer his closing argument. Let's hope among the jury, to quote the King, "There is none of you so mean and base, that hath not noble luster in your eyes," to see that doubt. Let's also hope Brice Matthews fares as well as Henry at Agincourt.

I filed my story and left the telegraph office for the street where Mojo waited.

"Mista Hal, Miss Randy dun tole me to tell you that you needs to stop and see Mrs. Van de Hoss at de hotel."

"Vanderhorst, Mojo. Mrs. Vanderhorst."

"Missus Van de Haws. She's wantin' to see you."

We walked the couple of blocks to the Mills House, and this time I took Mojo inside and told him to sit and wait at the porter's desk.

"Amm, Mr. Hinson," the porter said. "I'm not sure we can do that."

"Do what?"

"Allow this boy to sit in here."

"Listen, the last time we were here he was kidnapped on your doorstep by Klan thugs. He stays here, or I sic Mrs. Vanderhorst on you."

"Yes, sir. That certainly will not be necessary."

I smiled as I walked away. You have to know when to play your trump cards. I suspected the old *grande dame* would send shocks of fear through the hotel staff. I found her in the bar.

"Good evening, Mrs. Vanderhorst."

"Mr. Hinson. Please have a seat. You see I have a Manhattan in front of me. You and your charming lady have led me into bad habits. If I live long enough, I hope to become a regular alcoholic, as long as I am in the company of pleasant people. Please join me for a drink."

I did. The waiter appeared immediately, as if he had been standing offstage for several hours holding my drink. Fortunately, it was still fresh.

"While you were in the courtroom watching Mr. Matthews joust with windmills, Miss Dumas joined me for lunch. We had a lovely time and she has invited me to join the two of you for dinner as soon as this trial is over."

"I look forward to that. I'll have to warn you that her Meredith is an excellent cook, and you come to dine with some risk to your girlish figure."

"You flirt rather well for a Northerner," she purred.

"It requires the proper influence. Perhaps Southern women bring it out in men of either region."

"Your reward for your charm is this."

She handed me an envelope. I opened it and read the invitation:

Mr. Hinson,

You have seen one side. In order to offer an opposing perspective of the people in the area, please join us at Hyde Park Plantation on Saturday for an oyster roast. A boat will be waiting at 9 a.m. at Adger's Wharf for a trip up the Cooper River. Please bring an overnight bag. You are welcome to bring a guest.

Sincerely,
Brice Matthews

"I suppose you had a hand in this?"

"I warned you, sir, I have my hand in a bit of everything. In this case, I hope you will be able to see a gentler side of the people here.

I can promise you there will be no Klan on Hyde Park."

"Thank you very much. I hoped I might get a chance to talk with Brice in person. I'm sure this will be lovely. Now, if you'll excuse me, I'd better go tell Randy we need to pack."

"She's already aware."

I laughed. "The two of you are a pair to be reckoned with. I'll see you after the trial is over, if not earlier. Good evening."

"Goodnight, Hal."

CHAPTER FOURTEEN
Saturday
OCTOBER 8, 1910

Saturday morning came out the gate a winner. I awoke to feel the impression still intact where Randy had left the bed. Outside I could hear Mojo making a racket with Markus over some project already under way. The open window let in a fresh breeze that actually held a hint of fall. The smell of coffee crept up the stairs.

Randy presented me with attire more appropriate for a trip to the country, a sturdier pair of pants, decent hiking shoes and a Barbour jacket. I threw them on and went down the stairs smelling like I'd just stepped out of the tailor shop.

"It's nice to see you in something other than a coat and tie."

"Or nothing at all."

"I'm not tired of that. Not yet. You go in the dining room and have coffee and a beignet. Markus will drive us down to the wharf in about half an hour."

I sat and sipped the strong black coffee mixed with steamed milk that was a perfect match for the sweet New Orleans fritter. The morning newspaper was on the table. Randy had already been through it. The front page screamed, "Testimony Ends in Murder Trial." Randy and I had spent much of the previous night before the fire, discussing the trial. I gave her a carbon of my dispatch to the Tribune and she was pleased to read it ahead of the people of New York. The local paper carried much of the testimony, but the story seemed headed to a conclusion positive for the prosecution. It's a good thing the jury was sequestered.

A commotion came from the back and moved around to the front of the house. Part of the commotion was Mojo, the other part was another of Randy's surprises. She walked outside with me.

"A Stanley Steamer! You never said anything about owning a car."

"You never asked."

"I guess that's why you weren't impressed with Peurifoy's Tin Lizzie."

"It's an inferior machine. The Stanley is much faster. I like faster."

"I would imagine. How fast have you driven it?"

"You sure you want to know?"

"I don't know. Do I?"

"One day I took it out to Sullivan's Island and drove it out on the beach at low tide," Randy said. "I had it up to 60 miles an hour. The police would have arrested me if they could have caught me."

"Who's driving it to the wharf?"

"I am. Markus will drive it back."

"Let's try to keep it under 60."

"I'll behave like a law abiding citizen, even if I'm not." She smiled and grabbed her overnight bag. I did the same and placed both bags in the back of the car. Markus and Mojo climbed in the rear seat. Mojo had the same excited grin as when he was in the flivver. Randy climbed behind the wheel and I took the passenger's seat. She eased the car into the street, turned and headed down narrow Tradd Street and turned onto East Bay. We drove through Charleston's established homes, past the well-to-do. It was quite a show for anyone walking down those staid sidewalks to see a woman driving a male passenger with two young Negroes in the back seat.

We turned into Adger's Wharf, the dock where I had arrived a week earlier. I returned complete with an entourage, completely different from that newcomer to Charleston's shores. Mojo made a show of waving to the crowds of hucksters who were his former urchins-in-arms. A small river excursion steamer was docked partway down the pier, 35 feet long with a shallow draft. Randy stopped as close as crowd and cargo would allow. She left the Stanley running, set the brake and got out. I grabbed our two bags and Markus and Mojo climbed into the front.

"Now ya'll take the car straight home," Randy said. "Don't be driving around in broad daylight calling attention to yourselves. There's no reason to get anyone started. We should be back on the afternoon boat tomorrow, so meet us here then."

"Yes, ma'am." Mojo stood in the car with a mock salute.

We walked down the gangplank onto the boat. The tide was coming in, which would speed the trip upriver. There was one blast on the whistle and the hands started casting off lines. The skipper eased his boat away from the pier, turned the bow away from the sea and started up the great Cooper River. The sun was warm and the breeze coming off the water was so pleasant that Randy and I sought out the bow and took seats on a bench facing forward. She put her hands up to her head and pulled out hairpins, letting her tresses fall to her shoulders. She ran fingers through her hair and shook her head in a way that seemed to not just her free hair, but her feelings. One hand shot from her hair and she brought it down and slapped me on the knee. I jumped a little and she laughed.

"Mr. Hinson, I do believe a marvelous day lies ahead of us."

She stood and took my hand to lead me to the bow railing. We leaned against the metal and looked over the water to the land as the boat sailed further inland. The Cooper River was certainly different from sailing up the Hudson. On the Hudson, the river is framed by high banks of stone cliffs rising from the water. On the Cooper, the water meandered inland, framed only by large oaks and occasional plantations. The water was different, with patches of green or blue, depending on the interaction of the tides. As we moved upriver, the water changed to pure, with no taint of salt, and sometimes appeared almost black where it rested calmly under overhanging oaks. We moved upstream, past the brackish water, and Randy turned tour guide.

"The mileposts of this river are marked by the plantations and the families that have owned them for generations. Most people think of Charleston and the South for the Civil War, but most of these plantations on the Cooper River are far more deeply tied to the Revolutionary War. This is where the Swamp Fox, Francis Marion, fought the British. At least eleven battles were fought along the banks and on the Cooper River plantations. The British left a lot of burned-out homes, and more than a few sad ghost stories behind."

We moved further up the river, and the banks closed in along a branch that flowed from the east. Closer along the banks, I could see the occasional alligator sunning in the open, and I made a mental note that swimming on this trip was off the agenda. Randy continued.

"We're coming up on Quinby Plantation. One of those battles happened here. General Marion and his forces raided the British, killing forty-some and capturing more than a hundred prisoners. One of the mounted commands was under Light Horse Harry Lee."

"The father of Robert E. Lee," I said, to show that some Northerners were aware of General Lee's family's military pedigree.

"Steal my points, will you?" She gave me a gentle shove. "Sometimes at night, they say, there are sounds of horse hooves pounding up the dark road to Quinby. They say you can hear the heavy breathing of a horse pressed hard, and then the headless 'British Trooper' appears at full gallop up from the bridge he was defending when he lost his head.

"Now we're near the end of our boat trip. On the right here is Silk Hope plantation, but it's known more for rice than silk. The plantation had one of the first rice mills to serve the plantations in the area. During the War of Independence, Lord Cornwallis encamped at Silk Hope, but he made frequent trips across the river to our destination, Hyde Park. The story of Hyde Park is that Cornwallis was so worried about being captured by Marion's raiders that he would never enter the house, but instead always sat on the piazza, or under the oaks with his horse nearby."

She finished as we closed on the riverbank. On the far side I could see golden rice in the fields that looked as though it was ready for harvest. Up on a bluff was a house bustling with activity. The house was spacious and inviting, and nothing as ostentatious as Peurifoy's. The boat pulled up to a dock and we walked ashore along with a few other couples. Brice Matthews rode up on a horse.

"Mr. Hinson, Miss Dumas, welcome to Hyde Park. I'm glad you were able to come today. If you'll walk up to the house, I'll take this horse back to the stable and meet you there. You must be hungry. I believe we can find a little something for you to eat up there."

"Thank you," I said. "The trip upriver was lovely in itself. We'll meet you at the house." Matthews turned his horse with slight pressure from his leg, his hand hardly on the rein. The horse made a lovely pivot and trotted for a few paces until Matthews put him into a canter down a path and into the woods.

We started up the hill. Randy had wisely worn a wool walking skirt, a pair of decent shoes, and a blouse covered by a short wool jacket. Unfortunately, one of the other ladies from the boat had chosen to wear a hoop skirt and had a difficult time navigating up the pathway. At the top of the hill we turned to look back. The river curved below us, framing rice fields golden with ripened grain.

"It's a pretty color, isn't it?" Matthews said from behind us. He wore jodhpurs and a tweed jacket, and quite comfortably looked over the scenery. "The rice is a week or so from harvest. That color is why it's called 'Carolina Gold.' Even if it didn't provide a few extra dollars for a poor defense attorney, it would be worth the growing just to see it this time of year."

The color of the crop resembled something pulled from a painter's palette. There were sixty acres between the hill bottom and the river, surrounded by hump-backed earthen dikes. Golden fields, dikes, the green of grass and a brilliant blue sky; it was a portrait I'd love to have on my wall, one I could spend a long time getting to know.

"Come along," Matthews said. "Let's join the crowd. We don't want to be late when they start putting up the food."

The party was gathered on either side of two long tables. Some were already at work on the mounds of oysters being shoveled into the middle. Off to the side, a small crew was dumping burlap bushels of oysters over a low fire, then soaking the burlap and covering them until they began to open slightly. Then shovels came into play, to carry the cracked oysters to the anxious people waiting with shucking knives ready. We wedged ourselves between the other guests.

"Hal and Randy," Matthews said, "this is my wife, Laura." She was an attractive woman with knife in hand, eager for oysters and, like her husband, at ease in the environment and attire of their country estate. She waved over a young man who worked the edges of the crowd, carrying a tray with pints of freshly tapped beer. He sat several mugs on the table in front of us and cleared out of the way. The pace of the action at the table picked up, and it was all knives and elbows as we worked to separate the shells and suck out the oyster within.

"It's still a little early in the season," Laura said, while Brice built a pile of empty shells. "But these come from Bull's Bay, due east of here. I know they brag about their oysters from the Chesapeake, but I'll take ours over anybody's." She cocked her head at her husband. "Don't follow his example too closely. He'll stand there and eat oysters until the moon rises. We've got another Charleston favorite to follow this, so don't eat too many."

She could warn us but not stop us. The oysters were better than any I'd eaten, including my former favorites from Long Island. Randy dug in heartily, slurping and smiling, a happy girl from Louisiana on familiar ground. When the shells were stacked high enough to cut off the view of the other side of the table, the work crew came and pushed the empties through holes in the middle of the tables into drums positioned beneath. There was a lull while two huge, steaming pots were carried to the table and the contents dumped in the center.

"Randy, we thought we'd show you our version of the Louisiana crawfish boil." Laura and Randy now stood next to each other. "It's pretty much the same as what you serve, except instead of crawfish we use shrimp around here." She stood in front of a delicious pile of shrimp, potatoes, corn and sausage steaming fresh from the pot. Everybody started in on the shrimp with the same vigor and lack of delicacy as was shown for the oysters. As beautiful as the surroundings were, no one found anything interesting beyond the tables. After half an hour with satisfied grunts for conversation, the feasting slowed.

"By God, I surrender." I staggered back from the table. "I'll be the first to throw in the towel. Brice, I'll put your fare up against anything I've eaten on any shore, anywhere on this planet."

The servers passed around hot towels dunked into steaming water with lemons. We scrubbed ourselves clean up to the elbows.

"Let's have a seat over here on the grass." Brice led us to a cluster of Adirondack chairs overlooking the rice fields and I fell into mine, remembering in time that my belt should stay fastened. The rest of the party also left the table, and a few set up easels to paint, others opened books, still others struck up casual conversations, all content to settle down for a rest after lunch. Matthews relaxed into a chair and described the earthen dikes and the system that controlled the water flooding the rice fields.

"There are breaks in those dikes," he said, "where we have devices called trunks. We open the trunks on a high tide to flood the fields, and drain the fields by opening them on low tides. Most of the plantations you passed on the way up the river grew rice at one point in their history. It was Charleston's cash crop and made the city rich. Most of the plantation owners built expensive homes along the Battery. The reason these plantations were so valuable is because they are far enough up the river that the water is pure and not brackish. Any salt in the water would kill the rice."

"But if this is a tidal river," I said. "Does the seawater ever come this far up?"

"Rarely, thankfully. Only in a severe hurricane does the surge force salt this far up the river."

He talked on, sounding more the farmer than the lawyer, which was a bit disconcerting given the trial at hand, but then George Washington always considered himself a farmer and he didn't do too badly in his second job. He described details of the upcoming harvest and how the workforce had transitioned from slavery to wage workers. And then he got to his feet.

"I should pay attention to my other guests," he said. "Feel free to walk around and introduce yourself. It's our usual odd collection of artists and writers, a few free thinkers. I doubt you'll find them any too strange. Most will be leaving in couple of hours on the returning steamer. I was hoping you two might join us for a horseback ride late this afternoon. Your bags have been taken to a couple of small cabins, down that path." He pointed to an oyster shell walk that disappeared into the woods. "You can settle in there. I've put riding boots and jodhpurs in there for you. Randy, I hope you won't be offended, but we don't ask women to ride sidesaddle here."

"What a relief," Randy said, shading her eyes against the sun. "I've ridden for years, and have always admired women who could fox hunt sidesaddle, but it was never anything I have wanted to try."

"Good, then we'll meet you at the barn. Around four?" We

nodded and Brice and Laura headed off to their other guests.

I turned to Randy. "I didn't know you could ride."

"You never asked."

"That's twice today. And me a reporter. Will you always remain cloaked in this aura of mystery?"

"That is my hope. To keep you interested."

A group of people were perched in chairs on the bluff overlooking the rice fields. We got up and went to their circle. The men stood, looked at Randy and smiled. The woman who had hobbled up the hill in her hoop skirt turned to see us. Her eyes fell on Randy.

"You gentlemen can sit down," she said, dripping venom. "No need to stand for a whore."

My mouth went off before I could stop it. "The whore is with me," it said. "They obviously didn't stand for you."

Randy shot me a dark look and I shut up.

"Mrs. Holden," Randy said with honey, "we've never met, but I do appreciate your husband's contributions to my business. He's a valued and regular customer. I now understand why. Good day, gentlemen."

She turned on her heel and walked away quickly but without hurry. I had to hustle to catch up. She didn't stop until we were alone. "Randy," I said and she turned on me.

"Don't you *ever* call me a whore again. You know better. In one instant you confirmed what they expect and belied what you know is untrue."

"It was reactive," I sputtered. "Pre-conscious. I was simply flipping her accusation back at her."

"*Pre-conscious?* Then in your sub-conscious, I'm your whore?"

"No, Randy. Spare me the drawing room Freud. I do not think you're a whore. You know I don't." She tried to run away but I stopped her, turned her to me. We were on the edge of the woods, where the path led to the cabins. "I think you are, no, I *know* you are a remarkable woman, a unique woman with whom I am falling hopelessly in love."

"Love!" She was exasperated. "Yes, that's what I thought it would come to. But somewhere between your heart and your pre-conscious head, you haven't really decided whether I'm your love or your whore. You have some thinking to do, because as your whore I'm going to cost a lot more."

She jerked away from me and ran down the path to two small cabins clustered under branching live oaks, hunting cabins with front porches, supports and rails fashioned out of plain cedar. With wispy smoke curling out of the chimneys, they looked very appealing. Randy took the first one and slammed the door eloquently. I took the second.

Inside the simple, one-room structure, the floor was covered with handsome woven Indian rugs from a western American tribe. The furniture was simple, made from cedar saplings and cushions obviously crafted with care. Two large leather chairs flanked the fireplace, and directly across from the fire a large double bed was placed to provide a view of the fire dying down to embers. There were bookshelves lined with rather good novels, perfect for a night in front of the fire. Someone enjoyed spending time here.

As Matthews promised, a pair of polished riding boots and some breeches rested on a bench. A shirt with an attached collar and a tweed coat hung nearby, a note pinned to the lapel.

"Hope these fit . I believe we're similar in size. B.M.," it read.

I dressed, and when I walked out the door it was with the appearance of a perfectly attired ratcatcher. Thinking I might catch Randy, I went to her cabin and knocked. No answer.

The sun was still above the treetops, but only a couple of hours of good light remained for riding. I took the path and turned to the barn. Randy was already there.

"Hey, you two," Laura called from the barn, where she and the groom had finished bridling the horses. Two were already outside, tied to a cedar-railed hitching post. Brice led the last two out.

"Those two are for ya'll." Laura pointed to the hitched pair. They appeared to be Percherons crossed with Thoroughbreds, tall and muscular.

"We do a little foxhunting around here. These fellows are pretty good over a fence, and we've got a few jumps built on a course through the woods. Do you jump?"

"Some," I partly lied. I'd run with the hounds once outside New York, but preferred playing polo to crashing through the woods dressed like a dilettante dandy.

"Randy?" Laura was trying to make sure we didn't kill ourselves.

"I used to ride a good bit in the parishes outside of New Orleans, but it's been a few years. I hope I'm adequate to these fine horses."

I looked at her and she gave back ice. We mounted and walked down the oyster shell drive to a sandy trail that reached into the woods.

"Ready to trot?" Brice called back over his shoulder.

"Ready when you are," Randy replied.

He set out, posting his trot nicely. We all kept pace as we rode through woods thick with large old oaks. They were so numerous it was a shame to imagine that one might ever consider them common. I rode up abreast of Brice as we moved along, and we turned onto another lane with a grassy carpet.

"This used to be a colonial highway," he said. "It runs through the plantation and once was one of the more important roads through the area. It's carried troops and commerce and a lot of stories. Ready to pick up a canter?"

"I'm with you," I said and he nudged his horse up and moved forward. I held back a bit to let him lead since I had no idea where we were going. He turned again back into the woods and I saw the beginning of the course Laura had mentioned. Thirty yards up was a jump, fairly simple, two logs mounted on top of each other. He set his horse and took it cleanly. I followed and felt the horse rise beneath me, cleanly sailing over the logs. As we cleared, my horse brought his head up and into my hands, he was very aware of what lay ahead, and I was beginning to wonder. I glanced back over my shoulder to see Randy clear the jump with a look of focus on her face. She let her horse go and rode past me, loosening her reins and letting her horse flow up to follow Brice, who was not waiting for anybody. Laura rode up beside me, I think, to be polite as we picked up the pace. The next jump was a combination of two jumps, spaced by about five strides. Brice took it cleanly. Randy set her heels and pushed her hands up the horse's neck, rising slightly out of the saddle in a two point. She cleared the first one and moved to the second. I had trouble focusing on the first jump, watching her most lovely waist and hips rise in the saddle. I touched heel to flank and moved up on the pair in the lead.

The course wasn't getting any easier. We sailed over a stone wall (odd I thought as I went over, since I had seen no rocks anywhere) with a log rider on the top. Brice had managed to make a water jump with a small ledge that dropped down into a stream. Oh, he was crafty, this one. I managed to survive each jump in turn and I wondered if the mild-mannered defender was in fact some demonic designer of courses intended to scare, thrill or kill his guests. We jumped and survived nearly two dozen obstacles by the time we headed back to the river and the home stretch seemed in sight. The last section was the grassy top of the rice dikes along the river. Randy looked slightly back at me. She smiled, but not in her eyes.

I moved up abreast of her horse, dropped my reins and leaned up on the horse's neck. The race was on. We both kept pace heading to the turn that would lead back to the barn. As I flew along, I noticed more than one alligator splash into the water. Coming in on the turn I saw Randy check her horse slightly. It appeared she was going to give me the advantage. As I turned forty-five degrees to her, she spurred her horse up, pulling its head on the right rein and moving its shoulder just behind my leg. I knew what a bump was, and this one was dirty. My horse was knocked off his stride and felt like he might go down under me. I kicked my feet out of the stirrups and launched off his back. The line of direction carried me straight into the water.

The water hit my back and I sank into the rice field. Anger launched me out of the water. I gathered my feet underneath and exploded to the surface dripping water and mud as I stood about waist deep in the field.

"Randy, what the hell ..."

The point of my anger stood on the bank, holding her horse by the reins. Her eyes showed no emotion, they looked beyond me. Turning to follow her gaze, I locked eyes with a twelve foot alligator that was moving slowly at me. I gathered myself to try to beat him to the shore.

"Stop." Randy did not change her focus, but raised her hand. I wasn't sure if the gesture was for me, or the alligator.

"Not today, brother gator. Today, he is mine."

Her hand was parallel to the earth, her eyes were black, and for a moment, I thought I saw a vertical pupil, eye to eye, the same as the alligator. I walked so slowly that the surface of the water remained unbroken. At the edge of the bank, Brice stood and offered his hand to pull me up to dry ground.

"That was kind of close there, Hal. Gator baiting is not usually one of the entertainments here. I sure am glad he wasn't hungry. Let's get up to the barn and get some dry clothes on you and a glass of whiskey in you."

We were all dismounted, walking with reins in hand up the hill to the barn. Brice and Laura were leading, I signaled to Randy to hold back a few strides.

When there was a safe distance between us, I asked, "What the hell was going on back there?"

"The first, knocking you off your horse, was an attempt to hurt you. The second, the alligator, was an attempt to save you. I'm glad the latter was more successful than the former."

"I don't appreciate you ..."

"Taking me so lightly?"

She stopped me there.

"We must learn respect for each other."

"You're a tough teacher."

"I'm just hoping you're not a slow student."

"Can you explain what was going on with that alligator?"

"Later."

We approached the barn and rejoined our hosts as we handed off the horses to the grooms.

"Hal," Brice said, "if you want to go back to that washstand, you can take first in line and sponge yourself down before the horses. I've asked one of the grooms to run up to your cabin for your clothes. He'll be back in a second. I'll keep the ladies up front here, free from any risk of indelicacy, while we sip a whiskey."

I walked to the back of the barn, stripped down and poured cold, clean water over me. My clothes arrived while I finished toweling off and I rejoined the group before they finished their first glass.

"That was quick, Hal."

"I was feeling the need for a whiskey more than a perfect scrub-down."

"Then here you are, sir, glad that you're able to down the bourbon, rather than the gator downing you."

"It was a little more exciting a ride than I had bargained for. I'd love to see more of the plantation, perhaps at a slower pace."

"And you will, perhaps we'll have a trot by in the morning, something slower to suit a Sunday. I'm afraid we raced through the plantation so fast, you probably didn't see much."

"See much? I saw the sight between my horse's ears, and the jump ahead, all the rest was a blur."

We laughed and drank a bit of the bourbon. It was a pleasant late afternoon and we pulled a few camp chairs out in front of the barn. It's never difficult for horse people to sit and swap stories. The light began to fade and Brice stood.

"I hate to seem like a bad host. I'm enjoying the conversation immensely, but I am imagining the two of you might enjoy your own company for the evening. You'll find a simple supper in both your cabins, I hope it's adequate. For myself, Hal, I must confess I have a little work to do tonight."

"Brice, it's been an eventful day. On any other night, I would hope to talk well into the evening. But I agree, and wholly support your priorities."

"I was hoping you would. Meet us back here in the morning for coffee and biscuits. We'll take a short ride before you catch the steamer back to Charleston. Carry this lantern with you to the cabin."

He handed a portable torch and the two couples took separate paths, we went into the woods, Brice and Laura toward the house. As we approached the cabins, lantern light burning inside cast an inviting glow through the windows. We stepped onto the porch, the sound of boots on old wood, one of the sweet sounds of country life.

"Would you like to come in? I think we might have a few things to discuss."

I opened the simple latch on the plank door and walked inside. There is no room so inviting as a rough hewn cabin lit by firelight.

The light danced along the walls. Two lanterns anchored light at two spaces, on a dining table and beside the bed. On the table was a tray, a bottle of burgundy, two glasses, a wedge of cheese and what appeared to be fresh bread. A handwritten note simply said, "Enjoy your evening, as another host once said: Come freely, go safely, and may you leave something of the happiness you bring."

"Ha! Not only is he a good host, he has a sense of humor. Dracula's welcome."

"I get the sense you may have more than a glancing knowledge of the occult."

"The so-called occult, by others is simply the search for a hidden wisdom, knowledge that exists outside of your science."

"Voodoo?"

"That's one name for an ancient body of knowledge. Almost every culture has a connection to the occult. Yours is probably to Druids, but you've doubtless turned your back on your pagan past and in doing so, have likely lost your connection to the unseen world."

"So you practice voodoo?"

"It's not so much a practice, as a part of who we are. In New Orleans, voodoo is deeply entwined in the culture. In the last century, Marie Laveau wove voodoo and Catholicism such that most people became practitioners of both. One person's religion is another's occultism."

I let that rest. Grabbing the wine, I opened and poured two glasses, tore a piece of bread and ate looking into the fire.

Randy sat beside me and sipped her wine.

"You seem uncomfortable."

"The day has had some interesting turns. My unintentional insult, your assault and now voodoo. Your eyes told me a lot about you today. I'm not sure I can be comfortable with the combination of passion and the occult."

She smiled, "Some of those combinations aren't too bad."

"You mean?"

"No, Hal, I have not practiced any voodoo on you. What happened between us is the natural attraction of a man for a woman."

"Thank God. I can understand that."

"Don't underplay your knowledge. You've been around the world, seen people and cultures that most people only read about. You shouldn't pretend to be intimidated by a girl from New Orleans."

"You've already shown more complexities than any person I've ever met. There is a challenge to being with you."

"And you think there's nothing fascinating about a world traveling reporter? What do I know about you? Where did you get that little scar above your brow?"

My finger went to the small white line on the outer edge of my eyebrow.

I smiled. "No great feat of daring or honor. Just a boy trying to impress his father."

"How?"

"I was about eight, we were at our summer house north of New York. There was a pasture next to our property where the neighbor turned out his work horses. There was a pony in the herd. One day I got the notion that I'd show my father how a cavalry officer would command an attack on some Indians. I put on a blue coat, hopped the fence and then hopped on the pony. The pony stood still just long enough for me to get my father's attention, before he decided he was in command and took off. He jumped the rail fence. I didn't and went head first into a rail. When I came to, I was back in the house with my mother holding a cold rag to my head to stop the bleeding. My father stopped by later to suggest I take riding lessons."

"Was he always so cold?"

"I'd call it detached. It's not that he didn't care, he just didn't know how to show it."

"What does he do?"

"He builds things."

"Such as?"

"His most recent project was Pennsylvania Station."

"That's a pretty big accomplishment."

"He's not without accomplishments."

"You don't seem impressed."

"I understand the mark he's made on the city. He's a hugely successful man. After I finished school, it was my turn to detach.

Instead of going into his business, I became a newspaper reporter. He was not so proud."

"Surely that has changed."

"Some. Traveling with the former President seemed to change his mind about some things. I still try to get assignments that keep us a safe distance apart, half a world away is just about right."

The fire burned low. I stood up and threw on a couple of logs and prodded them. New flames cast warmth into the room. Outside the reach of the fire a chill seeped in to fill the corners of the cabin. With my back to the warmth I looked at the shadows.

"What do you see, when you look into the dark?"

"That which exists beyond the light."

I threw two more logs on the fire. The flames danced along the walls, long after we both faded into sleep.

In the morning I crawled out of a warm bed to stoke the fire, hoping to knock the chill out of the cabin. It warmed up as Randy finally awoke from the kind of sleep you only get in the woods away from all the sounds that can be generated by Man. She awoke slowly then continued to lie beneath the covers.

"You'll have to come out sometime."

"I will, I was just listening to the quiet, to the sounds of the birds, to the sounds of a peaceful morning. I could stay here for weeks, or more."

She pulled back the covers and fairly vaulted into the room. There was water in a washstand. The first splash to her face brought a small scream.

"I'm awake now."

I walked out onto the porch. A pair of fresh breeches and a shirt were folded on a bench next to the door. On the next porch, a similar display waited.

"I guess we were sleeping kind of deeply this morning. The clothes fairies delivered some fresh riding gear."

Brice thought of everything. The notion of putting on the slightly damp clothes from the day before was not appealing. We dressed quickly, pulled on boots and walked back to the barn. A couple of grooms were finishing the morning feeding. Horses were eating a bit of hay in their stalls. On a table to the side of the tack room was a silver service, coffee, cream and sugar and a plate of biscuits.

"Now *this* is something I could get used to." Randy poured coffee and buttered a biscuit. I joined her in the coffee. I always prefer my first cup plain before breakfast, and took this one on a stroll through the barn. It was well-made but not fancy, strong and functional, just as I would want one. I walked out the front as Brice and Laura approached from the house.

"Hallo! Good morning." Brice was in excellent spirits. "Ready for a rematch with Randy?"

"Brice, no, no, no." Laura said. "There will be none of that. You promised this was to be a slow walk through the woods this morning."

"I'm with Laura," I agreed. "I'm feeling yesterday's ride right down to my Achilles tendons. It's a beautiful morning and I'd like to see the plantation."

We sipped coffee and each downed a couple of biscuits. The groom led horses out one by one and tied them to the hitching post. When the last was out, we each took one by the reins and mounted. I rode beside Brice, and looked back at Randy.

"No funny business, you two," I said. Both laughed.

There was no shortage of trails. Brice explained the plantation was about seven hundred acres, nearly a thousand if you added the three hundred acres in the rice fields. We rode down avenues of oaks, these larger and older than many I'd seen. Wisps of Spanish moss gave them the aura of aged, bearded statesmen of bark and branch. There were tall stands of pine with thick trunks that reached up a hundred feet, the ground beneath carpeted with a thick bed of pine straw.

Far from any sign of habitation, we rode through a cluster of huge trees enclosing a few rough headstones.

"These headstones were part of a slave graveyard." Brice said.

"Some go back to the 1700s. Some have inscriptions, look at that one."

I dismounted and bent over a plain marker. The inscription was clear:

Joseph
friend and servant
Born 1790
Died 1880.
We all serve the Lord.

"My father's hand carved that headstone. Joseph was almost always by my father's side. They spoke as friends, not master and servant. There is much, Hal, to the relationship between blacks and whites in the South that you won't find at a Klan meeting, or in the cities. No one is defending slavery, but even here, there are bonds among men that defy the racial divide most take for granted."

I touched the headstone, stood and remounted. We rode along in silence.

"Was that headstone the whole purpose of my trip?"

"No," Brice said. "I'm not that directly manipulative. I invited you because I have read your articles. I like the way you think and thought we might be friends. I hope that can be the case after this trial is over. But, yes, after reading of your visit to Peurifoy's, I wanted you to see this place and the difference in our pasts.

"My father freed his slaves before the war started almost fifty years ago. Many left and he lost his rice crop, but many stayed and when the war ended, his house was one of few around here not burned by his own slaves."

Our ride had taken us back to the river. I heard a whistle blow a mile or so away.

"That's the steamer, heading back to Charleston. You'll find your bags at the dock ready to go."

"But we're wearing your boots and clothes."

"You can send them to my house in Charleston. It was the only way to get in a ride this morning and make the early boat back to town."

"Brice, Laura, we can't thank you enough for your hospitality and Brice, the insight. You are right on at least one point, there will be a friendship that will follow the trial."

"Then come again. I'll see you in court in the morning. I have a great deal of thinking to do today, and I do that best out here where it's quiet."

We dismounted and handed our reins off to the Matthews. He rode up the hill to prepare his last defense of Duncan. We climbed aboard the boat and made our way back down the river to Charleston.

CHAPTER FIFTEEN
Monday
OCTOBER 10, 1910

Nealy lay in his hammock looking at the note from Ida.

My dear Nealy,

Today we may know. Today this may be all over. Tonight you may be with me. Mr. Matthews has worked hard for you. I believe those white men on the jury have listened. But they scare me Nealy. They can send you home to me, or take you away. I will be there with you either way my Nealy, forever, on this earth or beyond.

My love,
Ida

He read it, put it down and looked out the window at the rising sun. He read it again. Tears came to his eyes. It somehow seemed worse to have hope, to think that they could ever be together again. At the beginning of the trial he had no hope. But like Ida, he listened to Brice Matthews in the courtroom and thought his defense had given the jury some reason to doubt the evidence. Now he had some reason to think that the nightmare of the past few months could be just a bad dream that would go away, like the sunrise dispels the darkness.

"Hey, Duncan. Get up. Yer lawyer sent this suit for yer big day. Get over there and clean yerself up so you don't stink up the courtroom."

The jailer hung the clothes on the bars of the cell and unlocked the door. Another guard stood ten paces away with a shotgun. Nealy turned away from them, walked to an open shower and turned on the water.

The crowd, trying to get public seating in the courtroom, formed a rambunctious line that stretched to the corner of Meeting and Broad and all the way down Meeting as far as the hotel. The courtroom filled quickly. Ida was in her solitary box. She must have arrived very early. I nodded and smiled at her and went to my seat. The attorneys on both sides were seated. Nealy was in his place at the end of the table. He was again wearing a suit and clean shirt.

"Rise." The bailiff called all to attention.

Watts entered and took his place at the bench.

"Gentlemen, good morning," he said. "Are you ready for your closing arguments? Mr. Peurifoy, if so, please begin."

Peurifoy stood and moved between the prosecutor's desk and the bench like he was taking the stage. He pulled himself up straight, hooked his thumbs in his vest pockets and walked pensively to the jury box.

"Gentlemen, I hope you had a pleasant weekend."

Matthews leaned back in his chair and ran his fingers through his hair. Peurifoy knew what he was doing, reminding the jury that they had spent the weekend away from their families all because of this black man on trial. It stank.

Peurifoy must have read my thoughts, a slight smile creased the edges of his mouth.

"Gentlemen, the State and good citizens of Charleston are grateful for your attention, for your part in bringing peace back to the city and putting a criminal behind bars."

Matthews put his chin down into his cupped hand. Peurifoy leaned in towards the jury box.

"Let me tell you why Daniel Duncan should go to the gallows. You've heard the eyewitness testimony of the victim Mrs. Rose Lubelsky, a woman not only attacked in her own store, but a woman left widowed by the same assailant." He let that sit for a moment.

"But why you ask? Why would he kill the widow of Max Lubelsky? Simple, to cover his tracks. He needed to remove the one person who might identify him as a suspect."

"But he couldn't kill them all. Three. Three different people identified Daniel Duncan as the man they saw in or around Lubelsky's store the morning of June 21st."

I looked at the jury. They were following Peurifoy, eyes fixed, as he listed the witnesses. One juror was actually keeping count with his fingers. Matthews was making notes as Peurifoy made his case.

"Our detectives described evidence recovered, clothing and jewelry from Duncan's tenement. You'll recall they testified the store looked ransacked. The defendant says he was getting married. He was also buying clothing, furniture and accessories that far exceeded his income."

Turning his back to the jury, Peurifoy raised his arm pointing toward Nealy, the finger directed in disdain.

"In the words of the widow, the woman savagely beaten, you heard her say, 'I am sure as I am sitting here that he is the devil. I thought he was going to tear me to pieces.'"

Peurifoy turned again to face the twelve.

"Gentlemen, for three weeks this summer this town lived in fear. Our police department and detectives scoured the state looking for suspects. When the defendant returned to attack Mrs. Lubelsky, the widow of the man he killed, he sealed his fate. She survived, that was her fate, to testify in this court against the man who killed her husband."

"You've heard the evidence, the witnesses, the physical evidence left at the scene. This is a case of luck and hard work. Luck that Mrs. Lubelsky survived and hard work by the Charleston police department. There is only one logical verdict here. Guilty. Daniel Duncan is guilty of murder. Thank you."

Peurifoy returned to his chair and sat facing forward. Murmurs began to swell behind him. He turned, leaned on to his elbow and looked across the courtroom at the defense table.

"Quiet," Watts pounded his gavel. "Mr. Matthews are you ready?"

Brice Matthews stood, placing both hands flat on the desk. "Yes, Your Honor."

He reached over and placed one hand on top of Nealy's, then turned toward the jury. Peurifoy followed him with eyes now narrowed to slits.

"Gentlemen, instead of a closing, I have a confession."

The courtroom was silent.

"I met Daniel Duncan the same day you did, the day the trial started. I assumed if the police arrested him, he must be the one. I was appointed to this case. I didn't ask for it, didn't want it. Would you?"

Several shook their heads, signaling no. Brice propped his foot on the edge of the jury box and leaned forward.

"This is what you call a high profile case. The State picks a top prosecutor and I'll give Mr. Peurifoy his due, he's a great prosecutor. The newspapers cover every detail, including those released by the prosecutor."

Peurifoy almost stood up, it was a reflex, but one stopped by a hot glance from the judge.

"The police, well they threw everything at this case. Then on July the eighth, poor Mrs. Lubelsky is attacked and a mob hands over a defendant. Seems pretty tidy to me."

Several heads nodded in agreement.

"Then I met the defendant and the closer I've looked at the facts of this case the more I was convinced that he might not be the Devil, as described, or a murderer, but he might just be a man who was in the wrong place at the wrong time. He might, consider it, he might just be innocent."

Matthews walked to the table and picked up a book.

"I've been a lawyer for a number of years. The law is not perfect. Sometimes mistakes are made. The State vs. Howard Hamilton, Orangeburg, 1905; The State vs. Joseph Middleton, Charleston 1908; The State vs. Frank Bonneau, Berkeley 1904. Three cases, gentlemen, in this decade, three men convicted of murder on circumstantial evidence. All three were executed. And all three were later proven to be innocent."

"What you gentlemen have heard is circumstantial evidence in this case. It is evidence not based on pure fact. It requires a leap of faith to connect that kind of evidence to an actual crime, to the crime in this case of murder. Faith, gentlemen, is best left to church, not a court of law."

"If Daniel Duncan had savagely beaten Mrs. Lubelsky, where

was the blood? How could he have beaten her with a slat, run from the building at the same instant and not show a speck of blood?"

"And how, for that matter, could he beat her, run out the same door after her and not be seen until he's halfway down the block standing stock still in the middle of the street, while he reports seeing another man leave the door of Lubelsky's shop?"

"Where, is that other man?"

"As for direct evidence. There was no witness to the murder of Max Lubelsky."

"Of all the articles of clothing they pulled from Duncan's tenement, they found no evidence of blood from an attack even more grievous than that upon his wife. And you can believe me, if they had found any direct evidence, it would have been here in court."

He had the jury and the court's attention.

"Gentlemen, you heard the description of the original suspect. You heard the testimony of the so-called 'witnesses.' No witness described anything unusual about the appearance of the suspect. But even you, gentlemen, noticed the scar that runs across Duncan's face, sitting all the way across a courtroom from him. For all witnesses to miss that one clear, distinct mark, raises questions about the credibility of the identification.

"And let's talk about identification. Why, of all the suspects arrested and held and shown in lineup, why was Daniel Duncan the only one dressed up in a suit to match a description? The 'witnesses' identified the clothing, not a suspect.

"The first description of the suspect. It was a mulatto. Daniel Duncan is not a mulatto. He's black.

"Then, there are the conflicting reports on the actual condition of the store on the day of the murder. You heard me ask Joel Posner, twice, if he noticed anything in disarray. He said no. But somehow, in the time it took for Posner to run next door, seeking help from Charles Levin, and being denied, then rushing into the street to find the first available police officer ... the store changed. The police report clothing and money being scattered about the shop. How did that happen? I'll tell you gentlemen, someone altered the scene to make it look like a robbery."

A couple members of the jury were actually leaning forward.

"Did I mention Charles Levin? I'm afraid I'm at a loss to explain how a neighbor, a fellow shopkeeper, would turn his back on a severely wounded friend. And, if he did see a man standing outside with a wooden slat acting strangely, why not sound the alarm? I raise that, not necessarily to accuse Mr. Levin of any wrongdoing, but to indicate that there is some piece of this puzzle that does not fit. Something that makes me doubt if the right man is in custody.

"The man in custody is Daniel Duncan. The key identification, that referred to again and again by the prosecution was from Mrs. Lubelsky. Let me be clear, my heart goes out to Mrs. Lubelsky, a mother and now a widow with a world of problems to face. But let me put you in her scenario. You've been attacked, your head is still spinning, you're in shock and the police bring a *suspect* to your door. If the police caught him, he must be the one.

"But the police didn't catch Daniel Duncan. He was accosted by a mob on King Street the morning of July 8th. There is no direct evidence to link him to the murder, even if there was evidence that he attacked Mrs. Lubelsky. Gentlemen, there is simply no *evidence* of either."

"For weeks after the murder, Daniel Duncan walked up that street past that store. He was never once arrested, never once an object of suspicion. All the while the police arrested suspects from as far away as Bamberg. Daniel lived one block from the police station."

"And what of the two men in police custody at the time of the mob arrest? Prior to July 8th they thought they had their men. They were released. They matched the descriptions and neither had an alibi for June 21st. Where are they?

"In closing. I want to ask you to look across the room. Look at Daniel Duncan, not as a suspect, but as a man. That suit he's wearing. It's the suit he saved his pay for weeks to buy. It was to be his wedding suit. He was a hard working man who was about to be married." Matthews turned to face the court. "That young girl was to be his bride." Ida lowered her head.

"Why, gentlemen, would a man with no record, a good job and future and a pretty girl commit either of these crimes? What the prosecution hasn't given you is a motive. Or at least not one fit to send a man to the gallows. Why would he attack Rose Lubelsky when she wasn't even a witness?

"If the police arrested him, he must be the one. I believe Rose Lubelsky made that mistake. I told you I made that mistake. Gentlemen, I ask that you consider the facts, and don't make the same mistake. Thank you."

Matthews eyed Peurifoy as he returned to his seat. The prosecutor was obviously furious. Peurifoy jumped back to his feet.

"Gentlemen, Mr. Matthews is asking you to accept a singular conclusion. That he is right, and Daniel Duncan is innocent, and *we* are wrong. *We* are the police, the detectives, the *witnesses* and the victim, a widow attacked and almost killed in the same spot where her husband was murdered.

"He makes a noble case. This poor boy is a tool of Fate, he is innocent and *we* are wrong. If he argues that circumstantial evidence bears no credibility, then I would counter that to believe him, you would have to believe that the whole of this community is involved in a conspiracy of wrongdoing. That everyone who has taken this stand has some reason to put an innocent man to death.

"I don't know about you, gentlemen, but I am outraged by the accusation. This trial is about murder, not conspiracies. To believe his case, you would have to believe that *we* are all wrong. To convict Duncan, then *you* would have to become part of the conspiracy of wrongdoing. Are you gentlemen a part of a conspiracy? I think not. Listen to the evidence. Daniel Duncan is guilty of murder. Thank you."

Peurifoy walked back to his desk and sat down slowly. Both men looked to the other. Both looked tired. This trial became more than either expected it to be. Now, both were finished.

"Thank you, gentlemen." Judge Watts was ready to charge the jury. "Mr. Foreman and gentlemen, the defendant here is charged with murder, the highest offense known to our law. The State charges that on the 21st of June of this year in this county and in this city that he feloniously killed and murdered the deceased by striking him with a stick. You have heard the testimony in the case and that is for you entirely to decide. If you are not satisfied beyond a reasonable doubt that the defendant here was the man who killed the deceased then you need not proceed further in the case but write a verdict of not guilty. If, however, you are satisfied beyond a reasonable doubt that the defendant killed the deceased then you will inquire whether or not he is guilty of murder or manslaughter because there is no plea of self-defense in the case at all. The defendant denies the killing and it is for you to say whether or not under the facts and circumstances as detailed in evidence whether you are satisfied beyond a reasonable doubt that the defendant did the killing or not."

Watts described the difference between premeditated murder and manslaughter and the distinction between circumstantial and direct evidence.

"If you find him guilty without a recommendation to the mercy of the court, the law fixes his punishment as death by hanging. If you find him guilty of murder and recommend him to the mercy of the court, the law fixes his punishment at life imprisonment at hard labor in the penitentiary. If you find him guilty of manslaughter, in that case his punishment would be at the discretion of the judge, no less than two years and not more than thirty.

"You will retire to your room for deliberations. I will expect to hear some word from you in one hour." He retired to his chambers. Nealy was taken out a door on the opposite side of the room to be held until a verdict was returned. The whole of the court was slow to rise. Some who had been following the trial since it began were afraid to leave, afraid to lose their seats just as the end was near. The notion of the end seemed to come down hard on Ida. Her head hung down, she appeared to be praying. I was neither brave, nor close enough, to intrude on the last defense she was offering up. Instead, I got up and walked up the aisle and out into the afternoon air. I thought about taking a walk to clear my head. That might be foolish, this may not take too much time. I walked a half a block in each direction to stretch my legs, most of which was in the street, the crowds had gathered thick on the sidewalk to await the verdict. I started back up the stairs and a voice yelled from the top.

"Jury's back!"

I raced the rest of the way up.

It took as long to get the judge and attorneys back in the courtroom as it did for the jury to come to its decision. The clerk called for the written verdict, which was handed over by the jury foreman. The whole of the court gallery leaned forward in their chairs, including the judge. Nealy was the only one not looking at the clerk. His head was turned to Ida and he smiled a nervous smile that she returned.

The entire room was hushed. The only sound was the rattling of the paper as the clerk opened the verdict that was written upon it. In a load, clear voice, he read: "The State vs. Daniel Duncan: indictment for murder – *guilty*."

The courtroom exploded in every corner. A squad of deputies swooped down on Duncan and circled him, all but blocking him from view. Lubelsky's widow wailed and was escorted out by some friends. There were a few scattered cheers. Watts pounded his gavel to restore order.

"Gentlemen of the jury, we want to thank you for your service to the community and apologize for the separation from your families. These are difficult and weighty issues that have been put upon your table. As you have found him guilty without recommendation for mercy, then the law is clear as to the next course.

"Daniel Duncan, please rise and face the court."

Nealy did so.

"It being solemnly demanded of the prisoner at the bar if he hath anything to say why sentence of death should not be passed upon him, he saith nothing further unless as he has before said; wherefore, it is considered by the Court, and pronounced as the judgment of the law, that the said Daniel Duncan be taken hence to the place whence last he came, there to be kept in close and safe custody until Wednesday, the 12th day of October next, and that on that said Wednesday, between the hours of ten in the forenoon and two in the afternoon, he be taken to the place of execution in the county, and there be hanged by the neck until his body be dead.

"And may God have mercy upon his soul."

DATELINE:
Charleston, S.C., October 10, 1910
Hal Hinson | New York Tribune

Death.

The word swept through this town, a plague of publicity. In some quarters, it brought cheers of celebration. In one small quarter, in one instant, in one glance before they pulled him from the courtroom, Daniel Cornelius "Nealy" Duncan looked into the eyes of the girl he would never marry and I saw the light of two worlds extinguished.

There was a mighty struggle in this small city. Not so much the battle between Good and Evil, although on the surface it would appear one of those lost horribly today, but a struggle between two men and the conflict of their time. I have met both and neither are wholly good, nor wholly evil. They share similar virtues in the love of the land, their horses, their homeland and heritage. They both share the fault of being human.

Both John Peurifoy and Brice Matthews entered into a trial with a preconception. Both came to this trial thinking that the defendant was guilty. One changed his mind. Neither came to this court with passion for the trial. Both left having fought harder than he had intended and both attorneys and those who watched walked away feeling that Nealy Duncan came closer to freedom than any expected. But close doesn't count, at least not to Nealy, because he is less than two days away from a noose.

When it was over, this trial was more fizzle than bang. Sometimes like life, when on your dying bed you wonder if it was all worth it, because in the end, it really didn't make a damn.

CHAPTER SIXTEEN
Tuesday
OCTOBER 11, 1910

Dawn came with little joy and a little pain. My head hurt, self induced.

Randy and I sat up late discussing how the trial ended, how close it may have come to sparing Nealy's life and drinking to our disappointment. But even good bourbon can't compensate for a bad verdict.

I heard the sounds of the morning routine downstairs and hauled myself out of bed. Into a quick shower with a couple blasts of cold water, a hot shave and a clean shirt and I began to feel human. A cup of black coffee would probably bring me back to something close to my former self.

The dining room was set for breakfast but Randy wasn't there. The molested morning paper was a sign she had been up much earlier. Meredith walked in.

"Meredith, where is Randy?"

"She said she had an early errand, for you to eat breakfast, she'd be back soon. Would you like your usual Benedict?"

I was lost in thought for a second, wondering where she might have gone so early. "No thank you, Meredith. Just coffee. I don't have much of an appetite this morning."

The paper was full of the usual post trial reporting. Peurifoy praised the fine people of Charleston and the whole county for persevering and bringing the difficult case to a just conclusion. Chief Boyle heaped praise on the fine work of his detectives and department for bringing the guilty man to trial. Absent from the quotes was Brice Matthews. I heard that after the verdict he met briefly with Nealy and then simply dropped out of sight.

I heard the door open and Randy entered the room. She poured a half cup of coffee and sat down next to me.

"Good morning, you've been out early."

"There are things to be done. I need to explain something to you. When we sat at this table the first night we had dinner together, you were talking about your visit with Ida, how sweet she was, how innocent and how crushing it would be for her if he were convicted. Now, he's convicted and as it stands she will never see him again in this lifetime."

Something began to concern me. I remembered the moment, remembered her running her finger around the top of the wine glass while she disappeared in thought. At that moment, she seemed to be forming some idea.

"That can't happen. She will see him one last time."

"What do you mean? The sheriff's not going to let a woman into the jail. Your good buddy Chief Boyle isn't going to get involved in something that smacks of humanitarian effort."

"Not they, Hal, we are."

I sat in silence, giving my best impersonation of a dramatic pause. "Wait one minute. There's a lot not making sense about what you're suggesting, not the least of which are the obvious little questions about armed guards, breaking *into* a jail, which is not usually the sane approach applied to jail breaking and involving a member of a national newspaper in the whole affair. This sounds a little farfetched to me."

"Are you finished?"

"Yes, ma'am."

"Here's the plan Mrs. Vanderhorst and I have decided on."

"I knew the two of you together could come to no good."

"Quiet. Tonight, Mrs. Vanderhorst is hosting a dinner party. She has not held one in several years, so it will be somewhat unprecedented and no one will be able to refuse her invitation. She is still a woman with some power in this town. On the guest list will be those involved in this case, call it a 'Toast to Justice' party. Peurifoy, Chief Boyle, Sheriff Martin, Mayor Rhett and enough other notables so that no one will suspect the key people and purpose. Dinner will be from six until about nine, plenty of time to accomplish what we need to do. At six-thirty several 'girls' from my brothels will drop in on the jailers with a little liquor. After a little entertainment, the girls will drop a sleeping potion into their drinks. As soon as they're passed out, I'll bring Ida in to see Nealy."

"And what am I supposed to do?"

"You'll keep watch. You'll take the front. We'll put Markus on one corner and Mojo on the other."

"You realize this is foolish."

"You realize this is the last time this girl will see the man she loves."

"Love is worth the risk?"

"Love is always worth the risk."

"Count me in."

" Now, if you'll excuse me, I've got plans to complete."

She walked out of the room and out the front door again. I sat and thought about whether it was better for Ida to see Nealy again, or just face having him ripped out of her life. That's when the wisdom of women came to me all over again. Randy was right, love is worth the risk, even if it's for fated lovers.

I put my coat on and walked out into a bright morning. There was a bit of warmth back, enough to remind me that this was a southern town on the ocean with all the heat and humidity that can come with it. Sheriff Martin had agreed to meet me. Details for the execution were being completed, but it was clear that he was not going to make it a public event. A limited number of people would be allowed to witness. I needed to be in that number.

Like everything else in Charleston, the city jail where Nealy was held and where the execution would take place was a pleasant stroll of a few blocks until you crossed that line that separated the civil from the unseemly. The block surrounding the jail was, simply put, seedy. Respectable people, who would not want to live next to a jail, ceded the area to those who would. Among those were several brothels, admittedly belonging to Randy. The jail itself was gothic, surrounded by a twelve-foot wall that would keep the execution from prying eyes. The jail wall would not screen the view from the nearby buildings with second story balconies.

I walked through the entry gate and was met by a guard.

"Hey, you," he said. "You can't come in here. We got business today."

"Sheriff Martin is expecting me."

"He's over there, by the gallows."

The courtyard wasn't big. On one end an upright structure was raised, resembling a ship's yardarm. It didn't look like a gallows, except for the rope. A noose makes a statement all by itself.

"Sheriff Martin? Hal Hinson. Thanks for meeting with me."

"Mr. Hinson, I hope you don't mind if I continue working. We're a little busy around here today. We need to do a few tests on the gallows here."

The noose was cinched around a burlap sack of grain that sat on a small platform five feet off the ground. Sheriff Martin waved his hand. A man stood by a small shed on the back of the vertical post holding the yardarm. The man nodded, did something and the sack suddenly jumped four feet to its apogee, then fell back and was caught by the noose. The bottom split out of the sack and grain poured to the ground. Martin went to the sack, looked up at the noose and nodded, satisfied.

"Hank," he called, "I want this tested at least two more times. Don't want nuthin' to go wrong tomorrow. Mr. Hinson, come along with me." We crossed the courtyard and went into the building. His office window faced inward, so we could continue to watch the grim rehearsal.

"Sheriff, I've never seen a gallows like that."

"It's something we borrowed from the sea. In 1820, some sailors were convicted of piracy aboard an Argentinean ship that docked in our harbor. Even though the ship was at dock, naval tradition dictated the executions had to be performed aboard ship. The men stood on deck where a noose was placed around their necks, the rope ran through the blocks at the yardarm and looped back down and tied to a heavy weight, lashed to the outside of the ship. The captain signaled the lashings holding the weights to be cut away, the weights fell into the harbor, jerking the prisoners into the air. Death comes on the descent, when the neck is snapped. We experimented with the method and by the middle of the last century all our hangings were performed using the dead weight method."

"And where is this dead weight?"

"It's on the other end of the rope, in that small shed. There's a four foot hole in the ground. When the executioner pulls the lever, the weight drops and then the prisoner is hoisted up until he reaches a peak and then drops. When it works right, you hear the neck snap."

"Very satisfying, I'm sure."

"It beats the alternative, when the prisoner hangs by the neck until he suffocates."

"Does that happen?"

"Rarely."

"Sheriff, I'm not sure I can thank you, but I appreciate you allowing me to be one of the reporters to witness the execution tomorrow."

"It was not my choice. I was told to."

"By whom?"

"Can't say."

"Did the unnamed party say that I was allowed to see Duncan today?"

"I was told you could, if you asked, but not to offer."

"Then, may I?"

He leaned back in his chair for a moment. His hand toyed with his rather oversized mustache, a gesture that appeared to be a habit. Something triggered when more than a few nerves in his brain were working at the same moment.

"Guard!" he shouted to someone outside his office. A skinny kid entered.

"Yes, Sheriff?"

"Take Mr. Hinson up to Duncan's cell. Give him 15 minutes, no longer. Then see to it that he leaves."

"Yes, sir."

I stood, not feeling any real reason to go overboard being nice to this man. "Sheriff, I'll see you tomorrow morning," and I followed the kid up the stairs.

"You from New York," the kid asked.

"Yes."

"You here just for the hanging?"

"I came for the trial, the hanging is the unfortunate result of the trial."

"You ever see a hangin'?"

"Never had the pleasure."

"Me neither. Looking forward to it. They say you can hear the neck snap from a couple blocks away."

We had come to the top of the stairs. His last statement carried through the cell area, including the cell where Nealy watched us from his hammock. The silence in the stare was painful. I turned to the kid.

"Why don't you wait downstairs."

"You givin' me an order?"

"Let's put it this way. The man who told the sheriff to give me this interview was high enough that the sheriff isn't going to mess with him. Do you want to mess with someone who gives the sheriff orders?"

"No, but I ain't takin' orders from you."

"You don't have to. You just have to give me the 15 minutes the sheriff told you to give me."

"Fifteen minutes. I'll be back. Not a second more." He turned, went down and took up post at a desk at the foot of the stairway.

I walked to Nealy. He stood and took two steps to the bars, put his hand through and took mine.

"Mr. Hinson, nice to see you. Thank you for coming."

His grip was firm, and he held my hand for a moment as we looked into each other's eyes. His were clear and calm, even peaceful.

"Nealy, you have no fear?"

"Mr. Hinson, to quote my Lord, 'It is finished.' In a day's time all the pain and worry of this world will be over. I will be with my Lord, and with my dear mother and sister. All the uncertainty is over. I know where I'm going and I'm prepared."

"You didn't mention your faith in our first meeting."

"I've always had faith. It's just at the end, when you know it's coming that you gain the clarity. I sat in church so many Easter Sundays hearing about Jesus, hearing about his death and the resurrection. I always wondered how he went willingly to the cross when he knew what was going to happen. He went because he knew he was going to be with his Father. He knew that joy was coming and it got him through the pain on Golgotha. I will not suffer as much as he."

I looked at him, at the cell. On one bar hung a suit of clothes. He held a photograph in his hand. He saw me looking and held it up.

"It's my Ida. She had this photo taken in her wedding dress. I'm memorizing her in the dress. It's how I will see her when she finally joins me in heaven. Leaving her behind is the only part of this that I cannot make peace with. I wish I could tell her that I will wait, until her time is through, to join me."

Tears formed in my eyes. I looked away to the window, clenching my jaw as hard as I could, swallowed and took a deep breath, "Nealy, you will see her."

He looked at me, as if I was crazed.

"Nealy, I'm serious. Listen closely." I described the basics of the plan. When I finished, there were tears in his eyes, too.

"You're taking a terrible risk for a dead man."

"I'm taking a risk for a man who is in love, and who will die. If we're lucky, we will all love, and then die, although most of us hope for a bit more time between the two. This is a scheme woven and executed by women. May God have mercy on all our souls, for we are powerless."

Though the tears were still in his eyes, he smiled warmly. His hand came through the bars and went behind my head. He pulled it to the bars of the cell until our foreheads touched. Our eyes were inches apart.

"You're a good man," Nealy said.

"You are the better man," I said.

I stepped back from the bars. Our eyes remained locked. My hand rose to meet his through the bars. I heard footfalls coming up the stairs.

"Say goodbye, Mr. New York, your time is up, just like his is. He's out of time and out of friends. His next date is with a noose."

I thought about hitting him, it would have been easy, but then I thought it might complicate matters in the hours ahead.

"See you later, Nealy."

Nealy smiled.

"What are you two talkin' about? There is no later ... he's got no later ..." I let the idiot babble as I turned and walked to the stairs.

I walked out of the jail and into an afternoon on the border of oppression. The heat settled down on the city. It was past noon and the temperature pressed ninety. I walked down Queen Street and entered the cool foyer of the Mills House looking for a late lunch. What I found shouldn't have surprised me.

In the dining room, surrounded by florists, waiters, chefs and other assorted but unidentifiable sorts, sat Mrs. Vanderhorst and Randy.

"Mr. Hinson, welcome to our little planning meeting. We're going over details for my dinner tonight. Will you be attending?"

She knew I wasn't, so this was my prompt for a public and plausible denial. "Why, Mrs. Vanderhorst, very kind of you to invite me, but I have a deadline tonight, a story that I must finish before morning. I'm afraid I will be unable to attend."

That got a nod of approval from Randy. They went on about their business. The old doll was having the time of her life, making quite a show of ordering food, offering instructions to chefs and servers alike. She had been here before. I retired to a corner table and ordered a club sandwich and a beer. After a few minutes, Randy slipped into the chair next to mine.

"Hiding in the corner?"

"Just staying clear of you two. I'm only one man."

"Funny boy, that fellow from New York."

"There are places where my *bons mots* are still being quoted."

"It's time to gather your wits, my friend. We've got a full evening ahead of us. I'm going to sneak out of here in a few minutes and run by to make sure the girls are all prepared. Let's meet back at my house by five. Markus will bring Ida to my house disguised as a charwoman. She will change there."

"Change?"

"Oh, I didn't mention? Into her wedding dress, there's to be a wedding tonight."

"No, you didn't mention that. You didn't mention that this idea, which was crazy from the beginning, has crossed into the realm of insanity."

"Did you see Nealy today?"

"Yes."

"What was he doing?"

She was leading me. She knew it. I knew it. "He was looking at a picture of Ida in her wedding dress. Not seeing her on their wedding day was his only real regret."

"So there," she smiled, stood and slipped away.

"So there," I said to myself, alone.

From the front, Randy's house appeared quiet. It was a pretty house, on a pretty street and decorated in all the trappings of taste. Inside, that facade fell aside.

"Mista Hal, where you been? We got bidness here." Mojo was in a high state of excitement. The house was in a high state of frenzy. Meredith had laid the table with a few finger foods, which had apparently been touched by more than a single hand, including that of a distinguished looking Negro who stood with a small plate and napkin in hand and a white collar on his neck.

I stepped forward. "Good evening, Reverend. I'm Hal Hinson."

"Mr. Hinson, I'm Ruffin Nichols. A pleasure to meet you. Miss Mary has said many good things about you."

"Did she mention that I was crazy?"

"Sir?"

"Crazy, Reverend, for allowing myself to get involved in this scheme."

"Mr. Hinson, if that's what it is, then I guess crazy is contagious and we may all be committed together."

"Hanged all together would be more like it, Reverend."

"The Lord works in mysterious ways. I have never presided over a wedding and a funeral for the same man on the same day, but it seems that will be the case. One will be a joyous secret, the other a public shame. I am proud to take part in the former."

"Reverend, when you put it that way, I'd have to say 'amen' to that."

At that, a commotion at the top of the stairs drew our attention to four women descending. In the lead was Meredith, followed by

Miss Mary, then Ida in a white wedding dress and Randy herding all forward. At the bottom of the stairs, she motioned us all into a circle.

"Ladies and gentlemen, let me introduce you to the bride to be, Miss Ida Lampkin, soon to become Mrs. Ida Duncan."

Ida was radiant. Her dress was cut to show her shoulders and décolletage, slim at her waist and flared at the hips. It appeared to be a light satin, not expensive looking, but she wore it like spun gold. She also wore the anticipation of a young bride, even knowing that this wedding night would be her first and last with her husband.

"Now that we're all together, let's go through how this is going to work." Randy described her plan. "Even as we're gathered here, the little party has started at the jail. There are two guards on duty tonight, instead of the usual one. One of the jailers has been around for ages. We already know he has a fondness for the bottle and the girls, as he is a regular customer. The other is younger, not too bright, but has already fallen under the charms of one of my girls, who has been 'dropping by' for the last couple of days."

She continued with the details and our assignments. "In five minutes a carriage will arrive in front. Miss Mary, Ida, the Reverend and I will leave in that. You boys take point. When you arrive at the jail, Markus and Mojo, you will each take the opposite corners. Hal, you will walk past once on the far side of the street to check the area for any guards or officers, then circle back past the front door. If the door is closed and there's a folded newspaper on the step, then we're safe to go in. You signal Markus and he'll signal us in the carriage. After we're in, we'll have fifteen minutes for the wedding. That's when the carriage returns and we have to leave. We go out the same way we came in. Hal, you stay one minute after we leave to make sure no alarm is sounded, then the three of you get the hell out of there. Markus and Mojo, if anything raises your concern, whistle once. If you see any police, anyone who looks official, whistle twice and we'll go out through the back alley. Now, that concludes the rehearsal party. Is everybody clear?"

Mojo snapped to attention with a salute, "Yes, Ma'am!" Markus and I smiled and followed suit. What else could we do? The plan sounded simple enough to work. If the girls were successful with the guards and assuming Mrs. Vanderhorst did her part in keeping the top officials at dinner, what could go wrong? That question has left the lips of many a fool.

I heard the carriage drive up.

"Markus, go check the street. Make sure no nosy neighbors are out."

He went out and returned a half minute later, "All clear, ma'am."

"Then my dear friends and conspirators, the game's afoot. Ida, fortunately the night is cooling off. Wrap yourself in this cloak to cover your dress. Now, let's walk out like it's a perfectly normal evening."

And they did. We went out the back door and caught the alley behind the carriage house so that we could progress toward the jail without calling attention to ourselves. After Broad Street, we headed up Logan. I left Markus at the corner of Logan and Magazine Street and Mojo walked with me down the street where I left him on the corner of Archdale. Walking past the front of the jail, I saw the door closed and a newspaper on the step. I signaled up the street. Markus caught the sign and waved down Logan where the carriage was parked.

Just to make sure, I walked up to the door of the jail and cautiously walked in. There was a table with four chairs. In two chairs on opposite sides, the jailers were face down on the table. In the other two chairs were two very attractive young women, showing considerable assets, sitting across from each other like they were playing bridge with two dummy partners.

"Good evening, ladies." They both stood.

"Mr. Hinson, so nice to meet you." They looked at each other and giggled. "We've heard so much about you." They moved toward me and I felt like I was about to be caught in a tough situation. "Are you alone?" queried the blonde, with ambitions that seemed contradictory to job security.

"Actually, Randy is right behind me." They drew back like vampires confronted with a cross. "But a pleasure to meet you, and thanks so much for your help tonight."

The door opened behind me and Randy fairly flew in, took one hard glance at me and the girls, then pointed up the stairs. "Ida, your fiancé is waiting. Let's go join him." She raced up the stairs followed by Miss Mary and the Reverend pulling up a distant third.

Randy turned back to the girls. "Constance and Charity, you've done a great job. Thank you, but don't get any notions about this one. He's mine. Now you two clear on out of here in case something happens."

"Yes, Miss Randy." Both walked out the door, closing it behind them.

"Now, Mr. Hinson, I believe we have a wedding to attend. Why don't you borrow those keys from the gentleman with his face on the table."

We walked up the stairs to find Nealy and Ida embracing through the bars. Miss Mary and the Reverend stood a respectful few paces back. When we walked up close to the cell, Nealy stepped back and smiled, first at Ida, then at me. I felt Randy's hand close on mine, tightly. If a ray of light had shot down from heaven, I would not have been surprised. The moment was blessed, worth every risk.

I walked up and unlocked the door. Nealy stepped out dressed in his wedding suit. With his right hand, he took Ida's hand. With his left, he took mine.

"Hal, would you be my best man?"

"You honor me by asking. Of course."

Then we formed up on the Reverend. Nealy and I to his right and Ida. Miss Mary and Randy to his left.

"Dearly beloved," Reverend Nichols began and my mind went to other times I'd heard those words. Never in a jail. I looked around the floor, empty cells, the other inmates cleared on this supposed deathwatch. A condemned man generally spends his last night in solitary. An execution can put a prison population in a nasty mood.

I came back to attention.

"This occasion marks the celebration of love and commitment with which this man and this woman begin their life together. And now – through me – He joins you together in one of the holiest bonds.

"Who gives this woman in marriage to this man?"

"I do," Miss Mary smiled through her tears.

The Reverend was on a roll. He continued the vows, praising

God and the glory of the union, but the time was running short.

"Ahem." Randy broke the runaway ceremony and glanced up at the clock. Message taken.

"Yes, of course."

"Do you, Daniel Cornelius Duncan, take Ida to be your wedded wife?"

"I do."

"Do you, Ida Lampkin, take Daniel to be your husband."

"I do."

"What therefore God has joined together, let no man put asunder. I pronounce you man and wife. You may kiss the bride."

And there, in the unholiest of places, beneath a bare single light, surrounded by faces gleaming with tears, Nealy and Ida consummated their marriage with a single, lingering kiss.

Time was short. I looked from the couple to the clock, then to Randy, who caught my eye. Nealy held to his wife with a force that might fuse them. Then they stepped slightly apart, clasped hands and turned to us.

"My dear friends. Tonight I have gone from a condemned man, to a husband. My one fear in these final days was that I would not see my Ida again. You have risked your safety, if not your lives, to bring us together and if I could live a hundred lives, I could never repay you. When you told me earlier, Mr. Hinson, that this was to happen tonight, I thought of taking Ida and running to a place where they might never find us. But if they did, it would only be worse. If they didn't find us, they would hurt who they could find.

"When you leave, you will take my love, but I will wait in heaven to see my Ida again."

With that, he walked over to embrace each of us, then took Ida's hand again and walked a few paces away where they touched foreheads and he whispered quietly to her. They kissed again and held each other tightly, then turned and rejoined us.

"Go safely, each of you. I am at peace. We will all see each other again, as our own fate is written."

His words seemed to have a calming effect on everyone. There were no tears. I had expected Ida to be wailing, had been prepared to help carry her from the room. It had been my one serious doubt about this plan. Now, she looked at him with a confidence that unnerved me. There was something I did not understand.

"Hal, you stay for a moment, lock up behind you and follow us out. Once outside, we all leave, as we arrived, separately." Randy shepherded her group down the stairs. I walked Nealy back to the cell and opened the door for him. He walked in, turned and put both hands on the bars and pulled the door shut with a loud metallic clang that echoed off the stone walls.

"Been a little exciting around here tonight," Nealy said. "Maybe I can get a little sleep now before my big day." He stuck his hand back through the bars. "Thank you for standing in as my best man, for making this night something better than what it was intended to be, for helping me face tomorrow. Now lock this door and get out of here before those guards wake up. I suppose I'll see you in the morning."

"I'll be here."

"Goodnight, then."

I turned the key in the lock, then walked slowly to the stairs before turning back and looking. Nealy was stretched on his hammock, looking at his photo of Ida and smiling.

Moving quickly down the stairs, I walked to where the guards were still passed out. One was stirring, so I didn't think hanging around was a good idea. I dropped the keys back in place and tiptoed to and through the door. On the sidewalk I let out a long breath. Everything had gone according to plan.

I heard a whistle.

Another followed from Mojo's direction.

I ran to the middle of the street and saw him running to me.

"Mista Hal!" He ran fast, and behind him came half a dozen men. From that distance I couldn't tell, but they didn't appear to be members of the Charleston social society out for an evening's stroll.

Mojo came abreast of me. "Mista Hal, I counts six."

"You go. I want you to run to Markus."

"No, I stays wid you."

"There's no time, and no arguing." I pushed him hard. "Please, Mojo, go! Get some help." He ran up the block.

The six fanned out across the street. One started a jog on the outside.

"Hey, I'm gonna catch me that little monkey." He was out in front of the rest of the pack. I cut the angle to catch him one on one. He wasn't slowing down and neither was I. When he was about ten feet away, I launched into the air and aimed my right foot for the center of his chest. It caught him totally unaware and he took the kick full, going down hard with the wind knocked out of him. But that was one down and in the time I took to deal with him, the other five closed in, circling around me. There were a couple of familiar faces and they were smiling.

"Where's that whore girlfriend of yours tonight? Don't think she's going to surprise us with a pistol this time."

They were starting to circle, moving clockwise. No one offered an easy target.

"Maybe when we're finished with you, we'll pay her a little visit."

Anger has no place in a fight. I wasn't going to fall for their taunts.

"Maybe we'll catch your little monkey, and hang him to go along with the nigger in the jail."

"Why don't you idiots just get on with it." So they did.

One produced something that looked like a homemade night stick and came at me with it raised over his head. He was easy, as he brought the stick down I stepped inside, caught his wrist and used his momentum to flip him. He went on his back, but the circle tightened and they were still moving around me.

The next one stepped in, raising his fists like a boxer. It looked kind of amusing. He led with his left, which I moved easily to deflect. But his moneymaker was his right. That caught me full on the side of my face and spun me around. The boxer had me facing away and went for the next best punch, straight to my kidney. I managed to stumble forward and not go down, but that drove me straight to the next attacker who lunged with a knife. I deflected the knife, drove my fist into his stomach and he doubled over. That left my back exposed. I saw a motion coming at my head and then the sap hit me just behind my ear. An explosion of light was my last sensation.

It was the next sensation that wasn't pleasant. My body felt like it was in some competition for pain. In the lead was my head. I struggled to pull enough of the pieces together to call it consciousness, but would be much happier to slip back into the black. It felt better there. Someone was trying to lift me.

"Hal. Hal. Please wake up. Hal."

I knew the voice. Something about it made me want to come back. There was something about it that didn't hurt. It was Randy. I opened my eyes. That didn't stop the pain.

"Thank God. Hal, I'm so sorry. Looks like they did a pretty good job on you."

Her face was close to mine. She looked worried. I still felt like I was being lifted. I looked down and saw two hands around my chest. Someone held me up. My arms weren't free. They were tied at right angles to the iron gates. After my buddies were finished with me, they tied me splayed between the gates of the jail. It might have looked like Samson between the pillars of the temple. It might have looked like Christ on the cross. But I felt like a limp scarecrow.

"Markus, hold him while I cut him down." Randy reached up and cut the ropes on one wrist, then the other. I sagged to my knees. Randy dropped down beside me.

"Hal, I know it hurts. You've taken a bad beating. But we have to get out of here. If those thugs have sounded an alarm, then the sheriff is going to make an unwelcome appearance soon. We don't need to be here for that."

"Markus, you get that side, I'll get this one."

The two of them supplied enough lift to get me to my feet. I was punch drunk and staggering. Thankfully, I only had to walk a few feet to her car. It was running and ready by the curb. They tucked me in the passenger seat, then both climbed in. When she hit the accelerator, I almost passed out again from the force of being jerked back in the seat. Markus held me in my seat and Randy drove with purpose. We were back at her house in minutes. They were a little more gentle getting me into the house. Mojo rushed us at the door.

"Mista Hal." He threw his arms around my waist. I cringed from the pain, but put my hand on his shoulder and let him pretend he was helping me to the parlor. Markus did the heavy work of getting me to the couch. Then they all circled in on me. Meredith arrived with a tray of towels and a surgical pan with water. Randy poured me four fingers of bourbon.

"Here, doctor says take a deep sip of this."

I did. "Thank you, doctor."

She took off my jacket, unbuttoned my shirt and started to tend my wounds, beginning with the gash on the back of my head. I held a bag of ice on that while she dabbed and washed the other cuts, adding iodine to my misery.

"You're really kind of lucky, Hal. They got in some good licks, but they seemed to work you over with a purpose and that wasn't to beat you to a bloody pulp. I bet the word was to hurt you, but not so you couldn't show up in public for the hanging in the morning."

"They must have done a little extra-curricular kicking after I was down. I think they cracked a couple of ribs."

"We'll bandage that up in the morning. You'll be able to stand and walk. It won't feel great, but the bandages will support your ribs."

I drank what was left in the glass.

"Patient needs more pain medication."

She smiled and stood, "Meredith, Markus and Mojo ... thank you. Now you'd better head off to bed. It's going to be a long day tomorrow."

They left and she poured a bit more bourbon for both of us.

"When those boys came running back in here and told me what was happening, I felt like the earth had fallen out from underneath me. I'm not sure I've ever felt fear like that. So in the future, Mr. Hinson, I'd rather you not play such rough games."

"I will try to keep that in mind, ma'am. You are a font for good advice this evening, like going to bed, if you'd be so kind as to give a guy a hand."

With Randy on one side and the banister on the other, we made it up the stairs. She tenderly helped me undress and get into bed. I put my head on the pillow and cringed. She smiled and leaned over, kissing me lightly on the lips. It was a sensation that almost trumped the pain.

CHAPTER SEVENTEEN
Wednesday
October 12, 1910

Sleep was stingy. It came in taunting bits, interrupted by shots of pain. When dawn began to show, I slipped off for about an hour, then awoke knowing my time was up. Randy walked into the room with a small tray holding coffee, juice and a metal syringe.

"Two of those things look like breakfast. What's the third?"

"It's not something I would generally recommend, but then this is not a general kind of day. It's a solution, with cocaine."

"A seven percent solution, Dr. Watson?"

"Since you've read Sherlock Holmes, he used cocaine for his amusement. This is medicinal. It will get you on your feet, knock down the pain and help you get through this day. As I said, it's not something I would generally recommend. I don't condone the use of drugs for pleasure, but they exist for a reason."

"I'm not going to act brave here. If it helps me get out of bed, then you're my Nightingale."

She came and sat on the edge of the bed, pulled up my sleeve and tied a ribbon just above my elbow, pulling it tight. When she saw a good vein, she gently pushed the needle home and slowly injected her medicine. I felt the effects almost immediately. The pain that had been competing for dominance from different parts of my beaten body, subsided. I felt in an instant like I'd had the most refreshing night's sleep in my life.

"That's pretty amazing."

"Don't get used to it. You *might* get one more injection, but that's it."

"I can see how this could become addictive."

"Yes." And she let it stop there. She stood up and gently ran her fingers through my hair. "I'll see you downstairs in a few minutes.

We need to plan our day."

Getting out of bed gave me a couple jolts of pain, a reminder to move slowly, but was far less painful than it would have been without Randy's medication. I threw down a half cup of coffee and stepped into the shower. By the time I'd dressed and started gingerly down the stairs, I felt like I would at least make it to the end of the day, which brought me to the point of the day. Nealy's execution.

Everyone sat at the breakfast table, looking as though they had just finished a full breakfast. Mojo wore the partial remains of eggs, bacon, biscuits and fresh jelly. I filled a small plate and sat down.

"We can be thankful to be here together today," Randy began. "By the end of the day at least one family will be torn apart. This will not be a pleasant day, but what we need to make sure of is that we're all back together here this evening, so let's be clear about a few things. Hal had a close call last night."

"I wouldn't call it close, seems to have been rather bang on."

"Always a joke from this fellow from New York. As I was saying, there are no reasons to take risks today. Number one, Mojo, you do not leave this house today."

"Aw, Miss Randy," was as far as he got. She looked full upon him and the tough kid became a little kid and put his head down.

"Markus, you shouldn't be too visible, but I do want you to arrange for a carriage for Miss Mary and Ida to follow the body to the cemetery.

"Meredith, there's no reason for you to go anywhere near the jail, it's no place for a lady.

"Hal, you have clearance to be a witness so you'll be inside the walls. Since I can't be with you, I'll be outside on the balcony of one of my houses that adjoins the rear of the jail's courtyard."

"Randy, I agree with everything, including the fact that this is no event for a lady ..."

"I'll be fine. My houses are safe. I pay a lot of money for that. Besides, it will give us a high view of the area, in case something goes wrong, I should be able to see it and you will have a safe refuge."

"I don't suppose there would be any point in my arguing?"

"No."

"Then I suppose we'd better do as we're told." With that I glared at Mojo, just to drive home his instructions.

We all stood up. It wasn't exactly a cheerful group. I went around the table and put my arm around Mojo. He put both of his around me and hugged. It hurt my ribs, but it was worth it. Randy and I walked onto the front porch. Nothing about the day was cheerful. Clouds gathered and winds blew in from the sea. The barometer was dropping, too. Randy saw me looking.

"That's going to need watching. There's some kind of storm coming. We'll know by tonight, but you can bet this New Orleans girl knows how to watch for signs."

"Hurricane?"

"Don't even say it. We're still in storm season. You don't ignore the warnings."

"That's a cheerful thought."

"Add it to the rest of the day."

We stepped out to the street. The jail was within walking distance, across that divide, just a few blocks. We walked to Broad Street and then up Logan toward the jail. Dark clouds forming over the city heightened the gothic look of the towers.

Around the building a crowd gathered, a surprising array of people. Well-dressed Charlestonians, churlish folk of the city and a smattering of people who drove in from the hinterlands. Hucksters were setting up wagons on the street opposite the jail. The execution was set for between ten and two. At this hour, it was still a bit early for the hot dogs and popped corn to be offered. We strolled through the crowd like it was the Easter Parade, passing close by the jail yard gate. A guard was posted, one of the fellows from last night, and he didn't look well.

"I'm Hal Hinson with the New York Tribune."

"I know who ye are."

"When are witnesses being allowed in?"

"Another half hour, at the earliest."

"How will we know?"

"You won't. You better be here then."

"Having a nice morning? How's your head?"

"How's yers?" He took a step closer to me.

There was a yank on my elbow. Randy gave me a look. We walked away.

"You can't let these yahoos know that you know anything about last night."

"Randy, it's all but over. What difference does it make?"

"The difference is that *I* still live here, and even after you leave I'd rather not be directly tied to our little scheme."

"That's a point, but I'd say whatever happens after is still up for discussion."

"That discussion may be the one bright point."

She took my arm and we walked around the corner of the jail, following the wall, which enclosed the yard, along a large courtyard. Across an alley stood the houses that Randy owned, the brothels that brought her influence, income and a reputation. We walked in as though we were stopping by for tea. The door opened into a large parlor that was well-decorated. On several couches, young women lounged in varying states of undress. There was not an unattractive one among them. My eyes lingered.

"Yes, they are pretty, aren't they?" She caught me looking, "You needn't act coy. They know they're attractive and they know you're a man. You should be glad I'm here to protect you. They know what they're doing. You wouldn't have a chance." She laughed.

"Yes, they are something. But this isn't my first time in a brothel."

"No doubt," she interrupted.

"With the intent, if I might continue, of walking out pure as the driven snow."

"So that's what you are?" The whole room giggled.

"Ladies, may I introduce Mr. Hal Hinson, my own personal virgin." They erupted in laughter. "However, we're here for more serious things."

She turned to one of the girls. "Mimi, would you send coffee up to the upstairs balcony?"

We walked up the stairs and down a corridor, surprisingly light in color and tone, and out a set of French doors onto a balcony. It was a surprisingly attractive setting, except for the fact that it offered a high reverse angle to the gallows scene I'd witnessed the day before. Below was the wall. Beyond that a large oak tree shaded the small shack and yardarm where Nealy would soon be hanged. I walked to the edge of the balcony and stared down. There was a flurry of activity around the gallows. The time drew near. Beyond the walls the streets were filling up too. Crowds came from near and far, not even to see the hanging, just to be near the spectacle of death. The Coliseum would still sell out. We have not come far.

I turned around. Randy was just behind me looking at the same scene. I expected to see fire, but her eyes seemed calm.

"I never cease to be disappointed in the actions of humans." She sat, picked up a teacup. "But I pretty much always know what to expect. I think, Hal, that you still think there is some inherent worth in Man. I accept that we are just a collection of base emotions. Were it not for love, love of the sort we saw in the eyes of Ida and Nealy, love that raises the spirit, love that binds souls, without that, or without the hope of that, my friend, there would be no reason to live."

"On that, we can agree, my dear," I still stood at the rail. "I do feel that there is, on occasion, nobility in this wasted race. I saw it in Nealy. He will hang in a short time, but he shows no hatred. When we talked yesterday, when I saw him last night, he showed a quality that gave me reason to raise my standards. His presence in this life will make me a better man."

She stood and walked to me, took my hands and pulled me close to feel her full body against mine. Then she kissed me with barely restrained passion.

"You are a better man, Hal Hinson, than many I've known. I don't think you need a whole lot of improvement."

I heard the sound of hands clapping and turned to look. On the balcony of the next house, John Peurifoy stood next to an attractive young lady. Before I could catch her hand, Randy grabbed her coffee cup and hurled it at his head. He ducked deftly and it sailed past to crash into a wall. He clapped twice again, then sat.

"Bastard." Now she was mad.

"Did you know he would be here?"

"That is my house. Yes, I knew."

"How long have you known?"

"Long enough to make sure you got the access you wanted."

"Quid pro quo."

"It's how deals are done."

Peurifoy looked at me and nodded his head. I returned the gesture.

"I'd better leave. Nealy should have at least one friendly face in the crowd."

"I'll meet you here afterwards. We'll have a carriage waiting to go to the cemetery. It's not far, but I don't want to walk through these people."

I kissed her cheek and walked back through the house, past the girls and into the street. The crowd had gotten much thicker and less civil. People had started climbing the trees overhanging the walls, young kids and a few young men, clinging to a chance to see a man die. I pushed my way through to the gate again. This time he opened it for me.

"How's yer whore?"

"How's your sister? I saw her in there."

He drew back to take a poke at me, but a bigger hand reached out and stopped him. It was Sheriff Martin.

"Mr. Hinson, I believe we've got more important matters before us than a few fisticuffs. Did last night leave you lacking?"

So he knew. Now he knew that I knew. Who else knew? I didn't care.

"The prisoner is in the process of being brought down. If you stand here, he'll pass you on the way to the gallows." The sheriff walked to where the officials and executioner were gathered.

Inside the jail's courtyard it was surprisingly calm. The din of the street could be heard but the wall worked something like a barrier. I looked around. No more than a dozen people were inside the confines, other members of the press and a few extra guards.

The jailhouse door swung open and unleashed an uproar.

From the trees the kids screamed to those outside the wall. "He's out! Here he comes!" Even though they couldn't see, the crowd noise swelled to a higher pitch, punctuated by occasional catcalls.

Nealy stepped out into the daylight. He squinted at the sky. Even though it was cloudy, it was the most light he'd seen for a few days. He looked around, gathering and savoring his last look. The bare tall wall in front of him was covered with bright bougainvillea, with beautiful flowers and painful thorns. His gaze lingered too long. A jailer shoved him from behind. Nealy stumbled forward. He was bound in leg irons, his arms were tied to his side. Walking was difficult. He made the slight turn on the path that would take him in front of me.

He had four guards around him, front, sides and back. As he walked, his head was high and he scanned the crowd. His eyes fell on me and he smiled. That sent a lump to my throat. He took a few more shuffling steps. I could hear the chains dragging. Then he kind of lurched sideways in my direction. I reached out and caught him, and clasped his hand. He slipped me a note. A guard jerked him upright, for an instant he stood.

"God bless you, Mr. Hinson. We'll meet again."

"Goodbye, Nealy."

A guard shoved him forward. I slipped the note in my pocket.

For an instant, I lost sight of the insanity around me. For a moment, as Nealy approached and fell into me there was a clarity and calm. He carried it with him. I glanced to the side, to the thorns on the bougainvillea and thought of a crown. It would not be out of place on his head.

The procession progressed and, along with it, the noise. The peace that had settled on me was gone, suddenly, replaced by the cacophony inside and outside the walls of the prison yard. I could hear the vendors hawking, the din of the crowd calling up to the trees, the boys in the trees calling out instant-by-instant reports of Nealy's progress toward his death. As they approached the gallows, the group spun around in formation and deposited Nealy beneath the rope. The gang of four stepped aside and the sheriff and executioner came in closer to the condemned man.

The sheriff raised his hand and the courtyard fell silent.

"Quiet, it's de sheriff," one young man yelled from a tree. All noise in the street stopped.

"By the order of the State Court of South Carolina, you have been found guilty of the crime of murder, and have been sentenced to be executed today between the hours of 10 a .m. and 2 p.m., and hang by the neck until you are dead."

A roar went up from outside the wall.

Martin held up his hand, and turned to Nealy. "Do you have anything to say before the order of the court is carried out?"

All sound was sucked from an entire city block. I could see the first sign that Nealy felt the impact of the moment. He swayed slightly, then pulled himself up straight, looked to the sky and focused beyond the wall, to all those gathered, to all of Charleston.

"I won't die with a lie on my lips," he said in a firm, clear voice. "I am an innocent man. I wait to meet you all in heaven."

The silence held. Martin motioned the executioner to come forward. He placed a black hood over Nealy's head, then positioned the noose around his neck and tightened the loop.

I looked up to the balcony where Randy stood. She was on the rail with her fingers to her lips in a state of disbelief. The executioner stepped back away from Nealy and put his hand on the lever that would drop the weight. There was silence still. Sheriff Martin looked at his watch, then nodded at the executioner. He pulled the lever, dropping the weight four feet and Nealy was jerked violently into the air. The whole courtyard heard the weight hit the bottom of the shaft. But no one heard the snap of Nealy's neck.

I immediately felt sick. Without the snap, there was no clear fracture of the neck and his spinal cord wasn't instantly severed. Nealy was still alive dangling from the noose.

His back arched and then he bent forward. Beneath the hood he gasped for air. He struggled against the noose to the point that he was swinging from the end of the rope. Every eye was fixed in sick fascination. Some turned away. The young guard who had been so tough the day before retched in the bushes. I looked to the balcony and Randy had turned her back to the scene. Calls from the street for reports went largely unanswered.

For almost a minute, the struggle continued. Inside the hood, Nealy fought for air, fought against the noose. He felt his eyes about to explode. Inside the blackness of the hood, he saw points of light as his eyes reacted to the loss of oxygen. What strength he had drained out of him, and he no longer strained against the rope. A calm came over him. In the blackness, a light grew and arms reached to hold him.

To those watching, they saw Nealy finally stop moving. He hung, a dead weight. Even then, the motion of his fight had created a pendulum and his body swung gently back and forth, now being pushed by the wind. No one moved. The guards looking to the sheriff were checked by his stern look. For ten minutes, there was neither sound nor movement save for Nealy's body swinging.

From the other side of the wall a voice called, "Cut the nigger down, let's be done with it." The sheriff held up his hand to those of us inside the walls. There was to be no action, not yet. I looked up. Randy had left the balcony. Peurifoy still sat there, but looking as glum as if he'd lost an election. He won the case and left the courtroom a local hero, but this execution had not gone well. The local papers were already pushing for electrocution as a new means to execute prisoners. It fit better with the new image of letting science do the grim work of killing people. Hanging was a throwback, or a holdback, for a politician.

The carnival atmosphere abated. I heard the sounds of people and traffic outside the wall moving again. But no one moved inside. I looked at my watch. It was twenty minutes since the executioner pulled the lever. I looked up to the sky and the clouds were darker. A light rain started. I looked anywhere I could as time moved at its painful pace, and Nealy's body swayed in the strengthening wind.

Thirty minutes after Nealy was jerked from the earth, the sheriff nodded. Two guards rushed into the jailhouse. Several minutes later they reappeared with a ladder and a doctor, who walked as if he had spent the morning drinking at one of the adjacent brothels. He climbed the ladder with the support of one guard and put his ear to Nealy's chest. Pulling his head away, he nodded at the sheriff.

Daniel Cornelius "Nealy" Duncan was pronounced dead. He had hung from a rope for thirty-nine minutes.

CHAPTER EIGHTEEN
Wednesday
October 12, 1910

The deputies cut down Nealy's body. They also cut a number of pieces of the rope and stuck those in their pockets, souvenirs for sale, mementos of an execution. Nealy was partly carried, partly dragged across the courtyard and placed in a plain wooden coffin. I walked over as they were nailing on the lid.

"When are they going to release the body?"

"Sheriff said give it a half an hour until the streets clear. We don't want nuthin' else going wrong today."

I walked out a back gate and almost directly into the back door of the brothel where I'd left Randy. The hanging seemed to have spurred business, or at least provided a reasonable excuse for well-heeled clients to slip out of the office or away from home for a few hours.

Randy was upstairs, still on the balcony looking vacantly over the jail at the threatening sky. The rain came down harder. She had been crying.

"That Peurifoy. That bastard. When they hanged Nealy, he stood up and gave one of those gentlemanly claps. Son of a bitch."

She was still in full fury.

"Did you throw something at him?"

"No, I threw him out. I sent one of our biggest bouncers, who grabbed him by the collar and crotch, dragged him through the house and tossed him into the street. He was described as outraged. I fully expect to be raided before the evening is over, so we might not want to linger."

"They're going to move Nealy in a few minutes. We might as well go now. After the funeral, I need to file a story."

"You can do that from the hotel. We should stop by and give Mrs. Vanderhorst the awful details."

"You can do that while I file. I don't think this is going to be a night to loiter outside."

"I've already sent word to Markus to start pulling the storm shutters and preparing for the worst."

We caught our carriage in front of the house. It was closed to block the view of the curious following the body through town. We arrived behind the jail just as the buckboard pulled out with Nealy's coffin. We formed up with the carriage Randy had arranged for Miss Mary and Ida. The procession moved up Meeting Street. Few people were out. Most sought shelter from the weather. Only a few people even paused to look at the funeral party, and those who did had little doubt it was the funeral for the hanged man.

The cemetery was part of Reverend Nichols's AME church. When Nealy's coffin was laid in the ground, Nichols read from a prayer book, and then dropped a handful of dirt on to the coffin.

Miss Mary and Ida followed. Randy and I did the same. Ida wept softly and placed two white roses on her husband's otherwise unmarked grave.

We rode back in somber silence, pulled up in front of the Mills House and dismissed the carriage. I told Randy I would file my story as quickly as possible and meet her in the bar.

"I doubt you'll have much trouble getting Mrs. Vanderhorst to come down for a cocktail," I said. "But let's try to make it quick, we're soaked and should get home before this storm gets any worse."

"A drink is a good idea. Don't linger too long. I'd hate to start a second one without you."

Bright Eyes saw me coming and waved frantically.

"Mister Hinson, they've just put up the hurricane flags. They say this storm is going to get a lot worse."

"That's not good news. Do you mind if I borrow a typewriter for a few minutes? I need to get a story out before the lines blow down."

"Of course. There's one in the office right here. Please use it."

I thanked Bright Eyes and gave her a tip. I think she wanted more, and I don't mean money. The ideas for the article were largely in my head. Even so, it wasn't easy to concentrate with her eager eyes on me the whole time. At 3:45 p.m., I filed the story to New York.

DATELINE:
Charleston, S.C., October 12, 1910
Hal Hinson | New York Tribune

The execution of Daniel Cornelius "Nealy" Duncan did not spark celebration in this city. By the time the young Nealy was pronounced dead he had hanged, struggled and suffered over the span of 39 minutes. It was an execution as bungled as the trial itself.

Justice in this case was neither better nor worse than that of ancient Rome. The state court of South Carolina and the Sanhedrin only served for the expediency of their masters. They who seek a sacrifice to calm the populace.

In his last words before execution, Nealy Duncan made a final statement of innocence. That conviction and his faith are what gave him the strength to face his death. Yet even in the face of death, he knew only compassion.

As he walked to the gallows he handed me a note.

Gentlemen: How can you have the heart to stand to see advantage taken of a poor man for nothing? But anyhow that will be all right. I leave it between you and the good Lord. He knows it all. Tell Mr. Frost who went down to the courthouse and kissed the Bible and said that I was the man he saw in the shop, which he knows is a lie.

But tell him that is all right. We will meet one of these days and we will talk the story over. I have no evil in my heart for him.

I must congratulate my jailors. During the whole time I was there, they treated me fine. Anything I wanted and asked for, they would let me have it, therefore, I ask the Lord to help them, that I may meet them in Heaven.

Tell my family and friends that I am at rest, because

I am innocent, and the Lord knows that I am today. They have taken advantage of me for something that I know nothing about. But that will be all right. I will meet you when the roll is called.

Daniel "Nealy" Duncan

Nealy Duncan never claimed to be the Son of God, but he learned at the foot of the Cross. Here in Charleston, they have washed their hands of a man who may merit being called a black Messiah.

If there is a Heaven, he is there tonight.

The lobby seemed a long walk to get to the bar. Randy and the old woman were finishing their first drink. I ordered a round for us all.

"Your story is over," Mrs. Vanderhorst said, "and this could be our last cocktail together. It didn't end well, but it ended as I might have predicted. I make no apologies for this town. It is filled with humans and fraught with the same failure of any gathering so ruled. But I sense that in the end, there is much good that will come from Mr. Duncan's death. I would hope that would include the two of you. A toast to two young and lovely people, do not waste a single precious moment in front of you."

"Why you charming old matchmaker, what you join together, let no man put asunder. I would imagine you will see us together again. It would seem a waste not to see you and Randy involved in any more of your devious plans again. But, for this evening, I just heard the hurricane flags are up, so I think we should all head to the safety of our homes and hunker down for a long night. Are you going to be safe here?"

"Hal, this hotel has survived a lot worse than hurricanes. I'll be upstairs soon enough to weather this storm. But thank you and please come see me soon," she said with a wink.

Outside the rain had slackened slightly, but the wind began to show a serious side. Small pieces of roofing, signs or anything else not secured were flying along the street like shrapnel looking for a target.

Randy took my hand, "Let's take a back route and stay out of that street."

She led off on Queen Street, cutting through alleys and through some gardens on an indirect approach to her house. One turn took us down a path that led through an ancient graveyard. The old oaks were massive. We were between buildings and covered by huge limbs. You could hear the storm, but there was a strange quiet in this little cove. I stopped and pulled Randy to me.

"It sounded almost like the old woman was marrying us in there."

Her eyes looked almost devilish, wild to match the wind, "Then take your bride." She laughed and pulled me backwards until she sat on top of an old grave.

"I have had enough of death today. We are alive. I want to feel you."

The kiss that followed was a sign. This was not lovemaking. It was a flurry of flesh, a wild affirmation of life that made me forget my pain – both physical and emotional. I tasted the bourbon on her lips and tongue as she tickled and then bit at my mouth. Reaching down, I lifted her skirt. I touched to feel her hot and wet with excitement. She moaned and pressed into my hand. Her hands grabbed my belt. In seconds she had me exposed. She pulled me on to her and into her in one fluid move. There was nothing polite, pure lust was unleashed. The tempo quickened until she clamped her legs around me, pulling me as deeply as possible. Her sighs were all I heard over the wind. Then like a storm subsiding, the fury ended.

I laid her down on top of the vault. She smiled hugely and dropped her arms. She pulled herself up and kissed me hard on the lips. Her hair was wild and tousled, a life-affirming harpy.

"Mr. Hinson, now that we've consummated our near-nuptials, I suppose we should go and tackle this hurricane."

She was back to herself. Full of life and in control. I kissed her and we repaired ourselves to go back into public view. Stepping outside our protected alcove we bent into the wind and hurried the few blocks to her house. The wind continued to build and the rain came down in horizontal sheets. We ran up the steps to the door.

Her house stood a good six feet above the ground. That gave the house a chance against a storm surge. Inside we were met by the assembled group and happy to be back among them.

"Mista Hal, is dis a hurricane?"

"Mojo, the flags went up about a half hour ago. The winds aren't strong enough yet, but I expect they will be soon enough."

The tough guy looked a little worried.

"Meredith, Markus, let's go through the checklist."

"Storm shutters."

"Done."

"Lanterns filled."

"Done."

"Bathtubs, water jugs filled."

"Yes."

"Ice box filled?"

"Yes."

"Extra food prepared for a few days?"

"Yes, including a couple of chickens roasted and ready for an early supper right now."

"Then I guess we're as ready as we can be. Let's eat something while we can."

Everyone headed to the dining room. I walked to the front door to have a quick look at the barometer. It had dropped below twenty-nine inches, a clear sign a bad storm was coming. The wind slammed the door behind me. I joined the dinner table.

"What's the reading?" Randy asked.

"Twenty-eight point seven five and still falling."

"We can be fairly assured it's going to get worse. If it weren't falling, in New Orleans, this little piddlin' storm wouldn't be enough to worry about. We'd be having a hurricane party."

"Dis ain't no party." Mojo looked around as the lights occasionally dimmed, a sign electricity would be leaving us shortly. Even Mojo ate lightly.

We quickly finish a supper of roast chicken and rice, with some beans canned during their prime from the summer. There was a banging at the door. I went quickly to see who was out on this kind of night.

"Miss Mary! What are you doing out?" She came in, soaked through and crying.

"Ida's missing. We got home and I went to lie down for fifteen minutes, I was so tired. When I came out of my room, she was nowhere in the house."

Randy and I looked at each other.

"Meredith, you take Miss Mary into the kitchen and get her a cup of tea and some warm clothes." They left the room.

"If you were guessing," I started.

"Nealy." She finished.

"There isn't much time before the worst of this storm rolls in. If the barometer's still falling, I'd guess the winds will hit hurricane force within the hour. Then it's a matter of time before the flood tide comes in."

"The fastest way is going to be the Stanley. Markus, please go get it started."

He left and we walked into the parlor.

"I'm going." She didn't wait.

"You're not, and here's why. There's a house and people that need someone here who knows how to handle a storm. They need someone to keep a lid on their fears. You could do that, or I could do that. But if my fears are true, I'm better equipped to deal with what we may face out there."

That didn't make her happy. But she couldn't argue either.

"You take Markus with you. He can at least help you if needed. And you better be back here in one hour, regardless of what you find or don't find, or I'll come looking for you ... and you don't want me coming after you angry." She laughed, breaking the tension. "But please, Hal, get back here safely."

I held her for a moment. Then broke away and grabbed a slicker off the peg by the door, pulled a hat down as low over my head as I could and headed out the door. Markus was in the driver's seat. The wind gained speed. I had to yell to make myself heard.

"Are you up for this?"

"Yes. I know this car. I'll get us there and back."

"Okay, as long as you're a volunteer. We're going to the cemetery. Let's go straight up Meeting as fast as you can go. We both need to keep our heads down for flying debris."

We set out with the top up, but it offered little cover from the rain blowing down the streets. Meeting Street was deserted. Markus could have set an in-town speed record, if not for having to break every few blocks to avoid a piece of roof or other flying projectile that threatened to crash into us. Even at that we were driving more than thirty miles an hour for some stretches. The wind was at our tail; every once in awhile a gust pushed the car forward. I was glad it wasn't blowing perpendicular to the car. We made it to the graveyard in less than twelve minutes.

The large, wrought-iron gate was unlatched, and the wind teased it back and forth. For a moment it made me think of Nealy swinging from the gallows.

"Drive through and keep going. Head for the cemetery." I leaned close and shouted to Markus. He sped through the old part of the cemetery. Around a slight bend, down a slope was the new section. Through the rain on the windshield, I saw Nealy's grave. She was there.

Ida wore her wedding dress. From a distance, she looked like she was kneeling, bent over the grave as if to speak to her husband. I rushed to her and knelt, putting my arms around her shoulders. She didn't move. I lifted her up. Her head fell back on my shoulder. Her torso leaned against my chest. A deep, beautiful crimson ran from her chest to the ground. A small hole over her heart released her lifeblood to mix with the rain. In her hand was a small pistol, her way to join Nealy.

I sat back on my heels, holding Ida. She was still warm, but she was gone. Gone to where there is no sadness. Gone to where she was in the arms of her husband. I held a shell.

Markus walked warily around the grave. He said nothing. Our eyes met and held for several seconds, they communicated everything we needed to say.

"Help me pick her up, please, Markus."

We lifted her and laid her back down on the wet earth. I glanced around and found the gravediggers' shack. The door was locked with a decent padlock on a poor latch. It was meant to deter, not stop anyone. I kicked, placing my heel right on the latch. The door flew open. We grabbed two shovels and walked back out where Ida lay. There was one choice. We couldn't carry her body back in a hurricane. There would be no chance tomorrow to bury her. She came here to die.

Both of us dug at the loose dirt that had covered Nealy only a few hours earlier. Even wet, it moved easily. Several feet down we stopped. Taking Ida by her hands and feet, we crab-walked to the edge of the grave and lowered her in. We both stood. I was at her head, Markus at her feet.

I lowered my head in the rain, bracing against the wind. "At death did you part. In death, may you be eternally together in happiness." From our bowed heads we looked up, then picked up our shovels and filled in the hole. When I finished, I tossed my shovel aside. It was pointless to return it to the shed. Neither the shed, nor many of the cemetery trees were likely to survive the night. If we didn't hurry, neither would we.

Back in the Stanley, two wet and muddied men hunched low and hurried for home. Swinging outside the cemetery, we hit Meeting Street and the winds head-on. The return trip would not be easy. Markus ran the car at a high rpm to make headway. The rain drove straight into us, making seeing difficult. Darkness approached and the headlamps were as hard pressed as the car to cut a path forward. As we pushed down Meeting, bright bursts and shooting sparks marked the arc of a power line, shorting out power to part of the city. Electricity is often the first casualty of a powerful storm and, block by block, Charleston plunged into darkness.

Moving south of Calhoun, we were making progress when a stray handcart careening down the middle of the road took flight and slammed into the front window. Markus swerved, blinded for a moment by flying glass. He stopped for an instant. Blood poured down one side of his face.

"You okay?" I leaned into him, pulling a handkerchief out of my pocket to put on his cut. It was a slice above his brow, bleeding but not badly.

"Yeah. Okay." It seemed to make him mad. He downshifted and put the accelerator down, spinning the rear wheels and launching us forward. He drove with a fury now, head low, ramming through the gears. We passed the Mills House in a blur. The lights were out. I thought for an instant about the tough old woman upstairs. Crossing Broad, the water in the street wasn't just from rain. The tide came in high, driven by the storm. Over the next few hours the surge would leave the town deep in ocean. We threw up spray and left a wake as we spun to the corner from Meeting and made a final turn to Randy's. We pulled in through the gate and I saw lanterns in the windows, beacons for our safe return. We bolted from the car and up the steps, crashed through the door with the full force of the storm behind us. Somehow Randy must have heard us coming through the roar of the storm.

Randy rushed into my arms. "You were almost out of time, Mister." She held me close, then stepped back to have a look. I believe she read the whole story from the state of my clothes.

"Ida?"

I shook my head.

Miss Mary ran into the room. "Did you find my Ida?"

I glanced at Randy, and then to Miss Mary and her face fell.

"Yes, Miss Mary," I said. "She's with Nealy."

Miss Mary sobbed quietly. I put my arm around her shoulders and walked her to the kitchen. Randy followed. Meredith was to one side tending Markus's cut. Mojo slipped in and I let him stay. I told the story as straightforwardly as possible, leaving out a few unnecessarily descriptive parts, and assured Miss Mary that husband and wife were now together, as they wanted to be.

"I knew them two had something planned," she said. "I saw it in their eyes last night."

She reminded me of the uneasy sense I had watching them in the jail. Miss Mary cried, moaning occasionally, shedding the tears of a mother, the hardest to watch. Randy caught my eye and nodded to the door. I left the kitchen, followed by Markus and Mojo. The three women stayed behind, to render the kind of comfort that no man can give.

Markus and I walked upstairs to change and clean up. I lent him fresh clothes. Mojo was in an excited state about the storm.

"Mista Hal. Whas gonna happen?"

"Run downstairs and tell me what the barometer says."

"How does I do dat?"

"Just read the number next to where the column of mercury is."

He came back a minute later.

"It say two-seven-nine-five."

"Damn, it's below twenty-eight inches. You can never really predict what a hurricane is going to do. The winds are definitely blowing above hurricane level, so it's only a matter now of how high the wind speeds go. Depending on where the storm hits, the worst part of it is the flood tide that the storm sends inland. It's possible that all of Charleston may be underwater before morning."

"Are we gonna drown?" His eyes showed fear.

"We should be okay. This house is built off the ground and if the flood comes, we'll move upstairs."

We walked back downstairs and joined the rest in the kitchen.

Miss Mary was calmer. Randy had put a little bourbon in a glass in front of her. While the others were taking seats to settle in around the table, Randy took my hand and led me out to the parlor.

"Thought you might could use a short drink, too." She poured me two fingers in a glass, got a little less for herself and settled on the couch. I told her the story with the details while she silently sipped her whiskey.

"It's terrible that those two young people are in the ground, instead of living their lives together. But there is a purity to their love that is almost to be envied."

"They are Romeo and Juliet, written in a different time. It doesn't make the ending any more palatable."

We sat and talked by the light of a kerosene lantern. When we weren't talking, we listened to the sound of the storm howling outside and wondering how bad it might become.

Just after ten o'clock, water began to seep beneath the door.

We gathered everyone from the kitchen and with our lanterns and a few rations, headed up the stairs.

It was no night to be alone. We all gathered in Randy's big bedroom. She had a sitting area where I dropped onto a small couch, set a lantern nearby and grabbed a book preparing for a few long hours. Randy plopped down next to me. The rest grabbed pillows and blankets and made their own niches for the night.

Mojo alternated between excited and exhausted, with the latter winning out after about an hour. Miss Mary read a Bible. I wasn't sure whether it was to find strength for what was to come, or what lay behind. Meredith and Markus took up spots between the motherless child and the childless mother.

Outside the howl had turned to a roar. The sound set a constant melody, punctuated by notes of destruction. Tin ripping off the roof was a loud metallic scream, followed by the clash of contact with whatever it hit at more than a hundred miles an hour. The great oaks surrendered their limbs with sharp sounds like rifle shots. Below us, the rising water streamed into the house, rearranging furniture and smashing Randy's collection of dishes and glassware. She seemed unperturbed and nestled against me, reading from the light of the same lantern. I leaned over to read the title on the spine of her book. "The Tempest."

"Was that selection by chance or circumstance?"

"It seemed fitting for the night. Nothing like a little levity in a storm. And you?"

"Seems Holmes is on the case of a mysterious hound."

She nestled against me for what would otherwise be a comfortable evening, were it not for the sound of the world being blown apart just outside our walls.

Around midnight, the wind began to diminish. It took only an instant for it to go from hell's fury to an eerie calm. We all looked at each other.

"The eye," Randy said as she stood up.

I walked to the window, opened it, then the shutters and pushed them back. Six faces pressed to look out, like voyagers from the upper deck of a ship. The oddity of the eye revealed a clear sky over Charleston. Stars shone, a gibbous moon lit the landscape below. It was a very different view.

The city was underwater as if Charleston had become some form of American Venice. The moonlight shone off the new canals. Damage was already looking severe. Huge trees were down across the streets as far as the eye could see. We all stared in silence, each trying to match what we were seeing against the image of just some hours ago. As we stared, the wind began to gust.

"Hal, grab those shutters and let's batten down. Here it comes again."

I moved quickly, snapping the shutters locked and closing the window. Within a few minutes, the winds were back to hurricane strength. Everyone returned to their places. If possible, the winds seemed to rise to an even greater pitch.

"Now we'll find out what this hurricane's got," Randy said as a gust shook the house. "The backside of the storm is usually the worst."

I knew she was right, but it didn't settle anyone's nerves to know that. Mojo moved over and settled with his back up against the couch. I reached a reassuring hand down and squeezed his shoulder.

No one was reading anymore. The sounds outside were too distracting. Each new one brought a jump from someone. Mojo was trying his best to be brave, but his eyes went back and forth from Randy to me, reading us both as a barometer of whether he should be concerned.

At the height of the hurricane, one huge wind shook the house and triggered an explosive snap as a nearby oak went down. Mojo was up and into my arms.

"Mista Hal!"

"It's all right, Mojo, that big tree must have known you were inside and decided to fall away from the house."

Shortly afterwards, the wind working at the corner of the roof, finally gained an edge, grabbed a corner and yanked. Everybody jumped as a section of the roof pulled clear exposing a corner of the bedroom to the sky and rain. We all shifted to the other side of the room and settled down around the bed. The sanctum was now disturbed and rain washed down the wall. We formed a tight circle with arms around each other, a lantern in the center. I was beginning to wonder if the storm might slowly dismantle the house. I wasn't sure if either the house or our nerves could take a whole lot more. Under my arm, I could feel Mojo trembling and squeezed him a little tighter. Something huge hit the house downstairs and a window exploded. He started crying, softly.

"Mista Hal, I don't wanna die. I jes got you, and Miss Randy. Ya'll de closest to fambly I evah had."

Randy slid to my side and we both held him, talking softly by his ear, so he wouldn't hear the wind trying to convince him, and us, that everything was not going to be all right. With the wind screaming in our ears, Miss Mary lifted her own voice into the din and began singing an old spiritual. The song spoke of trials and salvation. She sang without pause. She sang until the sound of her voice was stronger and more audible than the abating wind. I looked at Randy. She smiled. She knew we had weathered the storm.

Brice Matthews had not left town to take refuge at Hyde Park after the trial. He retreated to his home on the Battery. On the day of Nealy's execution, when he'd heard the reports of the poor boy's cruel death, he looked out his windows and saw winds whipping up the harbor. The storm coming would be horrific. He could read it in the clouds. He could read it in the falling barometer. This time he felt neither concern, nor pity for the town. He felt disgust.

The old pink house where he and Laura lived had been built well before the Civil War. The walls were three feet thick. The house had survived both cannon balls and hurricanes, he was not worried about this storm. The windows were shuttered and doors locked. In a dining room on the third floor, Laura lit candles and lanterns and set the table for dinner. Brice drank deeply from a glass of wine. Deep inside his house he could barely hear the storm. When it was over, he thought, they would both leave for an extended trip to Europe.

John Peurifoy sat on the veranda looking out to the river. He'd quickly left town after the hanging, only after stopping in the sheriff's office to suggest strongly that a raid on the brothels behind the jail was long past due. Sheriff Martin listened politely then showed him the door. He knew a bad storm was coming and far too many things had to be done before he got around to acting on Peurifoy's complaint. He'd been told of the prosecutor's exit from Randy Dumas's establishment.

Peurifoy was not happy. The hanging had gone horribly. He had been insulted and assaulted at the hands of a woman he considered little better than a nigger whore. He nursed his injury with whiskey.

Looking out on the Ashley River, the clouds were a dark gray, almost black. It fit his mood. He heard steps behind him.

"Mista Peurifoy, deys a bad storm comin' in. You want us ta pull the shudders an lock de place down?"

"Damn you, Pinckney. You want to tuck tail and hide just because a little rain is coming in? Get your ass outta here!"

Pinckney turned and started walking down the steps of the veranda. Just for measure, Peurifoy picked up an empty glass from the bar tray and hurled it in Pinckney's direction. It missed, crashing into one of the porch pillars. He laughed and turned back to his whiskey and the incoming storm. The wind began to blow harder and although he sat on the leeward side of the house, the wind was strong enough to be uncomfortable.

He walked into the big empty house. Darkness was falling, hastened by the dark skies. He went about the house turning on lights. Normally, his solitary enjoyment of the plantation was soothing. Tonight it was not quiet and being alone was not soothing. He walked to the highboy and poured a glass of wine and sat at the table where a cold supper had been left for him. He ate alone.

Peurifoy and the evening were becoming increasingly unsettled.

He walked about the house in a state of agitation. He returned to the highboy to refill his glass several times. On one of his circuits through the dining room, he heard a crack and the limb from a live oak came crashing through the window. Maybe Pinckney had been right. Damn him!

Opening the door he walked out on the veranda. The wind hit him full and hard. It was far stronger than just an hour ago. Looking down to the river, a flash of lightning convinced him of what was to come. He could see the waters rising, already flooding his rice fields. This was a full-fledged hurricane coming in. He walked to the edge and put his hands on the railing for support.

"Pinckney!" He called into the wind. No answer.

"Pinckney! Dammit, answer me." All he heard was the wind.

His fears were replaced by anger. He stormed down the steps and grabbed a whip as he passed the barn.

"I'll teach that surly son-of-a-bitch."

With his head bent into the wind, he pushed his way to the small grouping of shacks where the plantation staff lived. The wind was all he could hear in his ears. He felt a trembling in the ground beneath his feet. Behind him a two-hundred-year-old live oak crack loudly as the wind pushed it over causing its enormous roots to rip from the earth. As the massive tree came down, one of the ancient branches drove John Peurifoy's skull five feet into the ground.

CHAPTER NINETEEN
The Wrath

A perfect blue sky shone through where a section of roof should have been. Without moving, I ran my eyes around the room taking a head count. Randy lay next to me on the bed. On the floor of the big upstairs bedroom, everyone else was clustered nearby, sleeping in the shape best afforded by a collection of pillows and blankets strewn across the rug. We survived the night, and when the winds ceased howling in the early hours, each had drifted into their own exhausted sleep. Randy reached a hand up to touch my face, and I held her hand tightly before swinging my legs to the floor. That move seemed to trip a trigger.

"Mista Hal, dat some storm. We beat dat ole hurricane." Mojo was up, the frightened child of the stormy night gone, the cocky Mojo of old back. With everything the last twenty-four hours brought, the kid made me smile.

I took a play punch at him, which he deftly ducked.

"You and me, Mojo," I said. "Nothin's too tough for this team."

"Das right, Mista Hal."

The rest of the group woke. Outside this room, our worlds had been rearranged by events of the last day, but inside we were all together, all safe. It was time to go outside and assess the rest of our lives. For some, it was a simpler task.

"Whas for breakfast? I'm hongry."

"Child," Meredith said. "I swear the only time you ain't thinkin' about eatin' is when you sleepin.' Here, eat dis biscuit, put sumptin' in your mouth to keep quiet while we find out how bad this storm was."

Everybody was on their feet and I led the group out of the door and down the stairs. Rain had washed in where the storm had ripped a section of roof off the front of the house. Walking down the stairs it was plain that the flood tide had swept through the downstairs. As quickly as it came, the tide went back out, leaving a water mark about two feet up the wall. The moving water had rearranged furniture and left a trail and the distinctive brackish odor of what Charlestonians call "pluff mud" through the house.

Randy walked from parlor to hall to dining room with her hands on her hips. "It's not pretty, but nothing that we can't fix. Let's start with fixing breakfast. Markus, see if you can get a fire started to get some coffee going. Let's try to clean up the kitchen enough to sit at the table and eat. Miss Mary, I think you should stay here for at least a day or so until we find out what's going on outside."

"Thank you, Miss Randy, all I got left to go back to is the restaurant and it can wait a couple of days."

"Good, we'll be better here all together for now. Hal, you come with me." She walked to the front of the house, pulled back the bolt, opened the door and walked out onto the porch.

The street was unrecognizable. Several of the large oaks that survived centuries had not weathered the night. Their huge bodies were sprawled across the road, some tipped into houses leaving a crevice carved deep into the building. What the tide had brought in was left behind. Several small boats had been pushed from the harbor into the peninsula and somehow floated through several streets to find this one. Debris of homes and land was mixed with that of the ocean. Fish were left behind when the water receded. In the street a stingray tried to survive in the wet mud, its wings flapping, but it soon grew feeble and stopped.

"It's going to be awhile before your pretty little town is going to be pretty again."

"It got what it deserved. These people decided to play God. Last night God wasn't playing. Today, everyone is equal. Tomorrow, the class lines will begin to reform. In a few months Charleston will be Charleston again, both beautiful and divided."

"Sounds like you might want to get out of Charleston."

"Is that an offer, sir?" She smiled.

"Maybe." I smiled. "Look, I'm going to try to make it down to the newspaper office. I am here. I am a reporter. I need to find out how bad this hurricane really was and get a report back to my paper."

"That's not going to be easy. I'm sure all the telegraph lines are down for miles. You should at least come back into the kitchen and grab a cup of coffee and a biscuit. You're not going to find any food out there."

In the back of the house the crew started to reclaim the first room. It was going to be a lengthy process. I drank a good cup of coffee and ate a biscuit with a thick spread of Meredith's summer jam. Breakfast was a good idea. I felt almost normal, until I walked back outside.

Randy's house and the local newspaper office were a ten minute stroll apart the day before. The journey now took almost an hour. Landmarks that had become familiar for the past two weeks were all but removed. It was impossible to walk down the street. It required climbing over or around or through trees and other wreckage deposited overnight. The water hadn't just left behind sea creatures. There were snakes that seemed as disoriented as I was, moving as if they'd rather be back where they belonged. Some were downright angry.

I ducked to climb through a fallen oak branch and found a man's body draped over the limb. He might have been holding on to the tree. He wore the clothes of a mariner. How he got from a ship or the harbor to this limb was a story he'd never tell. His eyes were open, his face pale and features beginning to bloat. I dislodged him off the limb and set him in the open where those gathering the dead would see him.

The open part of Meeting Street had fewer downed trees, but an even more bizarre collection of detritus. Boats in all sizes, and one that might be called a ship, had washed all the way up from the harbor. The flood tide must have broken their moorings and they floated into town, careening off buildings until the tide left them where they landed. A dazed man came out of the cabin of the larger vessel and saw me, shook his head and disappeared back into the cabin. We were both removed from our natural element.

There were a few officials, police and deputies on the streets. Most were taking stock. I saw a pair of mounted officers with guns at their sides, who were obviously on the lookout for looters or those who might be trying to take some advantage of the crippled town.

The newspaper office was as I'd expected, filled with the reporters and editors trying to cover the biggest story in years. It was a challenge. All the technology of modern times was washed away. No phones rang. Just typewriters and yelling and a cloud of cigar smoke hung over the room.

"Hey, you the New York feller?"

"Hal Hinson."

"I'm Bob Lathan. Welcome to the News and Courier. Take a desk and a typewriter if you need one. We've got people out on horseback getting reports on damage."

There's one thing about newsmen. The coolness I'd felt when I arrived in town was gone. In the middle of a big story, all reporters just want to know the facts. In the middle of a crisis, rivalries go out the window.

"Thanks, Bob. What have you folks found out so far?"

He sat down on the edge of a desk and kicked a chair my way, reached into his coat, pulled out a fresh cigar and sent it and a pack of matches flying in my direction.

"We got word from down at the Customs House that they recorded wind speeds of ninety-four miles an hour before the anemometer broke. The flood tide put up to ten feet of water across the peninsula. The cops are still out trying to get body counts, so far there's a half dozen dead, but we're days from knowing how many people died. We got one passenger steamer tied up at the dock and a bunch of folks thankful they didn't leave out for New York last night. There's one other passenger ship that didn't make it in last night. She's the *Apache* and we don't know what's happened to her. About half the people got off at the Isle of Palms, we don't know yet what happened to those that didn't. Most of the roofs on the peninsula are off or damaged. You've seen what's in the streets. We got no electricity and the city's turned off the gas to make sure that there aren't any explosions or fires. I guess you figured we got no phones or telegraph. We don't know for sure, but it looks like the storm sent salt water way up the rivers and if that's the case this town just lost its rice crop for the year. She was a hell of a storm, but we're still standing."

He delivered that whole summary with his cigar in his mouth, grabbing and glancing at occasional dispatches or notes from young reporters passing.

"Make yourself at home. There's some lousy coffee back there in a pot."

He pulled the cigar out of his mouth, "Hey, Marion, this ain't no party kid, you're either writing a story or you're out getting info and I don't see you doin' either. Now get to it."

"That steamer that was headed for New York, when is it heading out?"

"Tomorrow if the harbor's clear. You leaving lovely Charleston?"

"The story I came to cover is over. That ship might be the quickest way for me to get this story out."

"Hey, Marion," he barked at the kid across the room. "You just got a harbor assignment. Go down to the *Mohawk*, tell the Captain he's got a special guest sailing with him tomorrow. Tell him to save a stateroom if he's got one. Marion, did I mention I want you moving now!"

The kid grabbed his hat and coat, stumbling on one chair and hit a spittoon in his hurry to get out the door.

I laughed as the young reporter flew out. "Thanks Bob. I doubt I could get on that ship without a little help."

"You can buy me a drink next time I'm in New York."

"That's a deal." I stuck out my hand. He raised an appendage about the size of a ham and gave me a friendly grip that left a couple bones unbroken.

I walked a block back to Meeting and stopped in the Mills House to check on Mrs. Vanderhorst. The lobby had suffered the same flood. It would be awhile before she could resume her throne. I found her after climbing a dozen flights of stairs, ensconced in her suite, unscathed.

On the street, there were signs the city was shaking off the shock and getting to the task at hand. Mayor Goodwyn Rhett stood on the top step at City Hall and gave an impromptu speech to a few dozen citizens. The police and fire department prepared to secure the town. Coming down Meeting Street were several teams of draft horses, in harness, ready to hitch to sections of trees. I made my way back to Randy's. The dead mariner had been removed. Crews were trimming limbs and clearing convoluted paths down the street that would at least allow pedestrians to pass.

I looked down, fascinated by some of the objects in the street, and heard a familiar voice.

"Mista Hal!"

I knew it was Mojo, but I couldn't see him.

"Mista Hal, up here!"

My eyes went up. Mojo was up on the roof with Markus, tacking a tarp over the section of open roof.

"You be careful up there, Mojo."

"I gots to help Markus. He needs a man's help up heah."

Randy was on the front porch, dressed in pants and one of my shirts, its sleeves rolled up above her elbows. She had dragged a couple of her oriental carpets out to hang on the railing and was busy scrubbing off mud.

"You look like you've got this under control," I called.

"Some of us had to work. We all can't run off and be big shot reporters filing stories to New York."

"Can't really file. All the wires are down. You were right. Only way to get a story out now is by ship. I'm booked on a steamer leaving in the morning."

"Leaving Charleston."

"For New York."

"On a steamer."

"With a stateroom." I let that one sit for a second. "It might be a nice trip if you'd come with me."

Randy walked slowly to me. Her arms went inside my jacket and wrapped around me. She smelled of pluff mud and soap.

"Does that mean I should start packing?"

"I recommend traveling light. I'm sure you can find what you need in New York."

She kissed me lightly, then leaned over the railing. "Markus, Mojo! You two come down. We need to talk."

CHAPTER TWENTY
Friday
OCTOBER 14, 1910

If you can choose your departure from a city, always leave her by sea. It makes for a softer separation.

The deck of the *Mohawk* was crowded. Randy stood by me at the rail as we watched Charleston growing smaller, prettier. The city had suffered grievous damage. Adger's Wharf was beaten. Bales of cotton stacked for shipment were washed ashore by the tide and now lay waste where the water left them. Pieces of wrecked ships littered the shoreline. There were reports that several ships disappeared during the hurricane. The Battery was battered, its metal railing bent and twisted. Whitepoint Gardens, where we walked that first night, would take months to repair.

By the time we were abreast of Fort Sumter, three and a half miles out, the city appeared largely unscathed. Charleston was still beautiful. She had a knack for keeping up appearances.

"Mista Hal!" Mojo ran up behind us. "Dem fish, deys racin' the boat."

"Those aren't fish, Mojo, they're dolphins, and they're mammals, like us."

"You a smart man Mista Hal, but I ain't no fish."

We laughed. What can you say? The kid was just funny.

"What kind o school you sendin' me to? Maybe you shuld come too if you tinks we's de same as fish."

"It's a boarding school, Mojo. I have a friend who runs a small school for boys. He likes a challenge. I think I'm bringing him his biggest one yet."

Mojo settled between us on the rail as we watched Charleston disappear from view. I took Randy's hand. We turned and walked together to the bow and an open horizon.

DATELINE:
Charleston, S.C., October 14, 1910
Hal Hinson | New York Tribune

The history of Charleston will have to add two calamitous events.

Both happened in the span of single day. Of Daniel "Nealy" Duncan, you already know. A man hanged as a matter of popular expediency. Yet even as poor Nealy swung from a rope in a stiffening breeze, Charleston was facing the verdict of a higher court. On the night of the execution a hurricane arrived hurtling wind and rain and tide upon the town. A wraith of horrible proportion tore through the streets in equal order. In this town there was no Passover. Nature doled destruction with an even hand.

It will be weeks before the extent of the damage is known. The human toll will not be small, nor will the financial. I can attest to the wreckage of homes and ships. I saw the destruction on the docks of the season's harvest of cotton. There are reports that the city's crop of rice has perished and with it, perhaps forever, the culture of the rice plantation in the South.

In a night, those comforts we take for granted were all swept away. The city that prides itself on its historic roots was returned to its past. It will be weeks before electricity and telephones are restored. Those who feign gentility will soon find calluses on their hands.

That Charleston will recover is without doubt. The city has suffered far worse at the hands of history. The question is whether Charleston will take pause, to reflect, to ponder the coincidence of events.

There are whispers beginning in the Negro community. They're already calling this the "Duncan Storm," Divine retribution for the death of an innocent man.

Will the lily-white presbytery of Charleston hear those whispers? Will they connect the acts of Man and the acts of God? In this case, a synergy of destruction, the dominos of Fate that were triggered by a dead weight.

EPILOGUE

Nealy Duncan was buried in Morris Brown cemetery in an unmarked grave. The cemetery of the AME church is but a stone's throw from the Jewish cemetery where the other victim of this story, Max Lubelsky, was buried. One could not create more appropriate irony.

I spent many months weaving the fabric of characters both real and fictional. You have shared your time with me in reading this story, so I will share some of the bare facts. Nealy was real, as were the Lubelskys. John Peurifoy and Brice Matthews were the attorneys in the case. The court testimony is largely the actual testimony. Ida was to be Nealy's wife.

Nealy Duncan maintained his innocence to the end. "I won't die with a lie on my lips. I am an innocent man. I wait to meet you all in heaven," were his actual last words on this earth.

A hurricane in fact followed the execution. To this day, it is known as the "Duncan Storm."

In May of 2009, a letter petitioning for the posthumous pardon of Daniel Cornelius "Nealy" Duncan was filed with the Governor of South Carolina and the South Carolina Department of Probation, Parole and Pardons.